DANGEROUS MINDS

A Claire Roget Mystery

Priscilla Masters

This first world edition published 2016
in Great Britain and the USA by
SEVERN HOUSE PUBLISHERS LTD of
19 Cedar Road, Sutton, Surrey, England, SM2 5DA.
Trade paperback edition first published
in Great Britain and the USA 2016 by
SEVERN HOUSE PUBLISHERS LTD

British Library Cataloguing in Publication Data

Masters, Priscilla author.
  Dangerous minds.
  1. Forensic psychiatrists–Fiction. 2. Personality
  disorders–Fiction. 3. Detective and mystery stories.
  I. Title
  823.9'2-dc23

ISBN-13: 978-0-7278-8598-2 (cased)
ISBN-13: 978-1-84751-700-5 (trade paper)
ISBN-13: 978-1-78010-761-5 (e-book)

Typeset by Palimpsest Book Production Ltd.,
Falkirk, Stirlingshire, Scotland.

DANGEROUS MINDS

AUTHOR'S NOTE

I thought it would make the reading easier if I outlined the basic detail and terms of detention of the various sections of the 1983 Mental Health Act.

Section 2:

Under these terms a patient can be kept in hospital for assessment for up to twenty-eight days. There are certain stringent conditions – the application must be made by two doctors who have to have seen the patient within five days of each other or, alternatively, the nearest relative. One of the doctors must be an Approved Mental Health Professional (AMHP), who must have seen the patient in the last fourteen days.

A Section 2 order cannot be renewed but may be transferred on to a:

Section 3:

Under a Section 3, the patient can be detained for up to six months for reasons of their health, their safety, or for the protection of the general public. This can be renewed for a further six months and thereafter for periods of a year at a time.

Section 4:

Is to be used in emergency situations, needs the recommendation of only one doctor, and is designed to detain the patient pending an assessment of their mental health state.

The patient can be detained for up to seventy-two hours.

Section 5:

Is designed to stop the patient from leaving hospital. It is known as the nurse's holding power. It can also be used if the patient is having treatment in a general hospital for a physical condition. Under this the patient can be detained for up to seventy-two hours.

A Community Treatment Order (CTO) enables the patient to remain at large in the community but they can be taken back to hospital if they don't meet the conditions of the CTO.

There are further stringent conditions for all of these detentions. This is an outline only.

Hope this helps.

ACKNOWLEDGEMENT

'I wish I loved the Human Race', from 'Wishes of an Elderly Man, Wished at a Garden Party, June 1914' by Professor Sir Walter Alexander Raleigh (1861–1922).

ONE

The envelope dropped through her letterbox with a dry rattle, landing face up. Square and white, with a decorative silver border, addressed in a neat hand to:

Dr Claire Roget
46 Waterloo Road,
Burslem,
Stoke-on-Trent, ST6 4UJ

Even the postcode was right. Curious, she picked it up, fingered it, felt stiff card inside. A party invite? She opened it, pulled the card out and spotted the church bells straight away. So . . . an invitation to a wedding then. How nice. Her initial emotion was pleasurable curiosity touched with the tiniest tinge of envy. Which of her friends was getting married?

She was no nearer knowing when she read the names: 'Mr and Mrs Kenneth Trigg . . .' She scratched her head. The name was sparking no recognition. She read on . . . 'are delighted to invite you to the marriage of their daughter, Roxanne, to Mr Jerome Barclay'. Then she felt it. Fear. Sour and corrosive as battery acid in her mouth. Jerome Barclay, one of her more worrying patients, diagnosed with a severe narcissistic psychopathic personality disorder. Unpredictable as a pit bull on steroids. Subtly lethal as a virus, deadly as an asp. And he was getting married? She had always believed he was dangerous. He had dropped sketchy hints of torture, deceit, murder even, but she had never been able to prove anything. All she knew was that he had a talent to unnerve, frighten, terrify – even her, who was trained to float over these emotions like a helium balloon; to look down and get an overview of her patients without feeling threatened by them. Fear? That was not part of the job. But somehow, out of all her patients, many of whom had histories of extreme violence, Jerome Barclay alone had needled her; crawled right under her skin like a parasitic worm. During consultations she had sensed the cruelty and malice that peered out from behind his blandly delivered statements and descriptions.

People around him seemed to have 'accidents' – his mother a serious injury to her face, his girlfriend 'accidentally run over'.

'I just didn't see her, Claire,' he had said, while his face displayed the underlying story. *'I wanted to know what it would feel like to crush her.'* She knew. Oh yes, she knew all right.

Years before his father had died from the wrong dose of insulin. And again it was a story he had related, laced with underlying menace. 'Such a tragedy for my poor mother. He must have got his phials mixed up.' Spoken with a bland smile which hadn't fooled her for a minute.

His brother had died young: diagnosis, a cot death. 'Poor little Peter. Just unlucky, I guess.'

She agreed with that statement at least. Unlucky to have had you as his older brother.

And the final nail in the coffins of his family members, his *poor* mother's 'suicide'.

'She must have been more depressed than I'd realized and her tablets just . . . available.'

He had all his stories off pat. But he didn't deceive her. Not for a minute.

It had seemed that with the assault on Sadie Whittaker, his ex-girlfriend, Barclay had finally come unstuck. Sadie had initially pressed charges against him, stating that she had seen his face through the windscreen quite clearly as he had borne down on her. But once out of hospital she had retracted this version, substituting it for the story that she had run out in front of him and he had had no opportunity to avoid her. As the incident had taken place on a remote road just south of Macclesfield, there were no independent witnesses. No witnesses at all. Without Sadie's clear allegation, the police had had no choice but to reduce charges from 'manslaughter' to 'driving without due care and attention'. The forensic car-crash team stated that there was no evidence he had been driving at more than ten miles an hour. He had had a fine and three points on his licence. Hardly a just punishment for what Claire believed had been a serious attempt at murder. But proof is all in English justice and, without a statement from Sadie, there was none. It wasn't exactly difficult to deduce that Barclay had threatened her – again. The game of 'Tease the Psychiatrist' had continued during his monthly sessions as an outpatient. To her he had hinted that the deaths of all around him – mother, father, brother; almost his girlfriend – were all his own work. True or false? She had left every consultation frustrated, uncertain and worried.

And at the back of her mind she had to remember: his attention-seeking personality meant that he would do anything to retain her attention. His hints *could* be all about that. She couldn't know. Not for certain. It could be the truth. Equally it could all be a lie. But her gut feeling was that he was allowing his psychiatrist a dangerous glimpse of the truth. For no other reason than his own gratification, he was wafting aside the curtain for just long enough for her to peep on to the lit stage and see that the sad saga of Barclay's bereavements was really a story of serial crime.

But she could never be certain.

Two years ago, Claire had decided enough was enough, that he was just playing with her, that she was actually achieving nothing by seeing him every month. In a quiet moment she admitted to herself that he was, perhaps, too clever and too devious for her. And so she had stepped off the merry-go-round and discharged him from her clinic. She hadn't thought he was a danger to wider society, only to those close to him, and she did believe he would, at some point in the future, reoffend. She couldn't see how checking up on him on a monthly basis could anticipate, possibly prevent this.

But now he was to be married. She looked back at the card in her hand. Why? What earthly (or hellish) reason could have made Jerome Barclay decide to get married?

Not love – that was for sure. That was outside his repertoire of emotions.

She was still holding the invitation tightly between her

fingers while she tried to work it out. Maybe it was simply that a wife would be another person to torture, to tease. Would some 'accident' befall her, like Sadie's? Next time would he be successful – again? Not simply major injury but death – again? But she knew. Whatever his plan was in inviting her to his wedding, it was a dangerous game to play. Because she was the one person of all who would see through his games. Read his intentions. Anticipate his moves. And, the trump card here, she was the one who had the authority to incarcerate him. Barclay was astutely slippery enough to have resisted admission to Greatbach so far. So why was he taking this risk? Why had he suddenly surfaced, broken cover? Like the shark in *Jaws* rearing up to expose bloodied teeth before disappearing back into the deep. But . . . she held it in her hand. This time he was inviting her to follow him.

She was well aware of the significance of the small white square of card she held between her fingers. He had thrown down the gauntlet. Whatever he planned, he was inviting her to observe events from a ringside seat. The question was: should she go?

She thought back to the last time she had seen him. Almost two years ago when she had told him, quite calmly, that his condition was unlikely to respond to treatment. The consultations were achieving nothing and so she was discharging him from her care. He had taken the decision without any visible reaction. His features had remained as impassive as the Sphinx's. Not a twitch of his shoulders, not an alteration in the size of his pupils, a flicker of his cold grey eyes or an involuntary jerk of his slim fingers. He'd simply stood up. Polite. 'OK, Claire,' he'd said very slowly and deliberately, so she could not mistake his meaning. His tone had been so heavy with implied threat. 'If that's what you think.'

And then he'd just walked out.

Was *that* why this invitation had been sent? Out of pique because she had dismissed him? She thought for a moment, her curiosity pricked.

If she went to the wedding she might find out. Learn some answers. She read the card through again, this time noting that the invitation included 'and partner'. Well, she didn't have one any more. If she went she would have to go alone. At the bottom was the obligatory R.S.V.P.

Response. It was what psychopaths fed on, like vampires on blood. Psychopaths are both the conductor and first violinist of the orchestra. The attention focuses on them. And to have their psychiatrist in the audience for their show was a coup, a feather in their cap as big as an ostrich's, waving hurrah to everyone.

So would she go?

She sensed that he already knew. And so did she.

TWO

8.45 a.m. the same day

She propped the wedding invitation up on the mantelpiece, feeding herself the pointless fable that she would decide later whether to accept or decline. For now she distracted herself. She had to get to work.

Greatbach Psychiatric Unit was a large red-brick building in the centre of Stoke-on-Trent, close to Hanley. Claire was a consultant psychiatrist at the unit, with a special interest in forensic psychiatry, in particular severe psychopathic personality disorder. Together with two other consultants, between them they had eight wards under their care. Two of them were locked – one male, one female. Inmates could be detained, under a Section of the Mental Health Act, for periods ranging from three days to a year, after which they would be reviewed. All these patients were deemed to be a danger either to themselves or to the wider community, so they were under close supervision, the staff specially trained to spot signs of worsening conditions.

The other patients had a variety of other conditions: depression, anxiety, eating disorders, drug or alcohol addiction, bipolar affective disorder, and so on, and some who defied any classification, which even Claire privately classed as 'nuts'. These she treated with a mixture of confusion and affection. It had proved an interesting, varied and unpredictable career choice. Claire loved the challenge while acknowledging that, unlike many other medical specialities, a cure was frequently out of reach. One had to use other phrases in psychiatry: management, safety, minimizing harm, protecting the public.

She dressed quickly in a corduroy skirt and light sweater and locked the house up.

Although she only lived a few miles from the hospital, the journey seemed to get slower week by week, the roads more congested and hampered by roadworks and a lane closed on the A500 – the 'D' road link between junctions 15 and 16 of the M6. She looked out of her car window at what looked like half the population of Stoke, sitting in traffic, just like her, fuming at the delay. Probably their thoughts were reflecting hers. She simply couldn't work out why a lane closure during rush hour was so necessary. Apart from a line of traffic cones there appeared to be no activity: no holes in the road or raised drain covers; no workmen and certainly no accident. No reason at all for the delay.

But eventually she arrived.

She found an empty space in the car park and headed towards the quadrangle.

Greatbach had been built in the late Victorian era, when mental institutions slammed the doors on their inmates, often for ever; this was their punishment for even minor deviations from what was deemed to be socially acceptable behaviour. Claire had glanced through its archives and unearthed illegitimacy, homosexuality, sometimes nothing more than high spirits, or what today would be classed as excitable or hysterical behaviour. At times even simply glancing through the archives she could make a diagnosis:

Sitting in the corner not speaking nor was the patient eating. At times a tear would roll down her cheek but when asked she said nothing.

Depression.

Or:

Following childbirth the patient appears unable to function,

crying out that the child cannot be hers as it has odd ears.
Refusing to feed it as she says her milk is sour.
Puerperal psychosis.

The list was endless, and Claire cried out for these lost souls so misunderstood, so poorly treated.

In the 1980s, Greatbach had been modernized and a couple of wings added, but most of these were for office staff or outpatients' clinics. Since then the move had been a steady swing from inpatients to outpatients. But the heavy Victorian entrance was still the only way in and the only way out, leading to a quadrangle overlooked by most of the ward windows and into a spacious entrance hall with a Minton tiled floor. A nice touch from the Potteries. She rarely stepped over it without an appreciation for its beauty.

This door was watched over by a porter who sat in an office behind a small window; he greeted her with a cheery, 'Good morning, Doc,' which relieved the gloom a bit. She wished him a good morning back and stepped inside, going straight upstairs to her office.

She spent a fruitful twenty minutes with Rita, her secretary, dealing with messages and fitting in appointments. Then she locked her bag in her office and headed for the wards.

Her first port of call was on the ground floor to see an inpatient, David Gad. He sat heavily on her conscience because he had the most profound case of depression she had ever known. Gad had attempted suicide more than sixty times. Each time he'd been admitted to the local general hospital, had some counselling and been discharged. But the repeated attempts had finally brought him to her attention and she had delved into his past.

He was eighty-five years old and had had a successful jewellery business in Hanley until he had retired aged seventy-five. It had been then that his suicide attempts had begun, increasingly determined, and although Claire knew something was at the bottom of it, she had never found out what.

David was sitting, perfectly still, staring out of the window. He turned around when she entered and his face was so bleak it touched her heart. He was a tall, slim man with an upright bearing and thick silver hair. He had hollow dark eyes and a hooked nose. His physical health was good but his face, in repose, was haunted and sad. It was a sadness that reached out to touch her, to swamp her even. It wrapped him in an impenetrable fog.

Sometimes there is no cause for depression. The sufferers simply experience profound unhappiness. If a cause can be found, it is much easier to treat with CBT. The new buzz word. Cognitive Behavioural Therapy. In other words, you talk it through and see if you can find a way through the human maze of an unhappy mind, encourage the sufferer to work things out for themselves. But CBT had not helped David Gad so far.

He had a family – she had seen him talking to his grandson, an earnest, dark-haired teenager wearing a *kippah*. There were numerous cards on his bedside table. One sported a dark red rose, its name underneath. Someone loved him. So why, she wondered, was this elegant, highly intelligent and courteous man so determined to destroy himself?

She sat down opposite him and he met her eyes. His were dark as ditchwater, quite unfathomable. He looked through her and beyond her, back into the past. They were tortured.

Then he spoke. 'Your job, I understand,' he said, smiling, 'is to prevent me from killing myself. Yes?'

'If it's possible,' she said cautiously. 'I'm only human, David.'

He gave a little smile at that. 'Ah yes,' he said. 'Only human – not God himself.'

She watched him curiously. He was adept at keeping something back.

'David,' she urged gently. 'Confide in me.'

He gave a great sigh. 'Is that the answer, I wonder? Would that give me peace of mind?'

She leaned forward, touched his hand. 'I can't see any other way I can help you. But if we don't find some solution, one day . . .' She didn't need to complete the sentence. He understood.

She left him thoughtful, but the card had evoked an uncomfortable memory for her.

Deep Secret.

The phrase tugged at her. We all have them, don't we? Grant must have done to have gone without a word.

The phrase held further resonance. Claire recalled her own deep secret, sneaking up to her half-brother's cot, hatred in her heart and a pillow in her hand, and prayed Adam would never know.

THREE

The day passed with a long ward round, interviews with patients' relatives and an even longer outpatient clinic, which took all afternoon. By the time Claire was heading home, the worst of the rush hour was over. It was the moment of brief lull between going home from work or school and going out again. It was the time when everyone is having their tea.

Except her.

As she drove Claire reflected on her work. The psychiatrist's job was full of pitfalls: the attempted suicides who were finally successful, the anorexics who tested their body beyond the limit. There were the schizophrenics who caused public disturbance and not infrequently committed headline-grabbing crimes, the bipolar patients who caused mayhem whether up or down. And then there were the alcoholics and the druggies.

The problems of mental health compounded and spilled over into vague symptoms that involved other specialists, who all complained in their turn: the gastroenterologists, renal specialists, neurologists, general physicians, and so on. And everyone in the general hospitals shovelled them as fast as they could right back to her.

She wasn't short of inpatient problems. Just beds. But at least while they were admitted she knew what her patients were thinking.

Not so with the outpatients, psychopaths like Jerome Barclay and another outpatient who was more overtly dangerous: Dexter Harding, who made her so twitchy she made sure he was never between her and an escape route. She had her finger hovering over the panic button during his consultations.

Dexter was an out-and-out thug who had torched a house, believing it was revenge on the girlfriend who had dumped him. But, in typically stupid Dexter fashion, he'd got the wrong house; as a result four members of the same family had died.

Inexplicably, in Claire's opinion, Dexter was walking the streets again, having been released, deemed no longer to be a danger to the general public. Now he was simply under a Community Treatment Order. He had to attend clinic every fortnight. He was not allowed to leave the country. If he even left Staffordshire, he had to inform his community psychiatric nurse, Felicity Gooch; and he had to report to her three times a week anyway. If he defaulted on any of these conditions, she had the power to detain him; but Dexter, stupid as he was, wasn't that stupid. He obeyed the CTO to the letter, turned up three times a week to speak to Felicity, and was as regular as clockwork for her fortnightly appointments. He was prompt and punctual, surprisingly polite, usually arriving with ten minutes to spare and accepting the proffered cup of tea with a thank you. But behind the façades of normality and politeness, Claire sensed something dark deep within him.

Not quite evil. That would take intelligence – planning. No. It was something else that she couldn't quite put her finger on. Something like hatred, which beamed out of him.

And she knew that she was on edge throughout his appointment when they shared the small space of a consultation room, which seemed to shrink even further in his presence.

She wasn't happy about Dexter being out on the streets at all, but she had no jurisdiction to keep him in. And even if she had had, the pressure on mental health beds was huge – they could have filled Greatbach four times over, and then some. Many patients attended the day centre – mostly those with severe learning difficulties or chronic conditions who needed support rather than close supervision. Others lived in sheltered housing, with resident staff covering the twenty-four hours in three eight-hour shifts. It wasn't a perfect system but, the way things were in the National Health Service, it was the best of a bad job. An affordable alternative. And there was a whole host of others who attended Claire's huge outpatient clinics.

Inevitably there were incidents.

Two months ago a mental health patient, not detained under a Section, had gone on the rampage in Cardiff. He had, from somewhere, found an axe; two people had lost fingers and another almost his arm before he had been restrained by the general public and the police. And only then (talk about shutting the stable door) had he been detained under a Section 3. Initially for six months, which would almost certainly be extended to years. He wouldn't be going anywhere soon. Reading the patient's history, in Claire's opinion he should have been detained under a Section 3 in the first place. He had had a history of extreme and unprovoked violence. But she felt some sympathy for the psychiatrist in charge of his case, who had been given a very hard time by the Press and the general public, who had firmly placed full responsibility at his door. The hospital had had to pay substantial compensation, which further robbed the struggling NHS.

Ah well – for once *not* her problem; it was time to go home.

The evening sun was golden through the car windows, so the city looked blessed with sunshine, even the streets of terraced houses looking almost festive against the backdrop of a couple of bottle kilns, their stumpy shapes unmistakable against the sky. Maybe it had been a golden September evening, just like this, that had given rise to the fable that the pavements in London were paved with gold, tempting people away from Staffordshire. And perhaps, enjoying the evening's beauty, even here, people walked the streets with a bounce in their steps. A few cyclists weaved energetically in and out of the traffic, their jaunty actions mirroring the optimism of the evening.

There was another reason why she felt good. She had resisted the temptation to text or phone Grant for almost a month. That felt like a feather in her cap, a gold star pinned to her breast. She was really pleased with herself for this one small achievement.

Grant had been her live-in partner for almost five years, and had been colourfully and energetically renovating and decorating their home until six months ago. Halfway through his project, he had abruptly and without warning abandoned both it and her. Inexplicably and out of the blue, he had jettisoned her and vanished, and she didn't know why. She still found it strange to return to the echoing floors and empty rooms after a day's work and be greeted by no smell of paint, no swatches of material to look at, no shade cards to study. No ideas for furnishings and colour schemes. Nothing. She had been left with a tidy, empty place, some of the rooms still undecorated and unfurnished, paint splodges on the floor that awaited sanding or a carpet to hide them. One room still had the ladders and paint pots ready for a final coat she did not have the heart to apply. And although she was a psychiatrist, a forensic psychiatrist at that, she had not been able to work out why he had gone. What the trigger had been. On that last morning Grant himself had offered no explanation. He had simply mumbled something almost shamefacedly about *having to go* – as though he was someone who was a native of a country at the top of the Faraway Tree. His land was swinging away and he had to just go with it. She was still perplexed and it had been that puzzlement which had left the wound so raw.

They hadn't argued. In the months preceding his departure they had reached an agreement, a bargain – she would go to work and earn the money and he would renovate their house. When children came he would be the house-husband. He had seemed happy with that. She didn't know why he'd gone. It didn't make any sense.

That had been a little over six months ago, in mid-February. And now it was September. The weather was cooling, the nights *drawing in*, as her mother would say, tight-lipped in disapproval of the approaching winter. Almost as though he was ashamed of his decision, Grant had sneaked round and collected his stuff when he would have known she was at work. She'd come home to miss it: his slippers, his clothes, one or two ornaments she'd given him. She'd gone from room to room, missing the few articles one by one. His teddy bear from childhood, a dreadful picture she'd always hated of an E-Type Jaguar. She would have given anything to see it back on the wall.

None of their joint belongings had gone, she'd noticed. Just his personal things: clothes, pictures, kitchen utensils. He was keen on cooking and she missed that too, though sometimes his dishes had proved a little too adventurous. Octopus biryani being one of them. Yuk. Even now she wasn't sure whether she would smile or retch at the recollection. She didn't know where he was living now and she'd never known his family, who lived in isolation somewhere in Cornwall. Apart from that unsatisfactory mumbled non-explanation, he had not been in touch. Not ringing. Not writing. Not even a bloody text message, for goodness' sake.

Humiliatingly, after three weeks of insomnia, she had texted him, asking him to come round and explain what and why, but he had not responded and she recalled someone telling her that boys didn't 'do' explanations. Clarity, she'd asked? It was a girl thing, her friend had said. But she was left unfulfilled. She wanted – needed – an explanation. Settlement. She needed to know why he had left so she didn't make the same mistake next time. If there was to be a next time. Was it because she wasn't pretty enough, she asked herself? Or was too short tempered? Or had halitosis? She breathed into her hands and smelt nothing but toothpaste. But she double-flossed all the same, booked in with the dentist for an extra scale and polish, and rinsed noisily and energetically with a mouthwash that guaranteed fresh breath.

Was it something more inherent in her personality? Was she boring? Too predictable? Too wrapped up in her work? Not sexy enough? She went through everything: the physical, the mental, the social; found no answers, texted Grant again. Please – at least tell me why?

She watched her phone obsessively for an answer.

Nothing.

She flicked the memories from her mind, turned into her drive and climbed out of her car, glancing around her superstitiously, as though by allowing her thoughts to dwell on two of her most concerning patients they would, by black magic, appear as suddenly and dramatically as Houdini bursting out of a sealed casket.

But there was no one, simply a few loiterers.

The empty house greeted her sullenly as she let herself in. Maybe she should get a cat, Claire reflected, hanging her bag on the newel post at the bottom of the stairs, bare until a carpet was laid. Something or someone to welcome her home, at least. Not this echoing, hollow emptiness. Perhaps a cat or a dog would relieve this feeling of oppressive solitude which she hated. She felt like kicking the bottom step. Even a bloody budgie to at least tweet a welcome home. She entered the sitting room, one of the few rooms completely decorated and furnished. Even the curtains were hung. Ivory silk with large red flowers, blending in with pale carpet and a three-piece suite. Large black television, silently sulking in the corner. She and Grant had splashed out on a huge screen for the nights they snuggled up on the big soft sofa and watched a thriller chiller or a romance or . . . anything really.

She missed him most of all at this point in the day, the moment when she let herself in to a house that felt dead. Like entering a tomb, shutting out the living world outside, the front door a stone sealing up the mouth.

She moved towards the faux-log gas fire, meaning to light it to bring some warmth and movement into the room, but she was distracted. The wedding invitation glared at her from the mantelpiece, demanding a response. She picked it up. She had to make a decision. Should she go to Jerome's wedding, suss the situation out for herself, or do the wise thing – leave well alone and decline. He was not her responsibility any more. She had discharged him and he had kept out of trouble since then or she would have been informed. Whatever her private misgivings and suspicions about Barclay, his police record held only minor misdemeanours. She read the invitation through again, more carefully this time, noting the names: Mr and Mrs Trigg, Roxanne, their daughter, the bride. It was silly to infer anything from a name and an address in the Westlands, the smart area of the city, where the houses were detached and the gardens large, but somehow she perceived Roxanne and her parents as being vulnerable.

The ceremony was to be held at The Moat House, Acton Trussell, a venue near Stafford, at Junction 13 of the clogged-up artery which was the M6. She'd been there to a wedding once before and a couple of times for dinner, but since then it had been upgraded. She sat down and looked it up on her iPad. It looked beautiful, boasting a Norman moated house, a modern, well-organized interior and an award-winning chef. Great combination.

She fingered the card again, went through the picture gallery of the hotel, now visualizing Barclay in each shot, trying to picture him as the blushing groom and failing completely. Barclay would smirk and mock. He would meet her eyes, knowing she would understand. This was all a play to him. She only hoped it would prove to be a comedy, not a tragedy. She couldn't help herself. She was afraid for these three people whose lives were about to be wrapped up in Barclay's.

She stared into the distance, trying to bore into Barclay's mind. Getting married? Why? He hated women, despised them, belittled them and tried to run them over when he was tired of them. He had been violent towards the two women in his life – his mother and Sadie Whittaker, the ex he had almost murdered. Barclay didn't form relationships, particularly with the opposite sex. He *used* them. So how was he planning to use Roxanne?

She sank further into thought, moving beyond her patient. There is nothing that rubs in the single state more than an invitation to a wedding. She allowed herself a minute's pity before reading the card through again and wondering why he had suggested *she* be invited. She half closed her eyes, blanking out the room and imagining the conversation: Jerome saying, mocking smile on his face, when asked by his future in-laws what family to invite, saying, with a mournful face, that he had no family. Barclay was good at faces. He could mimic any emotion as well as if he'd been to acting school, because it was that – an act. An expression applied to his face, a tear as fake and obtrusive as a painted Pierrot's. But convincing for all that. She could imagine his face when he said that his mother and father were both dead, his only sibling too. It would invoke pity. Misplaced. Claire believed he was responsible for all three deaths: his brother's 'cot death', his father from poorly controlled insulin-dependent diabetes (how easy to tinker with insulin), and finally, last to go, his sad, devoted mother from a presumed overdose. But all Jerome would say when challenged about the poor life expectancy in his family was that *he* was the victim here. 'Gosh, Claire,' he'd said, 'I've lost *everybody* I ever loved.' With his nuptials approaching, the phrase had a sinister resonance. And Barclay didn't 'do' love. And to prove that? There had been no grief, only challenging merriment in his tone. And why had his eyes sparkled at such tragedy?

Hah, she thought, suddenly savage, hating him not only for the crimes but for the slimy way he had slipped through any attempt to prove it. Victim? I don't think so.

She fingered the card. There was a kernel of truth in her imagined conversation. Family members to invite to the wedding from the Barclay side *were* sparse. She recalled now that he had an aunt who lived somewhere in the wilds of Scotland, but she was labelled as 'peculiar'. Claire wondered whether the peculiar aunt had been invited. She thought she had also heard mention of a cousin, but knew no more details. No names for either.

And so, when asked who he would like to invite to the wedding, she could just picture it. Jerome would have said. '*My psychiatrist.*' Pulling her out of the hat like a true psychopath. Events, acquaintances, anything you and I would hide beneath the carpet, they hang out on the washing line to blow in the wind. Displayed for all to see and make of what they will, taking pleasure in the puzzled reaction.

'*Her name's Claire,*' he would have continued. '*Invite* her *to the wedding.*'

Then something else registered and she realized why the invitation chilled her. It had been sent to her private address, not to the hospital. It hadn't even been redirected but had come straight here. Here, where she was vulnerable, and did not have the protection that Greatbach provided. She could not hide behind the security and numerous panic buttons, the locks and keys and CCTV everywhere, the eye of the porters watching every move. No. This had dropped here on to the mat, into the heart of her private existence, straight into a house with too many empty rooms where she now lived alone with no one to protect her. Not even Grant.

Though – and she smiled here – Grant wouldn't have been much protection. He hadn't exactly been the chivalrous knight-in-shining-armour type. He was the sort to let a mouse out of the trap because he was gentle and couldn't bear suffering. He wouldn't squash moths or spiders or use fly spray, but tried to catch them in his hand and let them free, out of the window. He had had a gentleness belied by his looks. Again she smiled. He looked like Blackbeard the pirate. A shock of thick dark curly hair, merry brown eyes, and something of the blackguard about him.

She smiled again. Grant had always had that capacity, to make her smile.

Her eyes returned to the card. She needed to make a decision. She either went or she didn't. But now she had invoked Barclay he stood before her, his face bland, as usual, giving no hint of the weird and complicated person that hid behind it.

During consultations Barclay had only really had the one facial expression – vaguely interested, polite and impassive. He only acted when he needed to. On that first meeting she had wondered why Heidi Faro, her predecessor, had singled him out for such attention. She recalled the precise words and phrases she herself had written in his notes.

An unremarkable-looking guy – of medium height, around five nine, five ten, medium build. Slightly pale skin, medium-brown hair, cut neat and short.

The words bored into her mind exactly, every phrase, every adjective. She could remember his clothes. He was neatly dressed. Never wore anything that would draw attention to him. He was bland, would melt easily into the background. Useful.

Loose-fitting grey chinos and a cream sweater, sleeves rolled up to expose sinewy forearms.

Most of all she recalled his scent. Sometimes in her sleep she would smell it and wonder why such a pleasant scent made her feel uneasy.

He smelt vaguely of cinnamon, as though he'd just drunk a cappuccino.

And, in particular, as her image flickered, she would recall his eyes. Always an important sign for a psychiatrist. It is hard to fake the truth that lies behind the eyes.

His eye contact was good. Forthright and confident. Possibly arrogant.

Psychopaths blink less frequently than normal people. They don't blink because they lack empathy, and it is empathy that makes us blink. If you doubt this, stare at a cat.

And she remembered his smile, slightly supercilious, as though he knew something she did not.

She looked back at the invitation and knew that, as he had almost certainly anticipated, she had made her decision. She was going to accept. Spy out the land, make her own mind up. Without wasting any more time, she sat down and wrote her acceptance.

Wriggling through the back of her mind was a worm of an idea. It was time she did something she should have done long ago.

Claire Roget and partner *will be delighted to attend the wedding of Roxanne and Jerome on Sunday 5 October at 3 p.m. at The Moat House, Acton Trussell, Staffordshire.*

Done. She felt better already. Nothing like coming to a decision. She spent half an hour sweating it out on the rowing machine which Grant had installed in the basement. Then she watched the News Channel, had a long soak in the bath, wrapped herself up in her bathrobe, watched a romcom and finally went to bed.

Triumphantly ticking another day off.

She still hadn't contacted Grant.

She left the envelope on the mantelpiece three days before posting her acceptance. He would get it on Monday morning.

FOUR

Monday, 8 September, 6 p.m.

She had just let herself in after an exhausting day. The phone was ringing. She was tempted to let it go through to answerphone – it was probably a cold call anyway.

But there was always the chance that it might be Grant. A chance slowly fading into nothing. 'Claire.' He had her home phone number too? 'So glad you're coming. I wondered whether you'd accept the challenge.' His voice, in an otherwise silent home, made her skin crawl. He'd known he didn't need to introduce himself. He knew he was right inside her mind. He crept around it, tiptoeing through her brain.

'It's just an invitation to your wedding, Jerome,' she said, struggling to find a tone that sounded normal.

'Ah, yes.' His voice was mocking, 'To the lovely Roxanne.' He continued in the same tone.

'Whose parents *were* farmers but have just sold all their land for fracking, would you believe, and the animals – oh dear – have all gone to the slaughterhouse. So they've plenty of money but no pets.'

This was so typical of his behaviour, the underlying cruelty, dangling a silver lure in the water. Was that why she felt like a fish swimming towards it, taken partly by the current, repulsed, fascinated, but unable to resist?

She had always had a curious nature.

'It'll be a modest but stylish affair,' he continued, 'no use splashing out on just one day, even though Kenneth and Mandy could *easily* afford it.' The malice in his voice was rancid oil.

She refused to rise to the bait and spoke calmly. 'Perhaps you'll send me your wedding present list, Jerome?'

He sniggered. 'Of course.' He sniggered again. A disgusting, high-pitched giggly sound which contained no mirth. She hated it. 'Mainly money. Always handy to have plenty of *money* behind you.'

She didn't react.

He did by sending another barb to hurt and show her that he knew more about her private life than she would like.

'Glad you'll be bringing a partner, Claire. I did wonder about that now you're . . . alone.'

She stiffened. How did he know these things? How did he know her address, her phone number, the fact that her partner had left? It had to be the Internet? Surely? How else could he know? She wasn't on Facebook – it wasn't a good idea for a psychiatrist. Too many 'friends', some of whom had extreme personality problems, like Jerome. But some of her real friends might have posted something – or even Grant himself. She never looked at the site. But maybe that was where the explanation lay. Social media? It had a lot to answer for.

'Remember this, Claire,' he continued softly, 'I've never been detained under a Section.'

It was true.

He continued with his goading. 'And I never intend to be.'

She still didn't respond.

'And whatever I do, *you're* going to have an uphill struggle trying to prove *anything* against me. Ever.' He couldn't resist adding, 'Whatever your suspicions, Claire, or whether they're right or wrong.'

She didn't react. That was what he wanted, so he carried on, still in that same mocking, challenging tone, trying to provoke her. 'Heidi Faro never managed to pin anything definite on me, and to be honest she was much cleverer than you, so I don't give much for *your* chances.'

In the same way that one doesn't move away from a cobra's dance, she found herself unable to make the obvious move: put the bloody phone down.

And he continued with his goading. 'Shame she had to die.'

Again she did not respond, though the words hurt as though he had picked off a scab and exposed raw flesh, started it bleeding again. She had always been fond of Heidi, and perfectly aware that her predecessor was more intelligent than her. From deep inside, her naughty voice spoke up in her own defence.

But she still got herself murdered, didn't she?

'You should have focused less on me, Claire, and put your own house in order. Maybe then he wouldn't have gone.'

She stiffened. Of all people, was it Jerome who could explain Grant's abandonment? She put a hand up to her face. What she wouldn't have given to be able to get even on this hurt, bang him up, prove he had assaulted his ex-girlfriend, pin something on him and watch him stew in a locked ward – or better still, in prison, which was where he really belonged.

Safely away from the vulnerable. But, like teasing a dangerous dog, it could be risky to goad him. If not her, then someone else might be on the receiving end of his displeasure. Finally she did put the phone down while he was still talking, and she sat in the dark for a while.

Why the hell was she going to this bloody wedding? Barclay wasn't even one of her patients any more. There was nothing more she could or should do. She certainly didn't owe it to him to play this part.

But then maybe she'd been wrong anyway, wrong on all counts. Maybe he was just an attention-seeking bully and a tease. Maybe Heidi had been wrong to follow him so closely, and maybe she had followed Heidi's supervision more out of respect for her esteemed predecessor and an acknowledgment of her terrible death than out of real evidence. Perhaps Barclay was simply a narcissistic personality. Nothing more. He just had a pathological need for attention. Like a disruptive little boy in class, he enjoyed making a noise. Perhaps he wasn't a real threat. It was all in her mind. It was a comfortable road to saunter along.

Three things held her back.

The vicious attack on his girlfriend was fact. Sadie had confessed to Claire that she'd known Jerome had run her over deliberately. 'He was watching me through the windscreen,' she'd said. 'I saw him laughing. And then . . .'

She'd met Sadie once. She was a plucky girl. She wouldn't have backed down from prosecuting her ex-boyfriend unless she'd been really frightened. And who would know a psycho better than his girlfriend?

His psychiatrist. That's who. Initially Heidi and then her.

The notes Heidi had left had instructed close supervision. Underlined. Heidi *was* smarter than her. In this she agreed with Barclay. And Heidi *had* felt the need to keep a very close eye indeed on her patient. You didn't just check on people every fortnight unless you suspected something *was* seriously wrong or was *about* to go seriously wrong. But, Claire thought, fighting back on her own behalf now: Heidi Faro might have been smarter than her, but Heidi was dead. Not so clever then. *She* hadn't sensed the threat in another patient, her killer. So was her judgement to be relied on at all? Claire straightened, feeling a surge of confidence.

But of course there were the untimely deaths of the three family members. As the saying goes: one death could be carelessness. Two suspicious, and the third . . .? Downright proof. But she had *not* been able to prove anything, and Barclay, as sole beneficiary, had gone on to benefit very nicely from his mother's 'suicide' and the sale of her house.

Something told her that Jerome Barclay had not done his worst yet. It was still up his sleeve. The trouble was, she did not have a clue what his worst could or would be.

To distract her from the pointless ruminating, Claire switched the television on. It worked until 11 p.m., when she took a shower and went to bed, reading a novel until she fell asleep.

FIVE

Outpatient clinic, Greatbach Secure Psychiatric Unit
Tuesday, 9 September, 2.00 p.m.

If Barclay was a rapier, subtle as a virus with the deadly bite of an asp, Dexter Harding was a lump hammer. The strict terms of Harding's Community Treatment Order would apply until he was deemed to be no threat to society. In other words, in Claire's opinion, that would not be until he was decrepit and staggering along on a Zimmer frame. In other words, never. If he broke any of the conditions of his CTO, Claire had the authority to have him detained all over again.

She couldn't wait. In her opinion he should never have been released from prison; he should have been detained for life. He had never shown any signs of mental illness. He was simply a thug.

His appointment was at 2 p.m., the first afternoon appointment of a very busy and overbooked outpatient clinic.

C'est la vie et la mort.

He was a big man, in jeans which never quite fitted, hanging below a large, low-slung belly which swung, ape-like, as he walked. The illusion of an orang-utan was furthered by his large, long arms and the slightly forward lean to his gait. Today his ill-fitting jeans were accompanied by a well-washed navy sweatshirt size XXL and grubby trainers. At thirty-one years old, Dexter should have been in his prime, but already his hair was thin and wispy. He had a pale, unhealthy complexion and was usually about a week off a shave. He was supposed not to drink alcohol but the scent of cider generally clung somewhere around him. That and body odour and cigarettes.

He had an ungainly shuffling walk, rolling from side to side with each step, landing heavily on his feet. Enough of a sailor's roll that if you watched it for more than a minute you began to feel seasick. His bulky presence seemed to fill the tiny consulting room and the rank stink of his trainers made the atmosphere even more oppressive.

They went through the same rigmarole every fortnight.

'How are you today, Dexter?'

He lifted his eyes; they were an indeterminate colour – brown, green, hazel, grey; a mixture of all these tones – which made it strangely difficult to see what he was thinking. 'I'm OK.'

His voice was always the same: part mumble, part slurred speech. Nothing hurried or precise. She had the authority to test his alcohol levels but rarely bothered. He was on enough medication to keep him vaguely sedated. More than a couple of ciders and he would probably pass out.

She consulted her previous notes. 'We enrolled you in a job training exercise. Did you go?'

She already knew from Felicity that he hadn't.

'I weren't great that day,' he mumbled.

'OK. Well that's your decision. But we don't want you just sitting in your room. We want you to get out and about.'

He gave a slow, lopsided smile. 'Do you? Why?'

Because it's my job. That's why. Don't think it's because I care. I don't really.

She'd seen some of the forensic photographs taken after the arson attack: four bodies, in various states of cremation, two of them children. The outside of the house had borne scars too, the roof having fallen in and heavy scorch marks rising like widow's peaks above the windows. When the glass had cracked, the flames had shot out.

Considering his mental limitations, Dexter had made a good job of arson, Molotov cocktails through both doors, front and back. The family had had no means of escape. It had been cold-blooded, cruel, senseless murder.

If it had been left to her, Claire had long ago decided, Dexter Harding would never have been free. She wasn't even convinced that his crime was the result of stupidity or any other mental state. He might have the intellect and instincts of a bull, but even he wasn't that idiotic. He'd known exactly what his actions would result in. Death. He simply hadn't cared.

'OK, Dexter,' she said wearily, 'I'll see you in a fortnight. Try and attend the day centre, even if you don't get to the job training.'

Well aware of the format, Dexter rose and shuffled out, leaving Claire with an acute sense of pointlessness. Another waste of time.

Thursday, 11 September, 9 a.m.

There was always a sombre feeling on this particular date, 9/11, the anniversary of the day the world had changed for ever as the storm clouds had broken over the twin towers. Everyone was aware of it, and even here, in Staffordshire, the heart of the UK, 3,346 miles away from New York City, Claire stopped and remembered those terrible sights, planes piercing buildings, the knowledge that as you watched people were dying horribly, people jumping like film stuntmen – only this was real. Armageddon. How would it feel if the attacks had been directed at The Shard or The Gherkin? Just as terrible, was her guess. Only nearer.

But she had work to do. Siona stopped her in the corridor and brought another patient to her attention. 'Hayley's put on a bit of weight,' he said.

Claire was instantly suspicious. 'How?'

Siona grinned. 'Good food,' he said, 'and plenty of it.'

Which didn't allay Claire's suspicions one little bit. Hayley Price was fourteen years old and had suffered from anorexia nervosa for the last four years. She had teetered on the very edge of life and death and had been forcefully tube- and drip-fed to preserve her life whenever her weight dropped to a critical level. Most anorexic patients are devious and deceitful and Hayley was no exception. She had tried every trick in the book to avoid eating. It had become a lethal game with her, to exist on a starvation diet. To hoodwink the staff she'd done it all; concealed weights on her tiny body, under the armpits or once in a sanitary towel which hadn't fooled the nurses for a second. Patients whose weight has dropped that low cease to have periods. The sanitary towel had contained a small weight she'd filched from the nurses' station. This is why patients with anorexia are always weighed naked.

So, instead of feeling reassured that Hayley was genuinely putting on weight, Claire was suspicious. What trick was Hayley up to now?

'How much weight?'

'Well, only a pound,' he said, 'but at least she's not still losing it.'

'I won't have time to see her this afternoon, Siona. I've a busy afternoon ahead. I'll try to get to see her tomorrow. In the meantime keep an eye on her, will you? Just be watchful.'

He grinned. 'Will do. But I do think we're winning this time.'

'I hope so, Siona.' She patted his shoulder. A bluff Welshman. Although he had been a psychiatric nurse almost all his life, he'd never quite lost the gift of optimism. She couldn't help smiling after him. He was a good sort. She'd miss him when he retired, which would be soon.

'Keep an eye on Hayley, let me know if you have any concerns and tell her I'll see her tomorrow.'

'Will do,' he promised.

It was almost lunchtime now. She completed her ward round, seeing the other patients, and went to eat in the canteen.

She would look into little Miss Price when she had time.

For now she had a few things on her mind, which her registrar quickly picked up on as she joined her at the table. 'Claire,' she said, 'you look preoccupied.'

Salena Urbi was a beautiful Egyptian doctor, who wore the hijab with deft elegance. She had a mischievous sense of humour but also an incisive wit, as well as sharp intuition when something was wrong.

But Claire didn't want to confide her misgivings about Jerome Barclay – didn't want to tell her that his infiltration of her home made her feel as though worms were crawling inside her head, that he made her feel vulnerable and alone. A psychiatrist with mental problems? Help. Salena reached out and touched her hand. 'Claire,' she said, 'what's wrong?'

And then it came out limply, baldly. 'My boyfriend's walked out on me.'

The brown eyes met hers. 'I am so sorry,' she said. 'Had you had a row or . . .?'

Claire simply shook her head. 'No. Nothing.'

'Do you know where he is?'

Again Claire shook her head.

'How long?'

'Nearly six months.'

'Blimey,' Salena said. 'You've kept that well-hidden.'

At that Claire managed a smile. 'Separating work from personal life?'

'Yeah. But . . . Hey – you know where I am. If you want to talk . . .' Again that mischievous smile broke out, 'or do a bit of undercover spying on him.'

Claire laughed out loud. Salena was about as surreptitious as a fire engine in full pelt, siren blasting. She was – to say the least – noticeable.

'I don't even know if he's anywhere round Stoke,' she said, 'so it'd be a bit hard.'

'Yeah. I suppose so.'

They ate in companionable silence until Salena excused herself and Claire was left on her own in the busy canteen, people jostling all around her. But she was unaware of them. Grant's abandonment had proved useful to divert her attention from her pressing problem. But now she was still chewing over the wedding invitation, her mind flicking back to the last time she had seen Jerome Barclay, searching for some clue as to what was his intent. There was another possibility why Barclay might have wanted her to be at his wedding that she hadn't considered. People do grow out of personality disorders. Was it possible that he had changed and was no longer the complete bloody psycho he had been? Was *that* why he wanted her there – to witness something? What? His epiphany? His conversion? His St-Paul-on-the-road-to-Damascus moment? Not judging by the phone call the other night. He'd sounded just the same: arrogant, attention seeking, without conscience. The hints he had dropped about his future in-laws and his bride-to-be had been at best disparaging. At worst, downright nasty. Or dangerous – for them. The question rankled. Why was he taking this step? She puzzled before coming to the conclusion. There is nothing like a face-to-face meeting to judge intent. Maybe she should invite him in, make him an appointment. She considered this option for no more than a moment. Remembering their last encounter she shied away from this step.

It had been two years ago. As usual he had swaggered in, sat down without being invited and asked her how *she* was. Neat.

'I'm fine,' she'd said shortly. 'And you?'

'Not so bad,' he'd said, fixing into her eyes.

'Work?'

'Yeah.'

'What?' She hadn't meant it to come out quite so harshly.

'Got my own business,' he said.

'Doing what?'

'Marketing.' They'd both been aware that his responses were answering nothing.

'Relationships?' They were the key to what was really going on in this psycho's life.

'Got a girlfriend. And before you ask, we've been together six months now.' But his facial expression was all wrong. He should have looked pleased with himself, maybe a little smug, but he didn't. He looked challenging, mouth slack, eyes watchful, unblinking. It was an insolent look waiting for a response.

'And you're living where?'

'Got a flat,' he'd said, 'in Hanley.'

'We'll need the address.'

He gave a comfortable grin. 'Why, Claire? So you can look me up?' His eyes flickered a challenge as dangerous as a lit match about to be thrown into a petrol can.

'We need to keep our records up to date,' she'd said smoothly.

He'd stood up then, leaned right over her desk. 'You don't *need* to keep an eye on me at all, Claire,' he said.

Oh but I do, was her thought response. Out loud she said nothing. He would understand her disagreement with that statement.

He continued. 'I've never *done* anything.' He was still leaning over her, still with that cocky smile. 'Not that you can prove, anyway. I'm clean. I don't do drugs. So what . . .' He shrugged. 'What's your problem, Claire?'

'I don't have a problem, Jerome,' she'd said steadily. 'But I do have a job to do.'

'Then do it—' a dismissive wave of the hand – 'by all means, but leave me alone.' Then he'd leaned in even closer and she'd smelt the cinnamon on his breath. 'I'm bored with coming here. Bored with seeing you. Discharge me, Claire.'

And she had. It was all smoke and mirrors, suspicions and imaginings. It was only after he'd left that she'd realized how completely he'd orchestrated the entire interview. She felt cross with herself. She was the psychiatrist, for goodness' sake. She'd wanted to discharge him, but in the end he'd as good as discharged himself. Then she felt crosser. What difference did it make? Really.

At the end of the clinic she went to the receptionist's desk. 'Jerome Barclay,' she said. 'Did he change his address to his new one?'

The girl shook her head. 'No.'

So now she didn't even know where he lived.

But now *he* knew where *she* lived.

SIX

For once she finished clinic early, but instead of visiting Hayley she wanted to get to the bottom of David Gad's story. It was too early to go home to the empty house; besides, she felt she had unfinished business with the elderly man who was trying to conceal such turmoil. She found him in his room, studying a card he had been sent. She stood in the doorway and watched him for a moment. His face was worse than troubled. It was anguished, unhappy, the card held tight in his hand. With a shock she realized that on the front was a swastika. He finally looked up; didn't speak for a full, long minute. Then, finally, he gave another great long sigh and shrugged as though to say, why not? He set the card, face down, on his bedside table, as though he did not want her to see it.

She settled down in one of the two armchairs that faced the window, the view a panoramic vista of Hanley rising up towards the ridge, the high-rise flats crenellating the skyline like medieval castle walls.

'Confide in me, David,' she urged. There was a moment's silence. Then his eyes met hers but he shook his head, frowning.

'How can I inflict it on you?'

'It's my job, David,' she said gently. 'I can't treat you properly unless you confide in me. I need you to trust me.'

She waited, giving him the chance to consider the options. She saw his face calm as he came to a decision. 'Have you the time, Claire?'

'Of course.' She knew if she let him down now he would never confide in her – and his next attempt at suicide might well be successful.

He leaned forward, touched her hand, smiled and said, half mockingly. 'Ready for my life story?'

She smiled back and nodded.

'Well then,' he said. 'I was born in Aachen.' He gave a little smile. 'A spa town, the westernmost town in Germany, with borders to Belgium and the Netherlands. My father was a baker in the town.' Another little smile. 'Not really just a baker, Claire. *The* baker. He was very successful. His bread and cakes were renowned. He made the best.'

His eyes clouded. 'As you know I was born in 1930. And we were Jewish. With '38 came Kristallnacht. We should have left then, but like many Jewish families we did not believe it would get any worse. We thought there might be a bit of bullying, that we Jews would be singled out for adverse treatment.' He raised sad eyes. 'Nothing more. We could not believe that our German friends and neighbours would turn against us. But they did, and those that did not, in their hearts, had to bury their friendship deep and pretend they hated, despised us. Or else face death.' Another sad smile. 'A friend of a Jew was treated as though they were Jewish by blood.'

Claire was sitting perfectly still, not wanting to break the spell.

'By 1939, war was declared, and we were quickly herded up and made to wear the Star of David. I remember my mother stitching them on and telling myself and my sister that we should be proud to wear this emblem, that it was a sign of our ancient race.' He smiled at her again, this time the memory of his mother tingeing his face with some happiness.

'My surname,' he said, 'Gad. One of the twelve tribes of Israel.' He laughed, enjoying telling the story of happier times. 'I'm afraid one of my forefathers was partly responsible for the sale of Joseph into slavery.' His face softened. 'But he was forgiven . . .' A toss of the head. 'And it was a long time ago. Anyway . . .' He waved the distant past away as though it was an unwelcome intruder. 'In 1940 we were taken to Buchenwald where my father continued his bakery business, but not for the townsfolk of Aachen any more. He cooked for the camp guards. Hmm.' He gave a cynical laugh. 'They didn't mind a Jew *cooking* for them.

'My sister and mother were taken away. I never saw them again . . .' He paused, this memory frozen into his mind. 'I

was spared, but only because my father begged that I would
be allowed to help him in the bakery.'

He looked at her, anguish in his eyes. 'In 1944 one day I
was helping my father and I allowed the oven to get too hot.
The bread burnt. The guards came in and accused my father
of having burnt the bread deliberately . . .' An expression of
disgust twisted his face. 'They accused him of trying to sabo-
tage the Third Reich. My father said it was his fault that the
bread was burnt. He wanted to protect me. They took him
outside and shot him.' His eyes clouded. 'It was a bright day.
The sun hot in a blue sky. My father's shadow fell across the
floor of the bakery. I saw his hands up. I heard his words. "I
apologize for burning your bread." I saw him crumple when
they shot him. I saw his shadow shrink to that of a dead man
lying in a pool of blood. *Blut*,' he said, his eyes haunted and
damaged. 'Claire, that shadow that fell across me is still here.
Touching me. Here . . .' He tapped his left shoulder. 'Here. It
has never left me, my father's shadow. As I get older it engulfs
me.' He was silent for a moment, his hand still resting on his
shoulder. Then he looked up. 'They left his body lying there,
on the floor, in the mud and sand. They told us all not to touch
his body but to leave it there.' He paused. 'Claire, do you
know anything about the way Jews treat their dead?'

'A little,' she said. 'Enough.'

'So you know that we Jews bury bodies quickly, only
touched by another Jew's hand. To see him lying there made
it so much worse. When they had murdered my father they
came back into the bakery and, laughing, slapped me on the
back. Some of them still had my father's blood on their clothes.
They told me that was what happened to a careless baker who
tried to poison the German people with burnt bread. I could
not breathe for terror. I wanted to tell them it had not been
my father who had burnt the bread but I. They would have
shot me too. And I was frightened. They were noisy – pleased,
no doubt, with what they had done, and they said that I was
chief baker now. They clapped their hands on my shoulder;
put a cap on my head and an apron around my waist. Claire,'
he said, 'it reached to the floor. They told me to be careful
not to burn the bread like my father. They left my father's

body to rot outside until the dogs took him. Have you any idea, Claire, what that means to a Jew?'

She couldn't find the words.

He leaned forward. 'Claire, do you understand now why I do not want to live this guilty life any longer. I close my eyes and I see my father. His shadow falls over me but he is not even reproachful. No one has ever been charged with that crime.' His eyes were closed now and she had a glimpse of the burden he had carried for more than sixty years.

She was silent for a minute. She knew full well that it was pointless reminding him that he had a family, a daughter, grandchildren: people who loved him. He already knew that, but she must find a way to break through this or he would, at some point, one day in the not-too-distant future, succeed in his attempts to obliterate the past. She could see now why his suicide attempts had been repeated and increasingly determined. She was silent for a while.

Then spoke. 'David,' she said, 'will you give me some time to think about this?'

His mouth was cynical. 'You think you can help? You . . .?' His voice faded. And then, 'I will give you the time until you, inevitably, send me home.' Then he leaned forward and patted her hand. 'You are a good doctor, Claire. But don't set yourself problems you are not able to solve.'

She was so deep in thought as she drove home that evening that the journey seemed short. It was only as she inserted her key into her front door that she realized: the roadworks on the A500 were not there, so the traffic had flowed like clockwork cars in a miniature town. The advice he had given her – *Don't set yourself problems you are not able to solve* – rang like a bell, resonating inside her head. David Gad was an intelligent man. How could she possibly solve his dreadful guilt? What hope did she have?

But, once inside, the front door closing behind her, the emptiness of the house hit her like a hammer blow spreading apathy and inactivity. David Gad had a grandson he was close to. At least he had someone. Whom did she have? Adam, her half-brother, and Grant. She needed to speak to him, without rancour or blame. She needed an explanation of why he had gone. Her girlfriend's comment that men 'didn't do explanations' was not enough for her. It still left her with a black hole, quite apart from the practical considerations – a half-finished house. Only his sitting down and talking rationally to her would help her find some sort of settlement. But without seeing him, how would she ever hope to achieve this? Sadly, mentally she ticked another day off.

Didn't phone Grant!

But it didn't make her feel triumphant. Just sad and confused and lonely. And vulnerable. She walked to the window which overlooked her drive and the street. Was Barclay out there, somewhere, watching her? Cars moved past, a few pedestrians chatting, speaking into mobile phones. Everyone walking, going somewhere. But one person was standing at her gatepost. She tried to tell herself that it was a kerb crawler. Nothing to do with her, but underneath her fear was that it was him. Barclay, watching and waiting for an opportunity.

Heidi Faro, her predecessor, had once told her always to face your fears and then you watch them shrink.

Not tonight, she thought, and drew the curtains tight shut.

She made herself a cup of tea and sank into the armchair, tucking her feet beneath her. She looked up and saw the wedding invitation propped on the mantelpiece and remembered the idea she had had. 'Face your fears,' she recalled. Then decided. She would do it. Soon.

SEVEN

Friday, 12 September, 8.30 a.m.

The next day she was inspired and went straight up to his room.

She took his hand, met his eyes. 'David,' she said, and almost flinched at his dead eyes. 'Your father knew the burnt bread was your fault, didn't he?'

He nodded, head down.

'He probably knew he would be shot.'

Again that hanging of the head. Shame.

She pressed on. 'He died so that you could live – not die yourself. He wanted you to live through the war, bear testimony, marry, have children. Maybe he even hoped for a grandson like . . .?'

'Ephraim,' he supplied. 'The same name as my father's.'

She nodded. 'David,' she said, 'if you kill yourself now, you betray your father's belief in you. If you die nearly seventy years later, Hitler and the Nazi Party will have finally won.'

He didn't respond straight away but stared out of the window, ingesting her words. And then, without turning back to her, he spoke. 'You're a very clever girl,' he said; then, turning to face her, she saw a flicker in his eyes. 'Sure you're not Jewish?'

'Not to my knowledge.'

'You have planted good seeds in my head. But Claire . . .' There was something else in his eyes now; something which made him ache and her afraid. 'They are still out there.'

Her mouth felt dry. She couldn't ask the question: Who? Because he opened the card which had lain on the table by their side. And she saw the swastika, the black spider, and knew someone had sent this. David Gad was watching her read the words.

We are still here.

It was so clever, so cruel, so malicious. Was she seeing him behind every bush, every tree? It could not possibly be Jerome Barclay. It must be someone else.

David Gad's face was grave. Then he managed a smile. 'And now . . .' He met her eyes without fear or any sign of intimidation. 'Now I must think. Now I must plan.'

She put a hand on his shoulder. 'Families are important, David,' she said. 'They are our balm.' She paused. 'You have survived. Your father wanted you to carry on the line. Ephraim is a fine boy,' she said, and again she saw that smile, stiff and rusty through lack of use, but unmistakably warm.

'Yes,' he said. 'He is.'

She left him then to his thoughts, but carried the phrase with her as she left the room. *Families are important.*

As she walked down the corridor, she caught a glimpse of bright September sunshine. For once she actually felt she'd achieved something in her day's work. She believed she'd found the key to unlock David's death wish. The question was, did she now dare to discharge him?

Or would his next attempt be his last?

She did not have time to ponder the point. Recalling Siona's words, she made Hayley Price her next priority.

She hadn't liked the girl from the start. A sly little thing, she'd thought. Sly and deceitful, mistrusting the vapid blue eyes, the hair – goodness knew what colour it really was, straggly bleached and dyed purple with bits of blue – and the numerous amateur tattoos and body piercings. Her history was poor. She had been born the daughter of a heroin addict. Father baldly stated as 'unknown'. She had been fostered from two days old but, even as an infant, had rarely fitted in. Subsequently Hayley had been passed from pillar to post, ending up in a small children's home in Hanley.

The Rookery had fewer than twenty inmates at any one time and the children there were entertained and well cared for. But young Hayley had the blood of a tearaway and by the age of eleven she had found drugs of her own. The trouble was that in many ways there is no such thing as 'recreational' drugs. Claire disliked the phrase. It sanitized them, made them sound fun. Harmless when they are no such thing. The truth is they interfere with the mind. And so Hayley had turned from a truculent, difficult teenager into a disturbed and troubled young woman with a complete lack of self-esteem and an abnormal attitude to food. She sometimes claimed she had conquered appetite. That she didn't need food. But it wasn't the anorexics' desire to look slimmer. There was no vanity there. She had simply lost the desire to eat. Trying to get her to even manage an intake of 1,000 calories a day – what most of us would consider a slimming diet – was like trying to coax a toddler to eat his meat or his greens. The food would go round and round in her mouth and Hayley would try everything she could to spit it out surreptitiously. She would tuck it in her cheek for minutes and at the first opportunity it would be in a flowerpot or out of the window or deposited under the sheet

if she was in bed or behind a cushion if she was in a chair.
She would do everything she could to avoid swallowing
because then she would have to vomit it up which was a) a
bit more difficult and b) a bit more uncomfortable.

This was how she dealt with every single morsel of food.

She had no family and no one to care for her apart from
her social workers. Her only known relative, her heroin-addict
mother, had gone the way of her kind – dying from an inhala-
tion of vomit before reaching her thirtieth birthday.

Frustratingly, Claire knew perfectly well that Hayley was not
stupid. In fact she had above-average intelligence. She could
easily have managed a university degree, perhaps in the Arts.
In spite of the dreadful hair, she had a knack for colour and – in
some of the art classes run by the Occupational Therapy Centre
– had produced some excellent drawings. But who was going
to encourage, support and finance Hayley through this? Also,
with the terrible L-O-V-E/H-A-T-E tattoos, various ex-boyfriends'
names which had been blurred in a vain attempt to scrub them
out, the scarring and piercings of nose, upper lip, eyebrows,
who was going to give her a job? She was hardly going to be
the front desk girl for some major company or organization.

Her background screamed at you.

So what was her future – if she survived? Right now she
was teetering on the edge. Her liver, heart, lungs and kidneys
were all struggling without nutrition. At fourteen years old
she had the porous osteoporotic bones of an unhealthy seventy
year old. Her exercise tolerance was nil.

And so, as she approached the girl's room, Claire felt frustrated. She could go so far and no farther. She was not a wizard.

Hayley gave her 'a look' as she entered. Claire could see
that, contrary to Siona's overoptimistic statement, the girl had
actually lost even more weight, and soon they would have to
make decisions. They disliked tube-feeding their patients. It
might bypass the immediate problem but did nothing to deal
with the underlying issues. The trouble was that Hayley was
not going to share those underlying issues. It was possible she
wasn't really aware of them herself. Hayley might not lack
intelligence but she did lack insight.

And there was something in the girl's eyes, as though she

had read what was in Claire's mind as she had walked towards her down the corridor. It was as though she had seen the hopelessness of her future.

She knew that Claire had nothing to offer her. No happy pills. No great future. No stable happy relationships. The only tiny silver lining Claire could even conjure up was that at least Hayley didn't have a series of manipulative, unsuitable relationships behind her. There was no 'boyfriend' pimping her around. And also, surprisingly, Hayley had been clean for months. She didn't 'do' drugs any more. Probably because most of them had to be ingested. She might be clean but it wasn't much of a silver lining.

Claire sat on the edge of Hayley's bed. The girl was looking pinched and tired. Both she and Claire knew that she was heading towards readmission to a general hospital, tube and i/v feeding. It was that or death. It wasn't a great choice for a fourteen year old.

She met the girl's eyes. 'How are you?' she asked shortly. It was formulaic. She'd never once known Hayley admit the truth.

She was in for a surprise. Hayley looked straight back at her. 'Not good,' she said.

Claire's ears pricked up. She tried not to show she was startled by the response.

The girl put a weary hand up. 'Don't tell me to bloody eat. My friend tells me I do not need to.'

Claire tucked the phrase away for future discussion. Who was this friend who was trying to kill her? But she had the feeling Hayley would not tell her – either because she did not want to or because there was no friend. The friend was herself. She had no other.

For the time being she focused on questions she thought Hayley would answer. She gave the girl a chummy smile. 'So how did you fool Siona that you'd gained weight?'

'Drank a load of water,' Hayley replied, smiling like a mischievous elf.

Hayley had been Claire's patient off and on for almost three years – ever since she had been a stubborn eleven year old. Claire had watched as the tattoos had bloomed and the piercings multiplied. She had watched the stubborn child morph into an adult who always felt like she was going nowhere. But she had never mentioned this 'friend' before and no one ever visited her. So was Hayley becoming psychotic? Hearing voices which forbade her to eat? If so, it was a worrying progression.

'OK,' Claire responded steadily, 'I won't tell you to bloody eat if you'll tell me who this friend is.'

As expected, Hayley simply pressed her lips together. Claire would have to be a little more subtle. 'Did the friend say why?'

Alerted, Hayley started then frowned. She started on the *You're the psychiatrist* line but stopped herself.

'I suppose,' she said quietly, 'it's because I have a death wish.'

'OK, well that's a start,' Claire said. Then, 'Why? And what can I do to replace it with a life wish?'

Hayley managed a watery weak smile. 'Maybe it isn't up to you,' she said.

The words were unspoken but hovered between them.

Then who is it up to, Hayley?

She was not going to get an answer, although the obvious answer was: *Me.*

It struck Claire then that Hayley's teeth were bright white, regular and even. The girl had never worn a brace as far as she knew. Ergo she must have been born and blessed with good dentition, because constant vomiting with the reflux of gastric acid usually played havoc with the teeth. That and the two fingers down the throat which pushed them out. And Hayley would not have had access to an orthodontist.

It was something on the girl's side but not enough.

'You're good at art,' she said.

Hayley's lips drew back. 'Oh per-lease,' she said. 'And where's that going to get me?'

Claire bowed her head. Hayley was right. Not very far.

'Is there anything you'd *like* to do?'

'Yeah. Like be a supermodel.'

It could be so hard to connect with these girls.

But – was this a clue? Was body image behind this destructive behaviour? It was worth pursuing. 'So is that why . . .?'

Hayley shut this one down. 'Not really.'

It struck Claire then that her patient was too weary to fight, argue or even talk.

The friend was winning. What she prayed was that the friend was something in Hayley's imagination. Not a physical presence. Please – not Jerome.

She drew in a long deep breath. Something had to be done but the girl shook her head. 'Don't send me to hospital. Please, Claire, don't send me in.'

Claire hesitated. If she didn't admit Hayley, there was every likelihood the child would die. The girl was not mad. She had – the magic word – capacity. She could make rational decisions.

Claire waited and Hayley chipped in again. 'You can't give me a life,' she said. 'You can't give me a future.'

'And can your friend?'

Hayley closed her eyes wearily. 'At least he stops me struggling.'

Claire moved her hands apart in an encompassing movement. 'But Hayley, you're young. You deserve a future. Boyfriends. College. Fun. Socializing,' she appealed.

Hayley simply shook her head. 'Not for me.'

Claire left her room feeling depressed. Her biggest fear was that Jerome Barclay was poisoning this vulnerable girl's mind. Don't be silly, Claire, she said to herself. Stop seeing him everywhere. How would he gain access to Hayley? How would he inveigle himself and pretend to be her friend? Does Barclay have magical powers?

But her self-lecture failed to cheer her up. Ahead lay case conferences, decisions. But in the end Hayley Price was right.

A future? Maybe not for her. Hayley never would have anything.

And so days passed.

EIGHT

Wednesday, 17 September, 2 p.m.

The day was taken up with overbooked clinics and an extended ward round which, as always, took twice as long as it should have done. She was currently teaching a group of fourth-year medical students from The Royal Stoke

University Hospital, trying to encourage them to understand
the blurred variations and presentations of mental illness. They
were keen and attentive and asked lots of questions, hence the
extra time taken, but scanning their bright eyes and eager
attitude, she felt it was justified. Time well spent. An invest-
ment into their future patients. They always cheered her, these
embryonic doctors.

Leaving the hospital that night she felt happy and fulfilled.

It was past seven when she arrived home. The telephone
was ringing even as she put her key in the door. Leaving the
front door wide open she picked it up. Hopeful. Perhaps it
was Grant – ready to talk at last.

It wasn't. She recognized Jerome's voice at once. He'd
waited a few days before ringing again.

'Claire,' he said in a voice soft as suede, 'I wondered if you
wanted a room booking at the hotel after the wedding?'

He couldn't leave her alone, could he? She was his professional audience. She recalled one of Heidi Faro's lectures she
had attended eons ago. '*The strange thing*,' she had said,
shaking her shining hair self-consciously, '*about narcissistic
personality disorder is that however dangerous it might prove,
they always want an audience. They want applause. They can't
do without it. Even though it may put them at risk, they will
want you to applaud their cleverness. Interestingly this need
supersedes their instinct for self-protection. However, as they
believe they can outwit everyone, they don't really think they
will get found out. They think they're safe. Because they are
the clever ones.*'

Claire jerked the memory away, alerted to the fact that
Barclay was speaking. 'Double or a single?'

She gritted her teeth. 'I – we – shan't be staying.'

'Oh. That's a shame. But you are *still* coming to the wedding?'

'Yes.'

'Good. I shall look forward to meeting up with you again.'
There was a pause. 'I've missed our little chats since you
discharged me. It'll be fun to catch up.'

She couldn't respond to this, nor to his next words, which
were spoken so softly she wondered afterwards if she had
imagined them.

'*The hungry child,*' he said. '*The doomed homeless man. The haunted Jew, the dangerous butterfly and the stupid clever.*'

And before she could respond, he had put the phone down with a quiet chuckle.

Claire reached for pen and paper. She needed to write these down before she forgot them. The hungry child. Hayley? Hayley, who had a friend who told her she did not need to eat.

The haunted Jew. David Gad who was sent a card with a swastika on.

The stupid clever. Dexter. Stupid. Was he really also clever? Her patients.

Then she wrote down two other phrases which described others of her patients. The doomed homeless man. Stan Moudel?

The expensive butterfly. Could that possibly describe Maylene Forsyte, a patient with a histrionic personality disorder whose behaviour was destroying her husband, Derek? Was Barclay orchestrating more of her patients' lives? If so, she feared for their prognoses. Her throat felt tight with apprehension.

She sank down on to the bottom step of the stairs as she tried to think this through, rationally. How did he know these patients and their diagnoses? How did he know her private telephone number? How did he know where she lived? How did he know she was now living alone? He didn't have supernatural powers. He didn't. The only solution she came up with was a member of staff.

But, more sinisterly, what was behind it? Why was he spying on her? What was he planning with this elaborate scenario he was building up? What was in his rotten mind?

She was too disturbed to stay in, alone, and it was only half past seven. She couldn't face a long, troubled evening. She needed to escape. She had membership of a local gym, though she hated the place, and while Grant had been at home she had rarely attended. She'd almost cancelled her membership but in the end had never got around to it.

Perhaps that was a good thing. It was an option. And a better option than sitting here alone, ruminating, worrying and wondering. Barclay was not supernatural. So how did he know these details about her current caseload?

She packed her bag, trainers, swimsuit and headed off.

NINE

She hadn't meant to go in to Greatbach over the weekend. Her instinct was to avoid the place. It was her weekend off. She was heading down to Birmingham later to visit a friend and then they planned to see a ballet at the theatre but, as she locked up the house, she realized she would be far too early. She passed the unit anyway, she reasoned. She would just pop in to see if there were any problems.

The unit was ominously quiet as she crossed the empty quadrangle, the shadows long, bending towards autumn then winter. In winter the sun hardly reached the area at all. It couldn't peep over the high walls so remained outside, leaving the quadrangle damp and chilly until spring lifted its rays again. Being the weekend, the numbers of inpatients were depleted. Many of them would be home on weekend leave, and consequently quite a few staff were also able to have their weekends off. The kitchens and cleaners were down to skeleton staff too, so at weekends Greatbach could feel underpopulated, like Stoke during Potters' Fortnight.

She approached the ward cautiously, aware of an eerie silence wafting along the empty corridors like a chilly vapour. Sometimes, at quiet times like this, she fancied she could hear the whispers of patients long since gone, the ones she had read about in the records. She heard their shrieks and sobs and hopeless screams, felt their desperation to get out, to escape. The corridors windows were high, giving only a view of the tops of the trees, and through them the sky, which was full of tumbling grey rain clouds that threatened to dump a good soaking later on. The car park was almost empty, quite unlike a weekday when it could be hard to find a parking space. The old days of protected parking spaces for consultants and senior staff were long gone. As she parked she saw in her rear-view mirror a black Volvo estate pull up behind her, driver concealed behind glinting glass. She didn't recognize the car. Maybe a visitor, she thought as she locked her doors and made her way towards the entry, glancing back only once. Maybe not a visitor. The driver remained inside, still hidden.

She visited each of the wards, peeped in through the windows. Hayley was sleeping. If she had had somewhere to go she would have been allowed out for the weekend, but there was nowhere. David Gad, in his chair, was deep in thought. Her patients were healing – or damaging themselves. She tiptoed away. The nurses had no crises to report. Her inpatients, at least, were supervised and behaving themselves. Her weekend went well, her girlfriend understanding but not probing, and after a brief description of Grant's desertion, they enjoyed themselves, eating in Rusty Lee's famous Caribbean restaurant before going to see *Giselle*. Appropriate weekend entertainment for a psychiatrist.

TEN

Monday, 22 September, 8.30 a.m.

On Monday she was summoned to the police cells, where one of her patients had been charged with affray and illegal possession of Class B drugs 'with intent to supply'. Not if she knew Stan. Stan was another of her patients who was admitted and discharged in a regular cycle. But as she drove to the station to assess him, she recalled Barclay's phrase: *The doomed homeless man*. It described Stan Moudel to a T.

Cold water trickled down her spine. She had comforted herself with the assurance that Barclay was not supernatural, but this was unnerving her. Could he possibly see into the future? Was he clairvoyant? Stan hadn't even been on the radar when Barclay had delivered his list. Common sense told her no. It was not possible. And yet, when she received the call that Stan was in custody, she felt a sense of inevitability. Knowing that Barclay had forecast Stan's crisis, she felt she too was acting in an orchestrated, pre-ordained act. Barclay was not pulling her strings, she told herself. He was not. And it was possible that his description had not foreseen this crisis and Stan had been referred to because he was part of her caseload. This was what she wanted to believe.

The police knew her well and briefed her with a certain amount of familiarity as they led her to the cell where she would make her diagnosis within seconds. Stan Moudel was suffering from acute paranoia following an ill-advised mixture of meow-meow, skunk and alcohol. He was cowering in the corner when she approached him, his hands batting away at something or someone invisible. Then he jerked his head around and started up a conversation with someone else, also invisible.

'Yeah, man,' he was saying when she entered the room. 'I'm good. I'm good. Yeah. How are you doin'?' The rapid gunfire conversation was accompanied by a series of jerks.

His eyes widened when Claire's presence finally registered. They had met before on a few occasions.

'How are you, Stan?'

'Not good, doc,' he said. 'Not good at all.' His eyes were still skittering around the cell, his face creased with fright. Who called these poisons 'recreational'?

She moved closer. 'What's up?'

'With me?' He jabbed at his chest then looked a bit caught out. 'Oh.' His gaze moved past her to the policeman standing in the doorway. 'Maybe. I guess I'm OK. Good.' He had all the signs of paranoia, the eyes darting at nothing and no one, staccato speech, inappropriate smiling, sudden grins, hiccupping.

She rested a hand on his shoulder. Stan had once had a life. A wife, a job, a daughter, a home. That had been when he was twenty-eight years old. Only four years ago.

And then he had been picked up on a drink-drive offence and had lost his driving licence. And like many, after that, his life had slowly unravelled, like pulling yarn from a sweater until all that was left was a pile of useless, crinkly wool.

Stan's life.

It was like the old ditty: *For want of a nail . . .*

For want of his licence his job was lost.

For want of a job his wife was lost.

For want of a wife his daughter was lost.

And, the final want: he had been kicked out of his house, making him homeless. The downward spiral had continued. Stan had found solace with drugs and ended up at Greatbach more than once.

Stan was not a bad man. Unlucky, yes. Weak, yes. He had an addictive personality. Hence the alcohol and drugs. And yet, to Claire, he had never been anything other than pleasant and polite.

They had tried many things to help Stan – finding him a half-decent bedsit, trying to find work, even a vain attempt at putting him back in touch with his now ex-wife and daughter. Which had failed. But he had always reverted. Back to the drink. Back to the drugs. Same old.

She smiled at him, recognizing the symptoms. He was coming down now, returning to reality. 'How do you fancy a little holiday at Greatbach, Stan?'

His grin was pathetic. At some point he had had an incisor knocked out in a fight he couldn't even remember. That and his nicotine-stained teeth – together with a poor state of hygiene and a dreadful state of nutrition, along with his generally dishevelled appearance – made him look much older than thirty-two. She felt more than a touch of sympathy for him.

Life could have been so very different.

'Holiday?' He hiccupped. 'Sounds a good idea to me, doc.'

She asked the police to arrange transport while she had a room prepared.

She drove back to the hospital, thinking about Stan, wondering where he had got the money from for such a lethal cocktail of poisons. There was one possibility she didn't even want to consider. And it led her straight back to Jerome Barclay's prophecy. There was one way he could have known Stan would soon be readmitted, but she didn't even want to consider it. Not now. Not yet. Not without further evidence. She could not descend into paranoia too and join Stan in this world where she saw demons – or rather, a demon – behind every tree. She smiled at herself. That would never do – a psychiatrist with her own psychotic diagnosis?

But even thinking about him had brought her to the realization that the wedding was fast approaching. She did not want to go alone. As soon as she reached her office she knew she could put it off no longer.

She picked up the phone.

ELEVEN

Luckily he picked up on the first ring. Or she might have bottled out. It had been a long time since they had spoken. She could hear the surprise in his voice. 'Hello there, sis. How're you doing?'

'I'm fine, Adam,' she said, more heartily than she felt. 'And you?'

'Yeah. Good too.' She could hear the question. *What is she calling* me *for?*

So she might as well get straight to the point.

'Adam, I wondered if you'd do me a favour?'

He was instantly wary. 'If I can, sis,' he said, caution slowing his voice.

Claire bit her lip. Had he, even as a small child, been aware of her jealous hatred for him?

'Go on then,' he prompted. 'What is it?'

'I wondered if you'd come to a wedding with me?'

Now he was curious. 'What about Grant?'

This was a humiliating admission. 'Grant walked out on me six months ago.'

Adam's response was predictably blunt. 'Why?'

'I don't know.'

'Well – shit – sis – didn't you ask him?'

She was stung. 'Of course I did.'

'Well, what did he say?'

'That it was time for him to move on. That life was too complicated.'

Nothing that explained his actions.

'We-ell.' For once even her younger half-brother seemed at a loss for words. Then his conscience kicked in. 'I'm sorry,' he said. 'I'd have kept a bit more in touch if I'd known you were on your own. I just thought that everything was – well – hunky-dory, you know?'

'Unfortunately not.'

'I thought you guys,' he said awkwardly, 'I thought you guys would be together for ever, you know.'

'Me too.'

His next words were spoken heartily. 'So when's this wedding?'

She told him and gave him a potted background, that Barclay was a devious psycho patient of hers, who now appeared to have acquired supernatural powers, knowing facts about some of her patients even before they had happened; that three of his family members had suffered strange and untimely deaths, and that she had concerns over this marriage and the safety of his bride-to-be and in-laws.

'Wow. He sounds . . .'

'I know.'

'So why are you going, sis?' He made an attempt at levity. 'It's not part of the job, is it?'

'No. No. In a way I'm going – to keep an eye out. To find out what he's up to. I need to know how he knows about my other patients. It suggests a breach of confidentiality. A leak . . .' She paused. 'Somewhere.'

'Someone on your staff?'

'I don't know, but he's a nasty piece of work, Adam, who hides it well, and I want to stop him committing any more crimes.'

'How exciting. Tell me what I should look out for. Is he likely to flip during the service? Start wielding an axe or something?'

'I very much doubt it,' she said, smiling. 'Mr Barclay is much more subtle than that, but that makes him dangerous. If he wielded an axe . . .' She couldn't help smiling even more broadly at the thought of Jerome Barclay 'flipping', to use her half-brother's words. 'If he wielded an axe we'd have him banged up for life, maybe even reinvestigate the suspicious deaths of his family members and get his ex-girlfriend to admit he did try to kill her. Oh no. Mr Barclay is someone who keeps himself well under control. I've never known him lose his rag.'

'Hmm.' Then cheerfully and with a tinge of optimism, 'Always a first time, sis.'

'Not with him. You can stay here the night before, if you like, Adam, so we can go together.' She couldn't stop herself from adding, with a note of bitterness. 'There's plenty of spare rooms. Ad,' she said tentatively, 'will you do me another favour?'

This time he was more sure, more jaunty. 'Two? In one morning? And on a Monday? You're pushing your luck, aren't you?' He was laughing. She could picture him. A tumble of coppery hair, thick glasses, a slightly hesitant air. Pale skin – as far removed from her swarthy features as was possible. She laughed with him.

'Yeah. Go on then, but you already owe me dinner *and* a bottle of decent wine.' He gave a mock sigh and grumbled. 'It's one of the worst things of being a student – having to drink cheap wine.'

She smiled. This was Adam, her half-brother, who seemed to be making a career out of being a perpetual student. She resisted the temptation to point out that actually he didn't have to drink wine at all.

'Don't let on that you're my brother.'

'OK.' He couldn't resist pulling her leg. 'But I'm not going to snog you during the first dance – or propose.'

She felt a lot happier putting the phone down.

Now she only had to think up a suitable wedding present. She was even smiling as she dreamed up the scenario. What do you buy a psychopath for a wedding present? A set of knives, a chopping block, a cheese grater, an electric drill? Chainsaw?

In the end she settled for a John Lewis voucher. Let the psycho choose for himself.

TWELVE

In the meantime she had a hospital to run, patients to see, targets to meet and her own personal life to sort out.

She knew she would do a better job at Greatbach if she could settle something with Grant. The entire unsatisfactory situation snagged at her, night and day. But she couldn't ring him. She wouldn't ring him. Her pride wouldn't allow her to. In moments of weakness she'd texted him once or twice in the early days and he hadn't responded. But she did need to talk it over with someone. Who better than her very best friend, Julia Seddon?

Julia and she had been medical students together at Birmingham. She was now a GP in a very busy practice in Hanley. She had never married but lived with another woman, an artist named Gina Aldi.

Monday, 22 September, 7 p.m.

They met at a wine bar a few hundred yards down the road from her surgery, which had recently started serving tapas, which suited both of them. Since Grant had abandoned his role as chief chef, Claire was finding it easier to pick at food rather than sit down to a full-blown meal, so the tapas appetizers were welcome. Julia strode in, wearing tight jeans, ankle boots and a multicoloured Fair Isle sweater, sleeves pushed up to the elbows exposing tanned, muscular forearms. Julia was an outdoor girl. Claire was surprised she hadn't chosen veterinary medicine. She greeted Claire with a kiss on both cheeks and a hug before sitting down. Knowing her friend's taste, Claire shoved a glass of Rioja across the table towards her. 'It's good to see you.'

'And you.' They clinked glasses.

Claire felt reluctant to start talking about herself immediately, so opened the conversation by asking how Gina was.

Julia grinned. 'She's great,' she said. 'Absolutely great.' She leaned forward eagerly. 'She's branched out into pottery, making plates, ginger jars, stuff like that.' She stuck her cocktail stick into a cube of *manchego*, speared an olive and popped both into her mouth, chewing happily.

'She has such talent, you know,' she said, smiling with pride. 'I'm so happy with her.'

Claire nodded in agreement and Julia continued, her eyes shining.

'We've bought a house in Hanley,' she said. 'It's a neglected old place but has a lovely garden. How's your place coming along, by the way? Has Grant finally finished painting the Forth Bridge?'

Claire had kept the news of Grant's departure from her friends, thinking that, possibly, he would be back before they found out and it would spare her the explanations. But she was realizing that was not to be the case. Grant was not coming back. As succinctly as possible, she told Julia the sorry tale, and watched her eyes widen, puzzled, before she made a sound of exasperation. 'What is wrong with these guys?' she said. 'Had you had a row or something?'

'No. He just upped and left.'

Julia put her hand on her shoulder. 'Oh poor you,' she said. 'Here's me extolling my domestic ecstasy and there's you suffering. I'm so sorry.'

'It's OK,' Claire said awkwardly. 'Really. I can't say I'm over it but I'm learning to live.'

'What about the house?'

'Half done,' Claire said ruefully. 'I haven't decided what to do with it. And to be honest, unless Grant makes a move and tells me what he's intending doing, I can't sell, move on, or complete the job. We're both on the mortgage. I'm not even sure whether the area will stand the house being done up to the nines. It's going downhill. The *ladies of the night* have returned.'

'Oh well,' Julia shrugged. 'This is what happens. Areas go up and some go down but Burslem will always win through in the end. Aren't they redeveloping the town centre? Doing some arts project?'

They talked for a while, discussing various changes taking place in and around Burslem, mutual friends and planned events, and then Julia returned to the subject of Grant.

'I should wait and see,' she advised. 'He'll have to get in touch at some point.'

'At some point. But when, Julia? I can't wait for ever.'

'Well – he'll want some sort of settlement, won't he?'

'I would think so. *He* did all the work. Look,' she said, 'let's change the subject? I wanted to run something else past you?'

Julia smiled. 'Go on.'

'You remember a few years ago my having suspicions about a patient of mine.'

'I do,' Julia said, frowning, 'but if I remember rightly you were wrong.'

'I was, but I wasn't wrong about his diagnosis, and Heidi thought the same.'

'Hmm,' Julia said dubiously. 'So?'

'He's getting married.'

'Yes. And?'

'First of all, he seems to know a little too much about my professional and personal life. Even about my patients.'

Julia's eyebrows lifted. 'And second?'

'He's invited me to the wedding. Don't you think that's a little unusual?'

'Not sure. Are you going to go?'

'Yeah. I'm taking Adam.'

'Adam?' It sounded an expletive.

'Yep. I'm building bridges.'

'Well good for you,' Julia said. 'I'll be interested to hear how you get on both with Adam and your psycho patient. Let me know, won't you?'

'Yeah. Of course. But . . . why do you think he's asked me?'

Julia laughed out loud and hid behind the usual. 'Don't ask me,' she said. 'You're the psychiatrist.'

Claire laughed too. 'This is when I wish I'd chosen a different career path,' she said. 'No one will ever give me an opinion.' She paused and then told her friend the contents of his telephone call. 'How can he know these things? Stan Moudel, the homeless guy, hadn't even been readmitted. And as for the expensive butterfly . . .' She thought for a minute. 'I'm not absolutely certain who he means.' She frowned. 'I'm assuming it's a patient called Maylene Forsyte. But why would he choose her?'

Julia looked worried. 'I don't know. Is she in – danger?'

'Not that I know. Maybe. Aren't they all?'

'Does he know anyone close to you?'

'Not that I know of.'

'Is he likely to harm you?'

'That's the trouble. I don't know.' She tried to lighten their mood. 'Not during his wedding. That really would be a first.'

They both laughed uncertainly at that, but Julia reached out a hand. 'Be careful,' she said, and Claire nodded. 'I will.'

They chatted until ten. Claire offered to drop her friend off but Julia declined. 'It's a nice night,' she said. 'I'll walk.'

It was only a short journey home but Claire was thoughtful. She felt very alone. Discussing her domestic problem with Julia had clarified the situation. She did need to speak to Grant – not pleading with him to get in touch, to explain himself, to come home. Nothing heavy – just a business call. She needed to know what his plans were and whether he was willing for her to put the house on the market. Unfinished?

No. The decorating must be done.

She turned into her drive and stopped. A car had pulled up right behind her, its headlights on full beam. For a moment she was both dazzled and alarmed. She climbed out of her car, shielding her eyes from the light, trying to see who was driving. For one heart-stopping moment she had wondered whether it could possibly be Grant, stopped by – at last. But he drove a battered Peugeot and this was a black Volvo gleaming under the lamplight. There was no sound coming from the interior but she could just make out the fact there was no passenger, only the male driver. She could see his silhouette. She waited, convinced that this was not someone who had pulled up by chance, just to use a mobile phone, make a call or send a text, or even waiting his chance to make contact with one of the Professional Ladies who sometimes hung around this area, but someone who wanted to make contact with her personally. She took a step towards the vehicle and heard it slip into gear and rev up the road. It was only as she inserted her key into the front door that she started to think. That had been deliberate, someone targeting her. And the only person she could think of who was likely to do that was Barclay.

She closed the door, deadlocked it and shot the bolt across before doing the same with the back door and the French windows. Even then she didn't feel quite secure. He was watching her.

THIRTEEN

She should have learned one of the cardinal lessons of psychiatry by now. She'd been a consultant for five years. Take your eye off the ball and mayhem results. While you are looking the other way the game continues. It's just that you are no longer an active participant.

David Gad, *the haunted Jew*, was still an inpatient currently having CBT, and this time he was responding well, apparently. But he was a man who kept his feelings buried deep, and since his confession to her he had said little more about his damaged past. When she had been in his room she had looked out for any more cards. She hadn't asked him because she didn't want to bring up the subject. But as far as she had seen there were none.

Hayley, *the hungry child*, continued to tease: eating one day, vomiting the next. They were monitoring her blood levels. If her potassium dropped below a certain level she would be transferred to the Royal Stoke University Hospital. It had had its name changed from the North Staffordshire University Hospital to distance itself from the ill-fated Mid Staffs. Hospital. But it was as though Hayley had an almost supernatural instinct for the cut-off point. When she was almost there she would eat – soup or half a piece of bread. Just enough to keep her with them, at Greatbach. She wore an air of defiance always, and Claire knew the phrase 'you do not need to eat' had had its effect. One day she would ask her which particular friend had fed her this mantra. She could guess.

But these days it was Stan, *the doomed homeless man*, who was the main worry. He was not responding to treatment as quickly as they had hoped. If anything he seemed a little worse. Claire watched him with concern. His mental state had improved but his blood levels were abnormal. He was losing weight in spite of eating and he seemed very tired, finding getting out of bed, washing, eating, even staying awake an effort. She watched him and worried. She asked him who had given him the drugs. His eyelids had drooped. 'Nice guy,' he said. 'Nice guy.'

'Did you have to pay him?'

Stan shook his head. 'No, man. Benefactor.'

'What did he look like?' She already knew the answer.

'Ordinary.'

That was just how she would describe him.

'Smelt like cake, you know?' Stan gave a toothy smile.

'How did you meet him?'

'Came up to me in the street – you know. Nice guy. Offered me some.' His voice trailed off. He was almost asleep.

More and more she found herself using Barclay's descriptions of her patients. They were astute. And that was bad, not only because it meant he had access, somehow, to their case notes, but also because this knowledge was influencing her judgement. Dexter Harding, *the stupid clever*, continued to turn up for his fortnightly appointments, and the consultations were of as little use as they had ever been. There was no progression, nor would there ever be. The fortnightly meetings were simply a loose check on his whereabouts.

Jerome Barclay – no description of himself, she noted – was keeping a low profile before his nuptials. Which suited her. Had it not been for the invitation card on her mantelpiece and the John Lewis debit on her card, she might almost have thought the wedding was simply the result of a nasty nightmare.

To be fair she had had her distractions. While Grant was still in her mind he was not as vivid as he had been. His memory was fading, or least less brightly coloured. Less real. It was as though he was floating downstream, away from her, sometimes snagging on a branch, staying there for a moment, smiling back at her, water lapping over him, before floating farther and farther away. She no longer woke missing his muscular body next to her in bed, or reached out to touch his chest in the middle of the night; neither did she wait for his key in the door or miss the scent of a house being renovated or the aroma of cooking, the spicy scent of his deodorant. The place seemed curiously sterile. Without photographs to remind her (all in a drawer), his features were blurring, and she had to think hard to remember what his voice had really sounded like, while the house waited, stagnant, for the next chapter in its existence.

She wasn't ready to meet anyone else romantically just yet, but she was learning a sort of contentment on her own. Maybe one day, she thought, I will find someone to replace him. And next time they will stay.

But there was the giant practical problem she had touched on with Julia. Though she had been the one to pay the mortgage, he had been the one who had done the lion's share of the renovation work – plumbing, some building work, electrics and so on. He had also done all the decorating. Both their names were on the deeds, and so if she sold she would have to get in touch with him, even if it was simply for a signature. But she had no address. She didn't have a clue where he was. His passport was gone, along with all his other possessions, clothes, CDs, et cetera, but she didn't know whether it was an accidental inclusion and had simply found its way in amongst his clothes, or if he had deliberately taken it. But it meant she didn't even know whether he was in the country. She'd never met his family, who lived somewhere in Cornwall, and they had few mutual friends. No one who would know where he was.

And then, without warning, she saw him.

Saturday, 27 September, 3 p.m.

It was a busy Saturday, the last one in September, and the cold had seemed to be creeping up the road, forewarning her that winter was in its wake. She had spent the morning clearing out her wardrobe, trying on clothes from the previous winter and deciding which could be carried on to this season. Some of the items, like her winter coat, were a little tired and would need replacing. It was a twice-yearly ritual with her; one she rather enjoyed: spring and autumn clothes selection. Top of the list of wants was a pair of high-heeled black leather boots. And so she had set out at lunchtime to the Potteries Shopping Centre in Hanley. There were plenty of shoe shops there and they had all their new stock in. She tried on a couple of pairs with wedge heels. Comfortable, but they made her legs look clumpy. However, she wouldn't be able to wear the ones with high thin heels every day or for long. And they would be too hot to wear around the unit. Now the ones with high thicker heels were the obvious choice. And two pairs fitted the bill admirably, but she couldn't make up her mind and she definitely didn't want both.

So she went for a coffee to have a think. She was queuing up at Costa Coffee when something alerted her to a couple in the corner, heads together. Thick, curly, black pirate's hair, a low voice. Casual jacket and jeans. Grant. Her heart twanged. She hadn't seen him for almost six months.

And the girl?

Quite a bit younger than him, mid-twenties at a guess, very slight, almost emaciated frame, shoulder-length raggedly cut blonde hair, lots of jangling silver jewellery, wearing a scruffy brown leather jacket. And periodically she jerked her head. Either disagreeing or a meaningless habit.

Grant, eyes fixed on the girl, oblivious to everything and everyone around him, moved his head closer and stroked her cheek.

Claire fled.

And the appetite for a new pair of black leather boots flew away.

She was shocked. She drove home too quickly, opened a bottle of red wine, drank an entire glass in a gulp, trying to blot out the picture of those two heads practically locked together. The care, the affection, the solicitude in the gesture of stroking the girl's cheek. She didn't remember him ever being that attentive towards her.

She had fooled around, pretending, pretending, that Grant

would come back. That he loved her – really. That he was just going through a crisis. And now she had seen the truth and it hurt like hell, as though she had had her guts pulled out, twisted and stuffed back inside her.

She took another sip of wine and half closed her eyes. So . . . The oldest story in the book.

He'd found someone else and hadn't had the guts to tell her.

Well, she thought, putting her glass back on the table so angrily that some of the wine sloshed over the rim and threatened the cream-coloured carpet, *you might have bloody well told me.*

She forced herself to watch a film in the evening, taking none of it in. And Sunday? A long walk through horrid cold rain. Then a hot bath and tears.

Monday, 29 September, 9 a.m.

She was glad to go back to work, but the feeling in her guts was still there, twisting, stretching, pulling, wrenching, which is why she was working with only half her attention. Dangerous.

Hayley was deteriorating, and at fourteen years old the child would die unless they intervened somehow. She called a case conference about her. The girl's blood tests clearly showed a deteriorating condition. This time Hayley had failed to rectify her state in time. She had gone beyond the point where a couple of hundred calories would pick her up. Her anorexia was now causing irreversible damage. If there was no intervention, she would almost certainly die within weeks. What they needed to decide was how far they should allow her to control her own fate. When and how they should intervene.

Capacity is a key factor in many medical decisions. *Does the patient have capacity to make a rational decision about their future?* is an important question. *Do they understand what will happen if they opt for Decision A?* – life. *Do they understand the consequences if they opt for Decision B?* – death.

Hayley was fourteen years old. They could have made her a ward of court. But she did have capacity – that magic wand.

She knew exactly what was going on and understood the consequences of her enforced self-starvation. They could have detained her under a Section to protect herself from herself. They could have force-fed her, but it was not a permanent solution. At some point Hayley would win her fight; ironically – the fight to lose her life. The question was – should they let her?

Claire eyed her colleagues around the room. Siona, a year off from retiring, had plenty of experience. He had seen cases like this over the years. 'Attitudes and treatments may change,' he'd been known to say, 'titles of illnesses alter over the years, but conditions are the same whatever you call them. Patients are the same as they always were.'

Privately Claire agreed with him. In many ways psychiatry hadn't moved that far forward. It wasn't quite as barbaric as it had been, but they still hesitated to use the word cure.

She turned her head to take in Astrid, the psychiatric nurse, a self-possessed young woman of twenty-eight or so, with sleek dark hair, a long neck and her face slightly upturned with a calm expression that made you think of a Madonna. She had classical features – a straight nose, high cheekbones, good skin, and yet she failed to make the grade as a beauty. Perhaps, Claire had thought, it was because she appeared so confident, had no apparent vulnerability, never admitted she was wrong, never had self-doubts. She was just too sure of herself. And she was cold. Her gaze slid over the girl and to Edward Reakin, Clinical Psychologist.

Edward smiled back at her. He was an interesting one, she reflected, smiling back. Claire had been one of the panel who had interviewed him for the job, and within ten minutes of reading his CV and one minute of meeting him in the flesh she had known she really wanted him as a colleague. He was clever. He had written books on the subject of personality disorder. Intelligent, clever books, with stunning insight and original thought. She had read them all and had admired his wit, his use of English, his clear descriptions of various classifications of personality disorders, and lastly his realistic acceptance of what could and could not be done for their patients.

And she liked his self-effacing manner.

He was around forty, divorced; usually turned up for work in a shabby, crumpled jacket and either trousers or jeans. He was five ten, medium build, grey, streaked hair, a face dominated by clear, warm, friendly grey eyes. The more she met him, the more she felt this warmth and liked him. So the smile she returned that morning was equally warm.

'I don't see that we have much choice,' she said slowly, 'other than to send Hayley to the general hospital, and if necessary have her detained under a Section 2 for twenty-eight days.' She couldn't resist tacking 'again' on the end of the sentence.

'We're not going to win here,' she said.

Edward spoke up. 'We've tried everything,' he said. 'One of the things that works against Hayley is that actually she's quite intelligent.' He said this almost apologetically. 'She has real insight into her condition. We can't hoodwink her.'

Siona spoke up next. 'I thought she'd put on some weight.'

'I suspect she'd done the old trick of drinking pints of water,' Teresa, the other psychiatric nurse, chimed in wearily.

'Fourteen years old and what's ahead?' Claire mused.

They all knew the answer to her rhetorical question.

Not a lot.

Astrid spoke up. 'So all we've done,' she said dismissively, 'was a waste of time. She'll bounce between here and the hospital until she dies.'

Edward jerked his head to look at his colleague sharply. 'Wait a minute, Astrid,' he protested. 'There's no point taking that attitude.' His grey eyes flickered over her and Claire knew in that exact moment that Edward Reakin did not like the nurse.

But Astrid was having none of it. 'Come on, Edward,' she said, spoiling for an argument, 'what good have we done her? She'll soon be in liver failure, for goodness' sake.'

Claire tried to pour oil on the troubled waters, butting in to avoid an argument. 'We have to keep trying, Astrid. We can't just give up.'

Edward turned to her, frowning but nodding at the same time. He steepled his long bony fingers together as he spoke. 'I have to say,' he said, 'on reviewing her case—' he turned

to Claire – 'and considering your efforts, I don't see what any
of us could have done differently.' He scanned the room,
looking at each person in turn as though searching their soul.
'Anorexia is a difficult condition to treat at the best of times.
We might all feel that we would like to intervene . . .' His
grey eyes grew steely. 'One could substitute for "intervene",
"interfere", but we can only go so far, and this is the reason
why sometimes these cases end in tragedy.' There was no
doubt who was the target of this comment – his eyes were
fixed on Astrid as he spoke. She recognized this and flushed,
squaring her chin and flashing her eyes away from him. No
one in the room could have misread the stubborn look. Or
the anger. She was not going to agree with the psychologist.
Claire felt grateful to Edward but was troubled by the obvious
conflict between the two. It had never registered before. Astrid
was a highly qualified, experienced and competent psychiatric
nurse. She had specialized in forensic psychology and had
worked in Category A prisons. It wasn't her experience that
Claire had doubts about, but her coldness – her complete
detachment from the work, or their patients as people. Astrid
knew her stuff all right, but she lacked a conscience, and
never admitted when she was wrong, as she had been on a
couple of occasions. As they all were sometimes. Psychiatry
is not an exact science, and attitudes change from decade
to decade. But Astrid's attitude might cause problems in
the future.

Eventually the decision was made to transfer Hayley to the
general hospital.

They had more patients to consider. It was time to move
on. 'OK,' Claire said both wearily and resignedly, 'let's move on
to Stan. Why isn't he getting any better?'

Teresa looked up. 'He had a fit in the night,' she said, and
Claire felt a heaviness press on her shoulders. This was another
battle they would probably lose.

They spent almost an hour discussing Stan Moudel's latest
lapse. They all agreed he was unlikely ever to come clean.
There seemed one option open to them. In Fenton there was
a safe house called The Sycamores. Those more cynical
amongst them called it The Psyche-o-More, but there was a

space there. Compared to his lonely bedsit, there was reasonably close supervision. If they could get Stan to agree to this they knew the police would drop charges and he would avoid a prison sentence. He would have to agree to be tagged for up to a year, but it was a small price to pay for his freedom and by far his best option. Claire scanned the watching faces. Astrid spoke.

'I'll talk to him about that today,' she said.

Salena Urbi was shaking her head, her long earrings dancing at the side of her face. She was wearing her hijab loose so they could see the shining black hair underneath. 'It would be a good solution,' she said. 'I've spent a lot of time speaking to Stan and I don't think he's going be able to resist the drugs. And with that . . .' Her dark eyes looked around the room with a hint of sorrow behind them. 'With that,' she continued, 'comes the clumsy petty crime. With the petty crime comes the arrests. Goodness.' She flashed white teeth. 'He doesn't even try to avoid it. The police can't fail to pick him up every time. Every time,' she repeated. 'It's ridiculous. But . . .' She leaned forward, eager to find a solution to this small problem, 'if we can put him in Psyche-o-More . . .' She couldn't resist a smile. 'And he can be watched – maybe, just maybe, we can keep him out of trouble.' She hesitated. 'Keep him away from whoever's supplying him.'

Claire liked the girl. One could not do this job without a huge dollop of optimism, equally as important as a spoonful of realism.

'OK. Are you all right with that then, Astrid?' The girl nodded, displaying neither enthusiasm nor a lack of it for her task. But Claire knew she would succeed. The girl had a very good record of success.

But Salena hadn't finished. Her eyes looked troubled. 'But this fit is a disturbing symptom,' she said. 'So before we send him to Psyche-o-More, we have to stabilize his physical condition. For now he goes nowhere.'

Later Claire would reflect on those four small words: *stabilize his physical condition.*

Her registrar had picked up on something she should have done. And would have done had she not been distracted.

For now she hurried on. 'Right then,' she said. 'Now David Gad.' She had filled them all in on his background and the reason behind his recurrent suicide attempts. 'He's currently having psychotherapy and CBT and then we think we can have a couple of tries at abreaction.' This involved administering an intravenous dose of a major tranquillizer such as phenobarbitone or sodium amytal, and under this influence the trauma was revisited and a different outcome or settlement substituted; thus, hopefully, giving the victim, finally, some peace of mind. In general it was a successful treatment used on the right patients.

'I think,' she said, 'when he's had a couple of weeks of this we can probably discharge him safely. We trust there will be no more suicide attempts.'

No one looked particularly convinced at her statement and she knew why. Gad had suffered from these memories for just too long. Nearly seventy years. A lifetime. The experience would have been deeply embedded. She knew that as well as anyone in the room, but . . .

'Does anyone have a better suggestion?' she asked crisply and, as she had anticipated, they all averted their eyes, except Edward who gave her a half-smile in tacit support.

Inwardly she sighed. However many multidisciplinary meetings they held, the buck stopped with her. The buck always stopped with her. Ultimately only she was responsible for all these decisions. Then she remembered one of the many laconic conversations she'd had with Grant. 'That's what you get paid for, my sweet,' he'd said in his lazy, detached way before pressing his full lips down on hers.

She squeezed her eyes tight shut against the memory, and when she opened them again Edward was watching her, his eyebrows slightly raised in the faint question, *Are you OK?* She looked away. She wasn't sure she wanted her colleague to learn about her sad personal life.

She regained control. 'Is there anything else anyone wants to bring up?'

There were general shakes of the head and she stood up, went to her office, and started checking her diary.

It was now less than a week until Barclay's wedding, nearly

seven months since Grant had gone. And since seeing him with that pretty, fragile girl, she had recast him as a coward. A coward to simply go, a coward to avoid confessing and a bloody coward now to leave her so much in the dark.

When he had first gone she had dropped into the habit of making up her own explanations. He was tired of her. The life of domestication hadn't suited him. He had someone else. He had felt insecure in the face of her career. He hadn't wanted stability and predictability. There could be a plethora of reasons. She could take her pick like choosing a bloom from a bouquet. But now she knew. And she had to deal with it.

Since Saturday she had deleted his number from her phone so now she *couldn't* ring or text him any more. She had caller ID on her landline as well as on her mobile and rarely picked it up, preferring to avoid cold calls and rely on answerphone. So now she felt as though she had built a small wall around herself. Hardly a fortress, impossible to breach, but behind that small wall she felt a little more secure. She was still hurt at his abandonment and lack of explanation, still to some extent damaged and insecure. In future liaisons she swore she would be more guarded, more careful. Keep her feelings wrapped up. Less raw. This was what she promised herself.

FOURTEEN

Tuesday, 30 September

The day was going well until round about three in the afternoon when she was passing the door of one of the interview rooms. It was propped open. The afternoon was warm and humid so the air circulation would have made the atmosphere in the small area more bearable. But as she passed she heard Astrid's voice speaking to Stan Moudel.

'You don't have a choice, mate. It's that or fucking prison. Get it? And you know only too well what happens in prison. You'll get buggered.'

There was a small noise from Moudel. More a whimper than a comment or a response.

'You're doomed, matey.'

Stan's response was another whimper and Astrid continued, 'So you going to go for it? Or take the alternative? Your choice, mate. Not mine.'

Claire stood outside, shocked at the girl's tone. So different from the cool, detached, controlled manner she normally displayed. She was bullying him. She hesitated for a moment. She had eavesdropped here and wasn't sure how best to deal with the subject. One thing was for certain. Astrid would get results all right, but Claire couldn't tolerate her method.

She must choose her moment to speak. There was something else. It was the use of the word doomed. The same word that Jerome Barclay had muttered. Maybe Barclay was not psychic. Maybe he had a friend on the inside, just like Julia had suggested. For the moment she continued along the corridor, but questions buzzed inside her brain like flies round a rotting corpse.

Hayley was sitting on her bed, a pile of magazines at her side. She was leafing through them as Claire entered. Fashion magazines full of celebrity gossip, new partners, new diets, new babies, new beauty advice, new quarrels, new splits, new exercise regimes and the odd wedding. Plus some horror pictures of plastic surgery gone wrong. Enough to frighten anyone off going under the surgeon's knife to look more beautiful. Judging by the pictures, the reverse seemed the case. Claire looked at the top one and smiled. Here was news guaranteed to warm your heart. Prince George two years on, a sister by his side.

She sat in the chair at the window and surveyed her patient.

'Hayley,' she said gently, 'we're going to have to transfer you to hospital.'

Hayley didn't look up but continued looking down at her magazine. No response, apparently. Then Claire saw a single tear roll slowly down her cheek. Hayley was shaking her head, her shoulders tensed. 'Please no,' she said. 'Please don't send me there. You know what they do? I'll have tubes sticking out of everywhere.' She gave a mischievous smile. 'Everywhere except my arse,' she corrected.

'*We* or rather *you* have three choices,' Claire said. 'You either eat or you go to hospital or you die.'

The girl's shoulders jerked up as though to say, '*And I care?*'

'*You* make the choice.'

And Hayley's shoulders drooped again. 'But . . .' she objected.

'Whoever is whispering poisonous words into your ear, listen to me. You do need to eat, otherwise your organs will fail and you will die.'

There was no response from Hayley so Claire continued. 'We'll make arrangements for you to be transferred this afternoon.'

There was a flash in her pale eyes, a moment of challenge. 'I thought you said I have a choice?'

There was despair in her voice. Claire shook her head. 'Not really,' she said, 'and neither do we.'

Next she had to tackle Astrid. She drew in a deep breath and walked along the corridor to the girl's office, knocked on the door and waited.

Astrid opened the door with a sharp tug and looked surprised. 'Claire,' she said.

'Do you mind if I come in?'

'Sure. Sure.'

Claire knew this was an awkward situation. She had overheard the conversation quite accidentally. She hadn't been snooping. But . . .

'Astrid,' she began, 'I overheard you talking to Stan earlier today.'

The girl's eyes flashed. She knew what was coming.

'The door was open. To be honest I was shocked.'

Astrid was defensive. 'It's the only way to get through to some people.'

Claire shook her head. 'It isn't the way,' she said. 'It may be that in the prison you were harsh with your inmates, but not here.'

She met Astrid's eyes and read defiance.

'You understand?' she said sharply. 'Not here. Not with my patients.'

The girl's eyes still flashed.

'If it comes to my notice that your treatment of our patients is not what I would expect, I shall have no alternative but to ask you to find other employment.'

At last Astrid was paying attention. Bristling, but listening.

'I shall document this conversation,' Claire continued. 'Take this as a verbal warning.'

She knew there was only one way to play this. Tough.

The right way. She was almost out of the room when she turned back. 'By the way,' she said, 'you don't know a guy called Jerome Barclay, do you?'

Astrid's response was predictable. 'Not that I remember,' she said coolly. 'Is he one of our patients?'

But Claire could be devious too. 'Not an inpatient,' she said.

FIFTEEN

Thursday, 2 October, 1 p.m.

And now it was four days before the wedding and Claire suddenly realized she should look for an outfit to wear. She didn't want to let Jerome down, did she? Her mouth twisted. So what was really behind this decision of his to invite her? She would know when she met the bride and she was curious. Would Roxanne Trigg be someone vulnerable, someone easily frightened? Or would she be Barclay's equal? Someone feisty and strong. Another psycho, perhaps, to join in the fun? There were plenty of cases where two were more than twice as deadly as one. Two people with evil intent could goad each other into deeper and deeper crime. Think Myra and Ian, Fred and Rosie, even Bonnie and Clyde, to name a few of the most notorious.

She'd soon find out.

But the wedding had had one good consequence. She had made contact with Adam, started to heal old wounds. And the tinge of regret that she was not going to the wedding with Grant was slowly fading. He had someone else now. He just hadn't had the guts to tell her, but had crept away, tail between his legs, ashamed and ultimately a coward.

She was quite excited about going to The Moat House. She had been to one wedding there as well as a couple of times for dinner before it had been upgraded. It was a smart establishment near Junction 13 of the M6 – Stafford South. It had beautiful grounds and was licensed for weddings. One of her school friends had been married there eight years ago. She had taken Grant's predecessor, a tall, handsome guy – over six feet tall – named Conrad. Now what had happened to him? Oh yes. He had joined the Forces and vanished from her life.

She knew how to pick them.

But her immediate problem was finding something to wear.

Claire had never liked shopping with a girlfriend – or a boyfriend, for that matter. She invariably got talked into buying something unsuitable, expensive and unflattering. And to top it all, they were usually the outfits she felt most uncomfortable in. So why the hell did she buy them? Coercion. That was why.

She had Thursday afternoon off and decided, instead of searching round the Potteries, with a vague chance she might bump into Grant and his lady again, she would head south to Eccleshall, a small town down the A518. There were three good dress shops there. She had bought a fabulous New Year's Eve party dress there, last December, a couple of months before Grant's desertion, and she thought one of the three was bound to have something suitable: smart – and a bit different. Also she'd noticed when there before that they had a lively hat-hire business. And so that was where she ended up on that warm October afternoon, thinking as she drove down the road, which followed the M6 southbound for a while, how curious it was that she was shopping for an outfit to wear to Jerome Barclay's wedding. Of all people! *Blood and guts*, she thought. Jerome Barclay, who had given her bad dreams over the last five years. And she was going with Adam, whom she had plotted to kill when she had been a little over eight years old.

How strange life was.

And Astrid? How should she deal with the nurse? Watch her carefully in case she was abusive towards a patient again. Beyond that, she was starting to believe that the way Barclay knew so much about her patients, both inpatients and outpatients, was that there was some connection between him and Astrid. How they knew each other wasn't clear. Maybe it was simply through work, but it stood to reason. Even the cynical but correct descriptions of her patients – the stupid clever, the haunted Jew, the hungry child, the doomed home-less man – were cold but true . . . if you forgot they were human beings. The phrases evoked Astrid's attitude, which she had kept carefully hidden. She would deal with it later. For now she needed to focus on clothes. What to wear to a psycho's wedding.

An hour later she was sorted. Black shoes (high-heeled but comfortable); a black and white jacket over a plain black dress that she could wear again. Instead of a hat she tried on what was called a scarlet 'fascinator'. It felt suitable headgear for a psychiatrist.

She looked at herself in the full-length mirror. Her hair, always blonde, had lightened over the summer and her skin was looking good. She would paint her nails the same bright scarlet of her fascinator and carry a scarlet clutch bag. She had lost a tiny bit of weight from around her middle – due, no doubt, to the time now spent at the gym instead of cosying up on the sofa with a bottle of wine after a two-course dinner that Grant had cooked. Her evening meals these days tended to be scratchy rather than Grant's favoured meat and two veg, and this too had had an impact on her weight. She looked more closely at herself. In her facial expression her look of unhappy confusion had been replaced with calm acceptance. She actually liked what she saw.

Teach me to accept the things I cannot change. A slight misquote from the serenity prayer seemed appropriate.

So she smiled at herself. Serenity felt so much better than puzzlement, or anguish, or grief.

The only thing nagging at her mind was that she would need Grant's signature to sell the house. So she would have to make contact at some point. Right now she wasn't absolutely sure she did want to sell up, but she didn't want any avenue denied to her for want of a signature. If she did decide to sell she wanted to be able to do it pronto, not wait around for a solicitor to track him down. As she'd seen him in the Potteries Shopping Centre, he probably wasn't living very far away.

She'd deleted his number from her mobile, but she could easily access it through an old phone bill – through an old phone, even, if she charged it up. She would prefer to write a letter, though – more formal; less of a surprise – to give him time to think up a response and, most importantly, to avoid any physical contact. She could choose her words carefully.

The problem was, she didn't have his address.

SIXTEEN

Saturday evening, 4 October

Adam turned up as arranged at seven. As she answered the door to him, Claire reflected that they looked nothing alike. He had coppery-coloured hair and green eyes; pale, freckly skin. He was tall and slight almost to the point of being thin, and was short sighted, so usually wore glasses. It was that or fumble around half blind, he was fond of saying. This evening he was casually dressed in jeans and a rugby shirt but, as he had climbed out of the car, he had manoeuvred a suit-bag off the back seat and a small attaché case. He grinned at Claire. 'Hi, sis,' he said.

'Hi, Adam.' She gave him an awkward kiss on the cheek. 'Come in.' She stood back and he entered the hall, sniffing as he stepped inside. 'Something cooking?'

She nodded. 'Nothing fancy. Just pasta – and some salmon.'

'*Just* pasta?' He had the bachelor's enthusiasm of being cooked for.

She laughed. 'Glass of wine, Ad?'

He followed her into the kitchen, stood, leaning against the cooker, and spoke uncomfortably. 'I thought Grant, maybe, you know. I thought he'd hang around a bit longer.'

'Ah.' She pulled the cork out of a bottle of Rioja and poured two glasses. 'Well, he didn't, I'm afraid. He just went.' They clinked glasses and she drew in a deep sigh. 'I think he's got someone else. I saw him in Hanley one Saturday. He didn't see me.'

Adam's face changed. 'Men are such cowards, sis. Duck away when there's something they don't want to face up to.'

She wheeled around, hearing something in his tone. 'Is there something you're not telling me, Adam Spencer?'

'No,' he said hastily. 'No. Absolutely not. No way, Claire.' His grin grew. 'Don't get all paranoid on me. *I* wasn't in Grant's confidence.'

'Neither was I,' she said drily. 'Let's change the subject, shall we, and talk about tomorrow.'

Adam was frowning. 'Claire,' he said tentatively, 'what I don't understand is, if you think this guy who's getting married tomorrow is such a nasty piece of work, why are you going to his wedding?'

'To keep an eye on him,' she said darkly.

'But you can hardly,' he said, even more awkward now, 'go up to his bride and tell her the guy she's just married is a psycho.'

'No,' she replied, calmly stirring the sauce into the pasta, 'I'm well aware of that. I just want to see her for myself. I think I'll know then whether she's in any danger. I want to know she can take care of herself, Adam.'

'Hmm. I'm still not sure about this, sis,' he said dubiously.

'Don't you worry.' She was spooning the pasta on to their plates. 'Leave it all to me. I know what I'm doing.'

'He's not such a nasty piece of work that he might – oh, I don't know – harm you in any way?'

'I think he would if he felt I was going to blow the whistle on him. But I've never had enough evidence. Not anything proven, anyway, of any crimes or assaults.' She met his eyes. 'And I've never been absolutely certain that he *is* dangerous. He could be just playing. You know? Cat-and-mouse stuff. It's more a feeling and as you know . . .' She turned around to face him, 'feelings don't put people behind bars.'

'Hmm,' he said, still dubious. 'All sounds a bit thin to me.'

She leaned across and touched his hand. 'It is a bit thin,' she admitted, 'which is why I'm glad you're coming. You'll have more of an open mind.'

'OK.' He focused one hundred per cent on his food. And that was the end of the conversation.

SEVENTEEN

Sunday, 5 October, 9 a.m.

B arclay's wedding day dawned bright and cool, the leaves just starting to acknowledge the month and recognize that autumn was beginning. They were pale, green leaching out of them leaving them yellow to brown; some were already starting to drop. Not with the vengeance of autumn, but drifting lazily downwards.

The wedding wasn't until 11, so they had time for a good breakfast and left themselves an hour to reach The Moat House in case the M6 was misbehaving – again – even on a Sunday.

Adam looked smart – handsome, even – in a dark, well-fitting lounge suit, white shirt and blue silk tie. It looked expensive. And Claire surprised herself by feeling a tinge of curiosity mixed with the unmistakable colour green of envy. Had *her* mother and *his* father bought him that?

He looked at her anxiously, passing a hand over his head to flatten the thick, coppery hair. 'Do I pass the test?'

She stuffed her feelings back inside her. 'Yes,' she said. 'You look lovely.'

'Thanks. So do you.' He fingered the tie, unwittingly answering her silent petty question. 'Got it with my first pay cheque, so it's got significance for me.'

'Oh,' she said, twice as heartily as she felt.

'I'm eking out my money by doing some part-time office

work,' he said, making her laugh with his expression of mock disgust. 'The things I have to do, eh?'

She felt like hugging him.

As she drove down to Junction 13 on the motorway, wanting to avoid Stafford town centre, she tried to explain exactly what it was that she found so threatening about Jerome Barclay. 'I'd heard about him before I met him,' she said. 'They told me that Heidi, my predecessor, kept a tight rein on him, and I was curious to know why. He did have a criminal record but they were minor offences. A bit of shoplifting, forged cheques – the usual. And in his notes there wasn't really much to suggest he was or could be dangerous. The only real thing was a pretty nasty assault on his girlfriend which had landed her in hospital.'

Adam frowned. 'He didn't go to prison for that?'

She switched lanes to overtake, keeping her eyes on the road, busy now with Sunday shoppers. 'She dropped the charges. She was lucky not to be charged with wasting police time. He tried to run her over. The only person who could know whether it was an accident or deliberate was her – and him. And she wasn't testifying, although she did confess the truth to me – that she knew it had been a deliberate assault.'

'Barclay had threatened her?'

'He didn't need to. She knew what would happen if she testified. She'd never be safe.'

Adan looked horrified. 'That's horrible. *Never* to be safe. What an awful way to live.'

'Mmm.' She risked a swift glance at him. 'He assaulted his mother too, but she also refused to press charges and the CPS advised the police that there was hardly any chance of a successful conviction. Again they dropped charges. You can imagine they were grinding their teeth by then. Then he told me tales of animal torture,' she continued. 'They were pretty horrible, Ad: slowly roasting a bird and lopping off a rabbit's ears. Animal torture's a well-known early sign of psychopathy.'

'Well, you're the doc,' was Adam's unhelpful contribution.

She frowned, wanting him to understand, but it is hard to explain the threat of potential. *She* knew what Barclay was capable of, but to try and convey that concept to a lay person like Adam? It was virtually impossible.

'His baby brother died a cot death when Jerome was eight.'

Adam gave her a swift look and she felt chilled. What did he remember? He'd only been a baby. Babies, surely, have no memory? Or do they? Maybe not a completely formed memory, only a sense of a threat. And could they know from whom the threat was coming?

She hurried on. 'And his father died with diabetes two years later. I spoke to Barclay's mother and asked whether she had any suspicions about either death. She said no. She said that Jerome had adored his tiny baby brother and his father. While she obviously doted on her son. But then she died too, of an apparent overdose.' She was now turning off the motorway. 'Too much coincidence,' she said. 'I don't believe for a minute that she took an overdose.' Then, turning to him, 'I believe that *he* was responsible for all three deaths. That's why I want to make sure his bride can look after herself.'

Adam looked alarmed. 'But you can't warn her off – can you?'

She was driving through the village of Acton Trussell now, chocolate-box pretty. Neat gardens and clean cars. 'Not really. Like I've told you before, we have be very careful to preserve our patients' right to privacy. So I'm not going to be stopping the ceremony.' She grinned at him. 'You can relax, Ad. I won't be standing up when they say the bit about "lawful impediment".' She gave him a winning smile. 'I'm just an observer. So – shall we go?'

They'd reached the hotel. They could see several morning-suited men noting their arrival, and a large black Rolls festooned with white satin ribbon. They parked up. Adam touched her sleeve and whispered. 'Will you point him out to me?'

'I won't need to,' she whispered back.

They weren't the first to arrive. They made their way through a small knot of people sucking on their cigarettes outside. Barclay didn't smoke so she didn't look for him amongst them. They walked through the doors. Claire scanned the guests waiting in the foyer. No sign of him. She turned her attention

back to the guests, standing around, and assessed them. They
were an ill-assorted crowd: most of the women were either
overweight or very skinny, with the poor complexion of heavy
smokers. Their clothes were gaudy and looked cheap and there
were some pantomime hats. The women looked as though
they had had a hard life in one way or another. The men tended
to be pot-bellied with coarse features, and a few had the red
faces of a person who'd already had a few beers. Their jackets
were stretched tight over their stomachs and conversation was
loud and raucous. Claire looked around uneasily. These did
not look like people who were going to be able to stand up
to a clever headcase like Jerome Barclay. She gave Adam a
swift, worried glance and placed her wedding card containing
the voucher on the table with the other presents. Then she
continued scanning the crowd.

Mainly Roxanne's family, at a guess. Barclay's, of course,
were all dead.

Most of the people seemed to know each other already.
There were gasps of delight as they recognized friends and
relations; a few wary glances; a couple of people pushing past,
anxious to renew their acquaintance with someone or else
avoid an ex-friend or unwelcome encounter. The words that
swept the air were the same as at any family social occasion:

Haven't seen you for ages.

You do look well.

Harry, hello there . . .! – and so on. Shrieks from the women,
firm handshakes from the men. A bit of back-slapping.

She and Adam stood, a small island in the centre, strangers
amongst friends, aware that they were being given the covert
once-over, unrecognized, then studiously ignored. Claire
caught a couple of their comments bouncing around the room.

Some friend of the groom, perhaps?

No, I don't know them. Do you? Faces looking over their
shoulders.

Never seen them before in my life . . .

Maybe from the groom's side?

There was an air of effrontery; of invasion – hostility, even.
Claire was glad she had brought her half-brother and squeezed
his arm with gratitude.

There was still no sign of Barclay.

'*Remember our pact*,' Claire whispered. Not wanting to expose her single state, she wished them all to believe that she and Adam were 'an item'. Adam nodded, understanding, and whispered back. '*Split my tongue if I let on.*' She winced. It had been a childhood threat. Nothing more. She never would really have done that.

And then his voice was right behind her, smooth as velvet, an inch from her ear. 'Claire. You came. How nice.'

She turned around.

Apart from the formal grey morning suit, Barclay was exactly as she remembered him. Quite bland features really. Unmemorable. Unremarkable. Grey eyes, brown hair, bland features. What was there to be so nervous of? Then she caught it, the faint waft of cinnamon, as though he had just drunk a cappuccino. She looked into his eyes and read his glow of triumph. Round One to Jerome Barclay. He couldn't disguise the delight he felt at her presence as a witness to his marriage.

Why?

Then she worked it out. *She* was the entertainment today. Not the bride or her gauche family. Not the farmers and peasants of the gathered witnesses but her, with her so-called expert knowledge of his psyche; probably the only one there who had any insight into his personality disorder and how he would use it not to build happiness in his new family but to destroy it. He had needed her here, the only one who knew about his crimes, because now she was even more sure that they had been crimes. He *had* killed three members of his family. He *had* almost killed his ex-girlfriend, Sadie, and the poor girl *had* feared and hated him so much that she had not only refused to press charges but had also aborted his child. The devil's child, she had called it. One might have assumed that after the accident she had feared for the baby's condition. But Claire knew that Sadie had had a scan and that, miraculously, the baby and her pregnancy were unharmed.

She saw Barclay's eyes flicker and dim. And knew why. One thing was spoiling Jerome Barclay's fun: Adam. He had thought she would attend alone. That would have made her extra vulnerable.

In this tiny area, *she* had triumphed.

He turned his pale eyes on to her brother then back on her. 'This is Adam,' Claire said brightly.

Barclay took it all in: the tall figure, smart suit, his colouring and . . . narrowing his eyes, Adam's youth. He licked his lips. 'How do you do, Adam,' he said steadily. And Claire knew he knew. He had guessed.

She had just lost round two.

'And Roxanne?' she said, looking around her.

'Oh,' as if he'd forgotten her existence, 'I mustn't see the bride just yet. It would be terrible bad luck.' He smiled and winked. 'Something quite awful might happen.' He turned to smile at them both. 'See you later,' he said, and walked away, a bounce in his stride.

As they took their seats, a woman scuttled up the aisle. Roxanne's mother, at a guess. Claire's heart sank. Her skirt was tight over an ample rear and her hat had a feather which acted as a beacon for ridicule. She was dressed in an unflattering shade of turquoise – too bright; her hat and shoes were an exact match, and a large, unwieldy handbag, dyed from the same batch, swung from her shoulder. She gave the assembled congregation an abstracted smile as she crept up the aisle and sat down heavily on one of the front seats after beaming at Jerome who returned the glance coolly. Appraisingly. The woman who was about to become his mother-in-law.

Claire glanced at Adam. His eyes were wide open, as though he couldn't quite believe what he was seeing. She raised her eyebrows for comment but he just shook his head, looking bemused.

And then the Wagner started up. Claire stood up with everyone else and turned her head for a first look at the bride. The woman who would be exposed to Barclay.

Roxanne Trigg was short and plump. She wore a toothpaste-white nylon dress with a long nylon net veil, carried by a bridesmaid in a cherry-red minidress. Both walked with a slow, swinging walk, in time to the music, Roxanne on the arm of, presumably, her father. Another man who would have been more at home sitting in the cab of a tractor than leading his daughter up the aisle of a smart wedding venue. His eyes were bloodshot.

Not from crying at losing his precious daughter, Claire surmised, more likely from the beers he'd just downed. She caught a waft of pub as he passed. Roxanne carried a bouquet of blood-red roses and nothing, not even the voluminous dress, could disguise the fact that she was about four months pregnant. She stared ahead of her, looking vulnerable and not quite happy. She already looked a victim, and the glance she cast around at the gathering was of panic and confusion, as though she didn't quite know what she was doing there. That confused look lasted all the way up the aisle until she reached Barclay's side, when that look of confusion morphed into one of complete and utter radiant joy. Claire gave Adam a concerned look. This was not a feisty bride who could take on Barclay's character without it destroying her. Neither was it the fellow psycho, someone with whom he could hatch plots and plans. No. In her mind the new Mrs Barclay was already cast as victim. And she was pregnant, so that vulnerability included an unborn child. Claire watched her stand at her husband-to-be's side, her misgivings compounding by the minute.

Now Roxanne had reached her intended, Claire caught the glance Jerome gave her. One of complete and utter contempt tinged with amusement, marked by a triumphant curve of his mouth. So her worst fears had been realized. What was in it for him? Would violence be enough? Would she end up, like Sadie, in hospital with broken limbs? Or would she share the fate of Barclay's other family members – dead? Baby too?

Claire nudged Adam and caught puzzlement and concern in his face too. He'd seen the look Jerome had given his bride and shook his head. 'See what you mean,' he whispered.

When the appeal went out, if any persons present know of any lawful impediment, Claire stiffened. Adam put his hand on her arm and gently shook his head.

What would she have said anyway? It was all conjecture. And she was bound to secrecy. Confidentiality. Not for the first time, the limitations of her role hit her hard. She was powerless to act or prevent a crime she could already antici-pate. She could practically see it happening.

Claire's fears were not allayed when Roxanne stumbled through her vows in an unmistakably rural Staffordshire accent and Jerome responded in pristine English, every enunciation a mockery of his bride's diction. And then, all too soon, the whole thing was over. Roxanne was Mrs Jerome Barclay. *God help her.*

To 'The Arrival of the Queen of Sheba', the couple walked back through the aisle of chairs and out into the hallway. Ready for the line-up. As he passed, Barclay met Claire's eyes and smiled. Anyone not knowing him might mistake that smile for happiness.

It didn't fool Claire.

Barclay aimed a self-confident nod of his head at her, which Claire returned. She knew exactly why she was there. She was there to entertain him. No understanding audience, no fun.

At the reception they didn't stick to the usual order of speeches, but opened with the best man's, who began with saying what a great friend Barclay was. (Barclay had a friend?!)

He continued with his speech, but it wasn't the usual leg-pull about what a great stud his buddy was, but a sort of eulogy – more suitable for a funeral than a wedding.

'*Jerome is a wonderful person. Good at figures.* (Titter titter.) *Clever in the extreme. He's had his difficulties and more than his share of tragedy.* (Claire knew all about that.) *People don't always appreciate what a deep and interesting person Jerome is. Some people are envious of him and others make up stories to cover their own inadequacies.*' (Had Jerome written this himself?)

The friend droned on. '*And then he has a stroke of good luck. He meets Roxanne* (here a ripple around the room from Roxanne's friends and family), *and life turns around for him. I can tell you in confidence that Jerome has told me his life changed for ever when he met Roxanne. So I'd like you to raise your glasses and toast Jerome and Roxanne.*' (A round of applause.) The friend sat down to a continued smattering of more applause.

Trouble was, Claire thought, the friend hadn't detailed exactly how Jerome's life had changed.

Next it was time for the bride's father to make his contribution to the ceremony.

She had misgivings as soon as he stood up. As he stumbled through his words, Claire's worst fears were realized.

He was poorly educated, his use of English displaying a lack of subtlety and understanding. His stumbling, halting words were an embarrassment, and his praise of his daughter toe-cringingly gauche and clichéd.

'My beautiful little girl . . . My sweet princess . . . My gorgeous daughter . . .' and so on. When he added to the eulogy about Jerome, Claire almost stood up, but the moment passed and she was still seated. Again glasses were raised. It was only when she met Jerome's triumphant stare at her that her heart started to hammer. She looked at Roxanne's mother and father. Nice people, she thought, without the guile to understand just what their new son-in-law's favourite game was. She looked at Roxanne, her face flushed with too much red wine and happiness, a stain on the bodice of her wedding dress. Claire almost stepped on her own foot to stop herself from saying anything. She was seeing threats everywhere. Imagining them. But to her the red wine stain over the heart was a portent of a wound to come.

Barclay stood up and Claire held her breath.

He opened in the traditional way.

'A word or two about my bride . . .' His eyes slid down the girl's figure. Was it only her who could see the derision in the look?

'And the child.' Barclay paused to look around him. Some of the guests were patently embarrassed by this reference to the unborn child conceived out of wedlock. These were old-fashioned people with old-fashioned values. Claire glanced at Roxanne. Her face was scarlet with embarrassment.

He was doing this deliberately.

Barclay continued. 'I met Roxanne at a rather down-at-heel nightclub in Hanley, appropriately called *Tramps*.'

More discomfort amongst the guests as Barclay continued, smooth as chocolate. 'Little did I know then of her family's good fortune.' His lips seemed to curl as he spoke the words. 'But then it's not a bad thing to have a few secrets between husband and wife, is it, my dear?'

Roxanne's eyes flickered across the room. She was squirming with embarrassment now, looking down at the table and her half-empty champagne glass with dismay.

Barclay then appeared to follow the traditional form of speech. 'I think you'll agree that Roxanne and our bridesmaid, Pippa, both look amazing.' But he'd managed somehow to turn the word 'amazing' from a compliment to an insult. Roxanne, however, now looked happy, and so did Pippa, who had long slanting, devious eyes. Claire took a good look at her. Trustworthy friend or . . .?

Barclay continued. 'I just know that Roxanne and I will have an interesting and eventful life together and I look forward to having a little son or daughter to *play* with.' Again a quick flicker of a glance at Claire.

She leaned back in her seat, took a small sip of champagne, testing every word, every phrase Jerome Barclay had used, and realized that they had all been selected for their ambiguity, particularly the word '*play*'.

She glanced at Adam. He too was looking and weighing up every word, his fingers coiled around the stem of the champagne glass. He gave her a swift glance and raised his eyebrows.

Barclay finished his speech with a grin. 'What jolly fun,' he concluded, and sat down, but Claire was chilled. No one in the room knew quite what to make of this quote. But she did. She knew exactly what he was saying. He was quoting from a poem which had frightened her as a child. Written in June 1914 by Sir Walter Alexander Raleigh, titled 'Wishes of an Elderly Man, Wished at a Garden Party, June 1914', the words chilled her, reminding her of paintings where animals' faces had been substituted for humans':

> *I wish I loved the Human Race;*
> *I wish I loved its silly face;*
> *I wish I liked the way it walks;*
> *I wish I liked the way it talks;*
> *And when I'm introduced to one,*
> *I wish I thought 'What Jolly Fun!'*

The poem had been illustrated with a picture of a sheep. As an adult, she could understand what had frightened her so much as a child. It was the sheer cynicism expressed, the alienation from all people, the rejection and mockery of polite society's mores.

While one could understand this sentiment at a garden party in the summer of 1914, she now wondered. Had Raleigh had some foretaste of the terrors to come? Had he mocked polite society for its coming disintegration?

She focused back on the present, whispered a quick explanation of the quote to Adam, who frowned, looked shocked, and asked if she was sure. She nodded.

Formality over, people were beginning to stand up, circulate. The smokers dashed outside; some headed equally speedily for the toilets. Claire sat rooted to the spot.

Adam leaned over. 'I'm going to stretch my legs,' he said. 'I'm feeling quite cramped.'

She smiled at him and remained seated. 'We should be able to go soon, Ad. Thanks again for coming.'

'It's been interesting. But don't you want to observe your patient a bit longer?'

'Well – yes – but there's not a lot I can do here and now.'

She scanned the room. There seemed a generally happy air. She couldn't see Barclay at the moment.

Only one woman seemed to have any grasp of the real situation. She was slim in a red dress with a navy coat over, no hat. No fascinator either. Just a worried expression, almost one of apprehension, as though she could see that this marriage would be troubled. She had red hair, expertly dyed and coiffured, and was aged about fifty. Her frown and general look of disapproval made her look older. She crossed the room in quick, impatient steps, her heels clicking on the wooden floor, Claire clearly in her sights, as she took a path as straight and direct as a crow's flight. 'How do you do,' she said without preamble. 'I'm Maureen. Kenneth is my brother. You're Claire, aren't you? You're a friend of Jerome's.' Her eyes, too heavily ringed in kohl, worried and concerned, said more.

Claire was about to say, 'Not exactly a friend, Mrs . . .' but she stopped herself. What exactly had Barclay told his wife's family about her? Had he mentioned the fact that he was under a psychiatrist? Had he confessed to the petty thefts that peppered his past and the unfortunate events that appeared to befall his family? How had he explained his mother's suicide, his brother's cot death, his father's death? Merely as a succession of tragedies? Had no one questioned these *coincidences*?

One of her queries was answered in Maureen's next breath. 'He said you were a psychiatrist.'

Claire nodded, cautiously. Adam had returned to the seat next to her and was watching the woman with interest.

Maureen's expression changed to one of acute concern. 'Why does he need a psychiatrist?' The question was blunt and it left Claire in an awkward position.

She started on the path that, 'I'm not at liberty to reveal . . .', but Maureen looked at her sharply. 'This is my niece he's marrying,' she said. 'My niece who . . .' Her eyes skittered across the floor to the bulky wedding dress and frothy white veil. 'Bless her,' she said. 'She isn't the brightest button in the box.'

Her eyes grew sharp and skewered Claire's. 'What should I know about my niece's new husband?'

This put Claire in a quandary. She could have an ally, someone who would watch over the newly married couple and the vulnerable unborn child. But she was bound by a professional code.

She could only drop hints. 'Keep an eye on him,' she advised. 'Look after your niece.'

Maureen looked at her for a long minute, searching her eyes for something. Finally she spoke. 'You don't understand, do you?'

Claire felt the impact of the question in the pit of her stomach. Adam was watching, silent, wary.

'My brother,' Maureen said, 'is unused to all this money. It's possible he will be – unwise.'

Claire frowned. Now she was worried.

EIGHTEEN

'Six months ago,' Maureen said, 'Kenneth won some money on the Lottery. He got five numbers right and won three million.'

'Jerome told me they were farmers,' Claire said slowly. 'He said they'd sold land.'

Maureen shook her head. 'Typical,' she said. 'Why tell a lie when the truth is so much simpler?'

Claire could have answered this one for her. *For sport.*

'Now do you see exactly what's bothering me?'

Claire nodded. She could already guess the answer to her next question. 'And when did she and Jerome get together?'

Maureen's lips tightened. 'Just after,' she said. 'Roxanne just . . . well, she just fell for him. She got pregnant pretty quickly.' She glanced across to the bride and groom. Roxanne had linked arms with her new husband. With his free arm Jerome was lifting his wine glass to his lips, watching the conversation from across the room. Claire knew him well. He would know exactly what was being said. But it was getting to him. When his shoulders were bunched up like that he was concerned. It was one of the few emotions he ever displayed.

Maureen too glanced across. 'Well at least he's done the decent thing,' she said dubiously.

The phrase had a discordant resonance with Claire. *When had Barclay ever done the decent thing?*

She eyed Maureen warily. 'Are they going on a honeymoon?'

'I think so, but no one knows where.'

It was tradition but it still made Claire uneasy. Foreign places can be a great backdrop for tragic accidents, Barclay's speciality. Far away from family, friends, or an English police force. Maureen melted away and Claire continued to observe.

The first dance was interesting, Barclay handling his bride, keeping her at least a yard away. It made the child bump even more obvious. Most of the evening, though, he simply sat, regarding the entire show as though watching an amateur dramatic performance or a child's dreadful birthday party, something to be endured, smiling patronizingly but looking bored. And making no attempt to hide it. Claire observed him for a while. He wasn't drinking much alcohol but was staying sober and watchful. He didn't really look across at Claire or at Adam but his eyes stayed on Maureen. If looks could kill, she would have been lying dead at his feet, burnt to a crisp by the hostile heat in Barclay's eyes. As the evening wore on,

Claire glanced at Adam. 'Let's go,' she said. 'I think I've seen and heard enough.'

'Suits me.' He grinned at her, affection leaking from his face. He bent over and kissed her cheek.

'Do we need to say our goodbyes?' He glanced in Jerome's direction.

'No. I have a feeling I'll be seeing something of him.' They threaded their way through the revellers. Claire knew Barclay was watching their exit.

Adam waited until they were in the car before asking anxiously, 'Did I do OK, sis?'

'Brilliant,' she said. 'And now I need to go home.'

As she drove them back to Burslem, Adam quizzed her. 'What do you think's going to happen? I mean, he's not just going to polish off Roxanne, the baby and her parents, is he?'

'Who knows?'

'No – but really?'

'I ought to warn her,' she said, 'or at least warn her parents to be on their guard, to watch out.'

Adam put his hand on her arm. 'Don't, sis,' he said. 'They won't believe you. It might even get you into trouble.' He did look genuinely concerned so she kept her thoughts to herself.

As they turned into her road, they saw a couple of girls loitering underneath the lamppost. It was a cool night but they were skimpily dressed. Adam gave her a worried glance. 'Is the area changing?' he asked delicately.

She nodded. 'They have made attempts to clean up the streets, but they don't work for long. It's just a place with a bad name. Maybe I should move on. If I can get hold of Grant . . .' She couldn't finish, suddenly feeling swamped by sadness. Maybe it was the wedding ceremony which had upset her. Or maybe just the fact that when Adam left she would be alone again.

Adam glanced across at her. 'Do you want *me* to try to contact him?'

'Adam,' she said, surprised and unused to this brotherly concern. 'You'd do that?'

'Sure. If it'd help you, sis.'

'No. It's OK. I'll wash my own dirty laundry.' Something

struck her then. 'Does . . .' The word stuck in her throat like a piece of dry bread. 'Does Mum know you've come today?'

Adam looked uncomfortable. He squirmed in his seat. 'I didn't say,' he finally managed. 'I thought it better not to.'

And between the lines Claire read the message only too clearly. When Monsieur Roget had left, her mother's dislike for 'The Frog spawn' had begun, increasing in intensity when she had married Adam's father, the reliable, English, uxorious David Spencer. And the dislike had compounded when Adam-the-perfect had made an appearance. Her stepfather had barely tolerated her. And Adam? He had been just too young to have any insight into the uncomfortable situation. Only ten when she had left to go to university. Claire had not so much slipped from favour, she could hardly remember a time when she had even been in favour. She tried, sometimes, late at night, to conjure up a loving mother and *papa*. But she couldn't. All she could recall were her mother's words.

And who do you think is going to support you through all that? Not Monsieur Roget, the frog, I can tell you. Her mother never even called him 'your father'. He was always Monsieur Roget, the frog. '*He doesn't want anything to do with you, Frog spawn.*' She had put her face close to Claire's to deliver her blow. '*He doesn't even send you a birthday card.*'

So Claire had been a waitress and a barmaid all through university, and worked through the holidays, avoiding returning to the home where she was so unwelcome.

11 p.m.

They were in the sitting room, having opened a bottle of wine, and were sipping it slowly. After the tensions of the day they both felt they deserved it. 'Thank you for coming,' Claire said again, aware that had Grant not left, she probably wouldn't have rung him and certainly not asked him to accompany her to Jerome's wedding. 'Thank you for being my escort.' She giggled. 'And well, just thank you.' *For not hating me as I once hated you,* she added silently.

And their silence built a bridge between the resentful and jealous older half-sister and the vulnerable child Adam had been. It soared over the sly pinches and imagined pillow-smotherings and rested on the sofa between them, peaceful and healing as a dove.

Adam started fidgeting. He wanted to go back to his pad in Birmingham and possibly whoever was there, waiting for him.

'I think I'll be . . .' He rose to his feet and she hugged him.

'Again, Ad,' she said, 'thank you.'

'My pleasure, sis. Maybe you'll come down to Brum and meet up with Adele?'

So that was her name. 'Sure. Love to.'

'And you'll let me know if you want me to help track down Grant?'

'Certainly will.'

She saw him to the door, watched him climb into the car and leave; she turned around, locked and bolted the door behind him.

Though she needn't have worried. Of all the nights she might have wondered where he was and what he was doing, tonight Jerome Barclay was spoken for. He would be with his bride. It was, after all, his wedding night.

As she dropped off to sleep, her mind seemed to home in on the unborn – both the child Sadie had aborted and the four-month pregnancy of his now wife.

How much of a danger was Barclay to his unborn child?

NINETEEN

Monday, 6 October

But life goes on. At least the wedding was over and done with. But in her quiet moments Claire's concerns for Roxanne Barclay and the unborn child grew. She understood now why Jerome had felt the need to marry his bride. And a sense of duty towards his unborn baby was nothing to do with it. She could almost read his mind. Three million was a lot of money. She needed to work out a way to somehow let him know that she was watching. It was all she could do. She had tried before to intervene, but no one had shared her misgivings. She also determined to keep a closer eye on Astrid.

In the meantime, life continued at Greatbach more or less as before.

David Gad had gone home and he was due at the out-patient department later on in the week. As far as she knew there had been no more postcards, nothing to remind him of the Holocaust. But when they had stripped his room they had found two photocopies of the release of concentration camp inmates. Folded into four, at a guess they too had been sent to him while he had been an inpatient. And who knew how many had been directed to his home, maybe precipitating the repeated suicide attempts. It was a cruel reminder, but Claire believed – hoped – that now they would stop. Barclay had other sport to pursue and, surely, they would keep him busy?

Stan's condition continued to cause them concern. He'd had no more fits but he wasn't well enough yet for them to carry out their plan to discharge him to The Sycamores. But at least Astrid was not still bullying him. When the nurse and Claire met, they skirted around each other warily.

Since Claire had had a word with her, she had been subdued and very quiet. Claire still wondered if it had been Astrid who had told Jerome Barclay about her caseload, but she was biding her time. She didn't want another confrontation.

And Dexter Harding, *the stupid clever*, was turning up for his appointments like a good boy. There was no warning that anything was wrong there. She had no concerns. No red flag waving. Later she would search her mind for some hint, some clue, that all had not been well in Dexter's mind; that something had been brewing up: a resentment, anger. A plan. What would cut her to the quick later was that the clues *were* there. She simply wasn't reading them. But there he was: bovine, stolid, answering questions without meeting her eyes. There was no spark. For once in his life Dexter Harding was being careful, guarded. And clever.

She almost forgot about Barclay too. Then, just over a week after the wedding, on a Thursday morning, Rita spoke to her.

'I've had a request for an outpatient appointment from Jerome Barclay,' she said, watching for Claire's reaction. Clang. The alarm bells were loud enough to wake the dead.

'Do you want to see him?'

'What exactly did he say?'

'Just that he was intending going away for a while and he would like to see you before he went.'

Going away for a while. Everything connected with Barclay made Claire uneasy. Even this simple sentence made her query his motives. Where was he going? Why was he going? And most of all, why was he telling her? Was it another of Barclay's teases?

'Slot him into next Tuesday's clinic,' she said. 'At the end so I can spend some time with him, find out what he's up to.'

The secretary clicked a few keys and smiled up at her. 'Done,' she said.

TWENTY

Tuesday, 21 October

Claire was distracted all day, knowing how the afternoon would end, Barclay's 4 p.m. appointment lying at the back of her mind like thick, dirty sludge. She kept looking at her watch, wishing the hands would slow. But for once her clinic was moving forward smoothly and roughly on time, thanks in part to two DNAs – Did Not Attendees – whose non-attendance gave her extra free time. But in one of the cases, his non-attendance would have to be handed straight over to the police.

Dexter Harding. As his appointment time of 3 p.m. swung past, Claire grew increasingly concerned. He had never failed to turn up before. She scanned his notes. She had been seeing him for nearly two years. In fact she could never work out why he had ever been released from prison and been placed under the Community Treatment Order, under her care jointly with Community Psychiatric Nurse, Felicity Gooch, rather than kept in.

It wasn't as though his initial crime had not been murder. He'd murdered four people. He wasn't even bright. He'd got the wrong house. An ex-girlfriend lived two doors away on the opposite side of the road and he'd got the number wrong. Dexter was like that: stupid. The family he'd actually killed were an Iranian couple and their two small children, who'd come to the country a few years before as political asylum seekers. Some end to their troubled life. It was pathetic and a tragedy. But somehow Dexter had convinced some poor sucker of a psychiatrist that he was suffering from mental delusions at the time and had believed that his girlfriend was possessed of the devil. Claire could hardly believe that one of her psychiatrist colleagues had swallowed the obvious fable. Needless to say, once at Broadmoor these delusions had miraculously melted away and Dexter had been discharged from there and put under her care. But the terms of the CTO at least recognized that Dexter was dangerous. If he hadn't turned up by the end of the afternoon, she would firstly ring Felicity to see if there was a valid reason for his non-attendance and, if she had no satisfactory explanation, she would ring the police and they would track him down. At least, Claire thought, she had the right to detain him. But for now she wondered where he was and why he had not turned up this particular afternoon. He wasn't so stupid that he didn't know what the repercussions were if he didn't attend. He must realize that the police would come battering.

Not her problem for now. She had enough to think about. She made a note to ring Felicity at the end of the afternoon and moved on to the next case. Perhaps she should have remembered Barclay's assessment of Dexter.

The other patient who had failed to turn up was much more difficult to classify. Maylene Forsyte had a histrionic personality disorder. She would do *anything* to gain attention. In fact, she was the worst case of pathological attention-seeking disorder that Claire had ever met. Thirty-five years old and very attractive, as they frequently were, blessed with long black hair and a naturally curvy figure, she led her husband a merry dance. It was often difficult to work out what was truth and what pure fiction, dreamed up by Maylene to make her listeners gasp and open their eyes wide. The anomaly was that sometimes Maylene's real-life experiences were more unbelievable than her fantasies. Her family really had been circus performers. She really had swung the trapeze aged six. She really had been engaged to a member of the travelling community aged thirteen. He really had been murdered in a knife attack when she had been sixteen. All these events were clearly documented. However, there was no documentation that she had ever been the mistress of a Saudi prince or that she had ever had a pet tiger. These were Maylene's little fantasies.

The trouble was that her second husband was the very antithesis of this fantasy life. Derek Forsyte was a foreman and shelf-stacker at one of the local DIY warehouses. The poor man had fallen madly in love and had told Claire on more than one occasion that he couldn't believe his luck when Maylene had accepted his desperate offer of marriage.

Luck? If it was luck it was rotten luck. The poor man had been swept up by the whirlwind which was his wife and hurled into a universe he simply didn't understand. The world of the fantastic rather than prosaic, where truth had no value or meaning, a world which flung money around, ignoring the fact that it too was simply a fantasy. Monopoly cash. He had told Claire that he felt so proud when he introduced his picture-perfect wife to his friends. What he couldn't possibly have understood was that those same friends probably pitied him his terrible, unpredictable, unhappy, insane life. But he couldn't see it.

What was also true was that Maylene's spending habits had landed the couple in some real financial trouble and, like Barclay, Maylene had come before the courts more than once – for shoplifting, failure to attend court appearances, defaulting on debt and non-compliance with conditions of bail. She was a complete fantasizer who was always immaculately dressed, wafting expensive perfume and wearing only designer clothes.

What was for sure was that Maylene, for all her irritating

ways, was not a danger either to herself or to the public in general – only to her poor long-suffering husband – so her non-attendance was not concerning. It just felt like unfinished business. Claire put a DNA sticker on the notes. She would ask Rita to send her another appointment.

Maylene, *the expensive butterfly*. Barclay's description, how apt. Phrases started to dance in front of her, Maylene's justi-fication for her expensive tastes. Claire had imagined Maylene had dreamed up the phrases.

You deserve nice clothes.

You owe it to yourself, and so on. Now she wondered. Had Maylene and Barclay possibly met? Had he been the one to encourage her expensive tastes, fed her delusions? Telling a woman she owes expensive clothes to herself in this case had been a red rag to a bull. An invitation. How much more so when Maylene would have agreed with him heartily without a word of caution or realism. Truth was, her husband simply couldn't afford it. Oh yes, Jerome was hovering somewhere near, a shadowy presence behind the scenes, little more than a silhouette against a thin curtain. But there all right. In his way Barclay was a clever psychologist, brilliant at sensing the most effective phrases to gain the result he desired.

Claire sat and stared at Maylene's notes, clicking keys on the computer, registering her failure to attend clinic and puzzling. Why had Barclay homed in on this particular patient?

But part of the trouble was that instead of focusing on Maylene, Claire was seeing things from Barclay's angle. Distracted by the fact that she would soon be seeing him, and at his request, so while trying to puzzle things out she was missing the danger of the situation. Her mind was too firmly focused on Barclay. Why did he want to see her? There could only be one reason. He wanted to parade something in front of her. So, for now, mistakenly, she was thinking about Jerome. Not Dexter Harding or Maylene Forsyte.

He sauntered in at 4.30 – half an hour late. This was one of his tricks – to keep her waiting, knowing that she would be conscious of every minute that clicked past. Roxanne trickled in behind him, in his wake. The poor girl was bloated with her pregnancy and looked fearful and unwell. For some women pregnancy is a gateway to beauty. For others it is the reverse, and Roxanne Barclay was one of these unlucky ones. Her walk had morphed into a waddle as she entered the room behind her husband. Her lip was swollen and her right eye too. Her manner spoke loudly of a battered wife: the bowed head, humble attitude; something shameful about them, believing, although they were mistaken, that it was all their fault that bad things tumbled down into their lives. All women subjugated by their husbands look the same. They all look like this.

She met Barclay's eyes.

Jerome had his habitual cynical smile pasted on as he greeted Claire. 'I must thank you,' he said carefully, 'for your most generous wedding present.'

Claire looked pointedly at his wife's face.

'She's got clumsy,' he said, 'since her weight and shape have ballooned.' He half turned towards her in his chair, twisting his body and speaking with loud deliberation as though to an elderly deaf person. 'Haven't you, my dear?'

Roxanne nodded, eyes watchful and wary.

Claire was going to get nowhere with her, so she turned her attention back to Barclay. 'Was there any particular reason why you wanted to see me today, Jerome?'

He didn't answer straight away, but was still gauging her reaction to his wife's facial injuries. Instinctively Claire knew he had wanted more of a response. He had wanted her to question Roxanne more closely. Perhaps Roxanne had been taught the correct answers. But Claire had already decided that she would not get the truth out of Roxanne. Even if Barclay hadn't been present, his influence would have lingered, clinging to the air like the odour from bad drains. His wife would still be frightened of him, even if he were out of the room. Claire already knew, without a doubt, that Jerome had not only assaulted his wife but was deliberately flaunting it. This appointment had been booked specifically to make her aware. That was the reason. She moved closer to him, folding her arms across the desk. 'You understand, Jerome, that if I have any concerns about the safety of people around you, I can have you admitted under a Section?'

He simply smiled. 'Concerns? Safety? Section?' as though they were a series of punchlines to schoolboy jokes. 'Oh, Claire, I think you'd need some *evidence* against me. *Firm evidence*,' he emphasized, 'or your judgement might be questioned.' He gave a little smile. She knew that smile. It appeared when he thought he had neatly outmanoeuvred her.

His attitude was still pleasant but there was always a veiled threat behind the bland words spoken so politely.

So again Claire looked pointedly at his wife, who met her eyes only briefly before, predictably, they flickered away.

And Jerome was forced into pursuit. 'Where would you get evidence from? You'd need a statement, you know,' he finished, almost gently.

He'd got her there. Police do need evidence, particularly in cases of alleged domestic abuse. The problem is this: almost always only two people are present. And in this case neither of those would be telling.

'So why did you request this appointment?' She already knew the answer. So she could see that he was up to his old tricks again.

But she knew only half the story.

'I thought it was time you met my wife properly,' he said.

There was no response to that.

Barclay continued. 'My wife and I,' he began, parodying the traditional wedding speech before veering off wildly, 'plus her parents, with whom I get on very well, are buying a boat.'

He met her eyes. 'We thought we'd do a little sailing.' His smile was mocking. Begging her to challenge him. He wanted sport.

And she knew. She could see it unfolding, right in front of her eyes. How easy it can be to tip up a boat.

'What sort of boat?' She couldn't keep the alarm out of her voice.

'Oh, just a sailing dinghy,' he said carelessly. 'You know, cross the Channel, stuff like that.' He smiled again. 'I thought you'd want to know that I'll be leaving these shores. After all,' he continued cheerfully, 'I am no danger to anyone.'

At his side Roxanne flinched.

His smile widened. 'If I *was* still under close supervision,

I wouldn't be able to go, would I, Claire? But you've discharged me.'

She could read his intention. To lay any tragedy at her door and blame it on her bad decision-making.

For a moment she was so taken aback she simply looked at him. Then, partly because she wasn't quite sure what action she could take at this point, she focused on: 'And what about the baby?'

Again, Barclay smiled. 'Babies are born all over the world in various conditions, Claire,' he said. 'We'll make sure we're around in the UK for the birth. Won't we, darling?'

Roxanne nodded and linked her arm in his.

It broke Claire's heart to see how hopeful Roxanne was looking. If she'd had a tail it would be wagging right now. She considered her position. Barclay was right. She had absolutely no jurisdiction over him. No real power. By discharging him she'd relinquished it, pronounced him healthy and safe to be at large. Barclay's case wasn't like Dexter's the bruiser, or even the suicide-by-anorexia Hayley, both of whom it was easy to see had to have strong intervention. No, Barclay was subtle and clever, and she feared both for his wife and his unborn child.

But she wasn't in a good position. If she alerted the police now they would ask her whether he was a danger either to himself or to the general public. She could prove nothing. It was all shadows, so her answer would have to be no.

Her only hope was . . .

'Roxanne,' she said, 'how did you hurt yourself?'

A frightened, chamois-like glance at her husband, who simply smiled.

He knew he had her.

'I'm just clumsy,' she said, voice stolid; not looking at Claire but at her husband, who was nodding his agreement. 'I walked straight into it.'

'Straight into what?'

'A door,' she said brightly, then dropped her eyes.

Roxanne was not a girl who was comfortable telling lies. Or imaginative enough to think of something more original.

Jerome continued, well in his comfort zone now. 'You see, Claire, as I'm not under a close supervision order, I really can wander the world at will.' His eyes sparkled with the challenge. 'And remember. I made this appointment entirely voluntarily. Of my own free will.' And, finally answering her question, 'I really just came to say goodbye.'

Claire hadn't quite finished with him. 'Tell me, Jerome,' she said casually, 'how would you describe yourself?'

'Sorry?'

'A controlling psycho? A clever manipulator?'

His eyes glittered. 'I really don't follow you, Claire.'

'The haunted Jew, the stupid clever,' she pursued. 'How do you know confidential details about my patients?'

'Hit the nail on the head, Claire?' His tone was insolent. 'Good descriptions?'

She ignored the jibe and pursued her question. 'How do you know? Who is telling you things?'

His return stare was blank.

She continued the pursuit.

'The expensive butterfly, the stupid clever?'

He frowned. 'I don't seem to recognize those phrases.'

'Your words,' she said. 'You spoke them on the telephone.'

'Lucky guess.'

Claire shook her head. 'Oh no,' she said, 'not a lucky guess. I will find out who is leaking confidential information.' She met his eyes. 'I will winkle out this informer.'

His response was another of those annoying smiles.

'Who is it? Is it Astrid?'

He frowned, mock confusion. 'Don't think I know an Astrid.'

'OK then, is there anything you particularly want to tell me about these specific patients?'

He couldn't hide his delight. 'Wait and see,' he said.

TWENTY-ONE

After they'd left, Claire sat for a while. She could see trouble ahead, but what could she do? Nothing. Her mind was working frantically but she knew her hands

were tied, both as a professional and as a bystander. Feeling
that it would be of future importance, she documented the
consultation even more carefully than usual: Barclay's wife's
facial injuries, *claimed to be accidental* (she didn't even bother
putting in the tale of the door), his intended purchase of a
boat and, more difficult to put into words, his general manner,
sleekly menacing. Then she tried to work out a way to document his inside knowledge of her other patients.

She shook her head and put her pen down, worried. If Astrid
wasn't responsible, who was? Someone very close to her who
almost seemed to anticipate events. They knew her caseload,
both in- and outpatients, so well. And why pick on those
particular people? She had hundreds of patients passing
through her hands. Was there something uniquely different
about those five?

She was perfectly aware of the pleasure Barclay derived
from baiting her. That was the reason for his attendance today.
The problem for her – as his psychiatrist, responsible for his
actions – was that, apart from having a spy in the cab, he now
had four potential victims: Roxanne; her parents, who were
almost certainly unaware of Barclay's true nature; and then
there was the unborn infant who needed protection. Claire
estimated that Roxanne was about five months pregnant. Unlike
Sadie Whittaker, who had aborted Barclay's child, it was too
late for Roxanne to have an abortion, except on grounds of a
foetal abnormality or maternal ill-health. She would have had
her first scan, which would have excluded abnormality (having
a psycho daddy didn't quite fit the bill), and she couldn't see
Roxanne having any problems with the child. So now only an
accident or a late miscarriage could result in Barclay's spawn
not being born. But then what? Was the baby going to be safe
with Barclay any more than its mother was? Claire's mind
explored all the dark possibilities. Another accident, like the
one that had befallen his baby brother? Or would Barclay
nurture his spawn? Who could know? Claire would like to
have the baby made a ward of court but she would never have
this. A case conference to discuss the child's future would
achieve nothing. Jerome Barclay had no criminal record. He
was too clever. In the eyes of the law he had committed

misdemeanours, not crimes. None of the petty thefts he had been convicted of would justify denying him the right to bring up his own child. Once Sadie had withdrawn her allegation of GBH, Barclay's record had reverted to 'clean'.

Claire had never seen the brutal side to Barclay. She could only imagine what he was like when he let go. Not a sudden snapping of temper, but something far more calculated and cruel. Roxanne would have warning. She would know it was coming, what was coming, feel the whoosh of air before his fist made contact, see the blaze in his eyes, the sadistic joy in his face. Oh yes, Roxanne would have forewarning all right. And seeing the fear on her face would intensify the pleasure for Barclay. But if Roxanne wasn't going to testify against her husband, they had nothing that would stand up in a court of law. Round and round Claire's thoughts went, always banging into the same brick wall.

Good and evil. North and south. Black and white. The law recognizes only stark facts; acts in the past – not the future.

What about Roxanne's parents? Could she rope them in to protect their daughter and grandchild? Claire felt her spirits drop. They were the sort of people to take their son-in-law at face value, think he was charming, hear his smooth phrases without realizing that he was mocking them. Like the poem he had quoted at his wedding reception.

I wish I thought 'What Jolly Fun!' Hiding his contempt behind a jovial-sounding ditty. It still made her shiver.

And the guests at his wedding reception – including Kenneth and Mandy Trigg – had stood up, laughed and clapped their hands.

Oh no. Not them. She couldn't rely on them to have insight into Jerome's devious maze of a mind. She was on her own here.

More than ever, Claire wished that Heidi Faro, her predecessor, had not been murdered and in such a cruel way, her throat cut in her own office, her body suspended upside down from a hook. She needed an ally and didn't know where to turn. At one time she would have spoken to a colleague, Edward or Salena, but someone was feeding Barclay with information and she didn't know who it was, only that it was someone close to her. Astrid seemed the most convenient suspect, but Barclay had information about inpatients as well as outpatients, and that precluded most of the nurses and doctors at Greatbach. Edward and Salena both took clinics and would probably have seen all the patients in Barclay's folio. To alert the police at this stage was out of the question. On her evidence there was nothing they could do. When she knew who it was, she might take it up with either the General Medical Council or the Nursing and Midwifery Council.

And perhaps she was wrong. Perhaps Barclay had no intention of risking his freedom with a criminal act. Perhaps it was all bluff. Maybe he'd got what he wanted – access to plenty of funds and a pliant wife, baiting Claire along the way, enjoying her confusion. Maybe that was enough. *For someone like Barclay*, a voice growled inside her, *there is no 'enough'.*

Was it possible then that this was nothing but an elaborate game of chess? Strategy: *Knight to f3?*

She looked down at the pile of notes. She needed to move on, dictate her letters. Barclay was not her only patient. She had a great pile of notes needing attention, a plethora of diagnoses: depression, schizophrenia, substance abuse leading to acute paranoia; the list went on and on, each one a problem. And then there were the inpatients. Hayley, patched up by the general hospital, probably about to be transferred back to her care, and Stan. She almost sighed at the memory of Stan's haunted eyes. She had always liked him, felt sorry for his downward spiral of life and current plight, but she feared there was little hope that he would reverse the cycle, find his lost self somewhere. David Gad had gone home and she counted each day, hoping he would not be readmitted, or worse. It had been a risk to discharge him, and if she'd got it wrong and there was another, maybe successful suicide attempt, blame would be laid at her door. These were the adversaries and the problems she *thought* she had. She discounted Maylene Forsyte and her poor, unfortunate husband, Derek. She didn't even spare them a thought. She should have remembered. She could not afford to be distracted.

And for now she had a more pressing matter. She must report the fact that Dexter Harding had failed to attend his clinic appointment. She allowed herself a minute to wonder why. What clumsy mayhem was he organizing now? Another arson attack? On the wrong house again? The thought of him blundering around, possibly plotting another bungled plan, was worrying. What she was forgetting was the basic rule of psychiatry. Of life, really. While all your attention is focused forward, you do not see what lies behind you or around you, left and right. Which means that danger can sneak up, put its hands around your neck and squeeze the life out of you before you are even conscious of its presence.

By the heavy feeling at the bottom of her heart, she knew that she was still grieving for Grant. So often lately she had almost wished she had a recording of his tuneless hums and whistles, the noises he made when he was absorbed in something. She wished she had a can of his own personal scent, a mixture of paint and aftershave, of wallpaper paste and glue, wood shavings and that male scent that men don't even know they carry.

Physically too, the house seemed so different – dead instead of alive. Too tidy. No cans of deodorant, no empty beer bottles. *Why don't you throw them away when they're empty?* Which had provoked a grinning response: *I always forget which ones are empty.*

No kitchen counter full of washing-up from the elaborate meals he insisted on cooking. *Can't we wash up in the morning?*

His truly appalling taste in music: *Is there a tune in this or simply a noise?* His response an even-wider grin.

She sat still, frozen for a moment, thinking, feeling her eyes fill with salty tears, trying to stem them. That was no good. Crying wouldn't bring him back.

Nothing would.

She wanted to ring him. Talk to him. At least she'd known (thought she'd known) she could trust him. Even though Grant had never been much interested in her work, his attitude and presence had been support enough. She hadn't wanted input from him anyway, just for him to be there. And now he wasn't.

She pulled her mobile phone out of her bag and scrolled through her contacts. No Grant. She'd wiped it off. But not from her mind. She could still remember it. Her finger pressed in the keys. But she knew she would not press Call; neither would she compose some sad plea under the envelope icon. She put the phone back in her bag and used the hospital landline to make another call instead.

TWENTY-TWO

Dexter Harding's community psychiatric nurse, Felicity Gooch, was a capable woman. Claire rang her mobile and got straight through.

'Dexter didn't come for his appointment today,' she said. 'Is there any reason why?'

'I haven't seen him since last Tuesday,' Felicity said slowly. Claire could hear the flip of pages as she leafed through her diary. 'I reminded him about his appointment today and he said he would be there. I'll go round to the hostel and see what's up. He's been behaving himself lately.' Her voice was thoughtful. 'I hope he isn't planning anything.'

'It might be an idea if you could come with him next time,' Claire said. 'I should keep more up to date with what he's doing day to day.'

Felicity groaned. 'It's so hard,' she said. 'I've got such a huge caseload that I can't keep tabs on them all the time. And Marilyn Evans is off on maternity leave and hasn't been replaced. Quite frankly, Claire, I'm tearing my hair out. I'm lucky that I do get to make contact with Dexter a couple of times a week.'

'I'm sorry to put more on you, but this is the first time he's defaulted. Now Dexter's about as subtle as a blind elephant. You should easily track him down.'

The nurse's response was a 'Hmmph.'

Something led her to urge the nurse. 'Find him, Felicity. Put it number one on your list or else it'll mean trouble.'

'I will, Claire. Sorry to grumble.'

'That's OK. I'll put in a request that you have some help.'

'That'd be great but . . .' Felicity laughed. 'I won't be holding my breath.'

She rang off and Claire made her way up to Rita's office. The secretary had gone home now so she simply put the Post-it note on her computer screen.

Can you send Maylene Forsyte another appointment?
She DNA'd today.

It was only as she stuck the note up that something registered. Maylene – *the expensive butterfly.*

Why had he picked on her?

Tuesday, 21 October, 7.15 p.m.

The phone was ringing as she let herself in. It was only as she picked it up that she realized she'd stopped expecting it to be Grant. So his voice put an earth tremor through her.

'Claire, I'm so sorry.' Husky, apologetic, familiar, welcome.

She was so shocked that she didn't speak and his voice came on again.

'Claire, I really am.' Then, as she still simply gaped at the phone, his voice became more urgent. 'Are you there, Claire?'

'Yes,' she said, 'I'm here,' and was stunned at the coldness and hostility in her voice.

'I want to explain.'

Nearly eight fucking months too late, she thought.

She felt anger then. Hot and wild as a forest fire. Then she managed, 'I take it you've rung because you want your share of the house?'

'Claire.'

He sounded hurt and she dived in. 'Well, what else can this phone call be about, Grant?'

'I want to explain,' he said again, and now she just felt irritated and foolish.

'You want to explain why you just vanished out of my life, Grant?'

'Well—'

'Oh forget it,' she said, and slammed the phone down.

She stood in the hall, surprised at her response. She'd really liked him. OK, at first she'd had her reservations, but later she

had grown to appreciate his virtues. They'd been together for
five years. Bought this house together. But then he had just
gone. Not explained, apologized. Nothing. Just gone. And that
she couldn't relate to. His pathetic, cowardly abandonment
had made her so unhappy, so lost, so unsure of herself. Work had,
initially, been difficult. Then a welcome distraction. And all for
. . . She blinked away the memory of him stroking the girl's
cheek. It hurt more than if she'd caught them in bed together.
She knew one thing. She didn't ever want to go through all
that again. That terrible feeling of being swept downriver on
a torrent of misery, unable to swim, survive, or reach the
river bank.

She took the phone off the hook and started to cook tea:
pasta, cheese, onion, tomatoes and bacon. Hardly tasting it,
she ate it, chewing mechanically in front of the television,
watching a medical soap, but hardly taking it in. She'd
always wondered what her response would be if he made
contact. Well, now she knew.

She simply felt cold. Numb. Devoid of emotion. So what
did that make her? As unfeeling as some of her patients?

Wednesday, 22 October, 9 a.m.

Rita put her head round the door. 'I've sent that appointment out to Maylene Forsyte,' she said cheerily. 'Let's hope
she comes this time round. But still,' she said, comforting as
a mother hen, 'she's not one that you're worried about, is
she?'

'No. Although it's not the first time she's DNA'd, I'm just
puzzled. And it's odd that both she and Dexter failed to attend
their appointments.' She tried to make a joke of it. 'Nice, easy
afternoon.'

'Yeah.'

Rita picked up her notebook full of messages. 'Oh, and you
have a message from your favourite patient,' she said.

'And that is . . .?'

'Mr Barclay,' Rita said, reading verbatim from her notepad.
'He wanted me to tell you that he's bought his boat and will
be sailing off into the sunset with his wife and in-laws for a

couple of months.' She watched for Claire's reaction. 'Did he mention it to you yesterday?'

'Yes – I just hadn't realized he'd be going so soon.' Something else struck her.

'He's learned to navigate in so short a time?'

'I think he said something about having someone do the sailing for him.'

And that was when Claire decided, as with the messing around by Grant, that she was sick of Jerome Barclay's games too. She had enough to focus on with her inpatients and the couple of missing outpatients. Let them sink or swim, she thought. It isn't my problem.

It would be an attitude she almost knew then that she would later regret. She had lost her grip and she kept remembering Grant's voice on the telephone. '*Claire. Please . . .*'

What had he been about to say?

'And the most important thing,' Rita said. 'Felicity rang. Dexter's still missing, I'm afraid.' She looked up. 'He's not been seen at the hostel since the weekend.'

'Oh, bugger,' Claire said. 'That means we'll have to involve the police.'

Rita nodded. She had been Claire's secretary for almost five years, almost since Claire had taken up the consultant post – two new girls together. The relationship had been close and successful from the first. She was an intelligent woman with impressive computer and typing skills and had an unerring instinct for knowing the patients, understanding their conditions, realizing what was a serious incident and what could be left to work itself out.

Claire could not have managed without her. She would have been diminished. The relationship between consultant and secretary is necessarily close. They know all their secrets – home, family – and because it is they who type all the letters about patients, they are party to all that too. Claire knew little about Rita's personal life, though. Only that she was married and had one son. Rita returned to her typing and Claire closed her office door. She needed privacy to make this call.

Dexter missing was top of the list of serious incidents. She

spoke first to Felicity, hoping he would have turned up, or that
she had some clue where he was, what he was up to, but she
had heard nothing. He hadn't been seen. 'Have you informed
the police?'

'Yep. They've put out a "stop and apprehend" and one of
them's coming round to talk to you.' There was a pause while
Felicity obviously juggled with her diary to find the name. 'A
Detective Sergeant Zed Willard.'

'Do you know when?'

'No. He just said he'd be getting in touch with you.'

Claire felt suddenly weary. And it wasn't just the complica-
tions at work. Her job had *always* been stressful. She had
chosen it because of the challenges.

No. It wasn't that. She was weary because she knew she
would have to meet up with Grant again – even if only to sort
out what to do about the house. She tried telling herself that
she didn't care about the house any more. It meant nothing
to her without him. And she didn't care about *him* any more
either, so . . . what exactly was the problem?

She knew full well what the problem was. Her damaged
heart.

Damaged initially by his abandonment and subsequently by
that tender image that had stuck to the front of her eyelids.
She dropped her face into her hands. The betrayal made the
hurt fifty – a hundred – times worse. No matter how many
times she told herself she had hardened her heart and raised
her defences, that he was not going to breach them again.
Ever. It still bloody well hurt.

2.30 p.m.

She just had time to ring the hospital about Hayley before a
case conference about Stan Moudel, whose condition now was
giving rise to serious concern. They were going to have to
investigate the cause of his deterioration. DS Zed Willard
would have to slot in wherever. She was not in the mood for
indulgence. She didn't have time to fret about where Dexter
was, why he had vanished from his hostel, where he was now
and what exactly his stupid, wicked brain was planning. If

anything it was a problem for the police. That much was clear under the terms of his CTO.

She rang the ward where Hayley had been and was told she had been transferred.

Good or bad news?

She was then passed from pillar to post until a young foundation-year doctor came on the line. She explained who she was and he cleared his throat. 'She's in trouble,' he said. 'She's been having cardiac problems.'

'Cardiac? At her age?'

'Arrhythmias. We're having a problem getting her to revert to sinus rhythm and keeping her potassium level stable. We're worried about her, Dr Roget. She's in an awful physical state.' He paused. 'We just hope we can pull her through.'

'Thanks.' Claire put the phone down. Another problem to worry about. She sat for a while, feeling both reflective and sad. Fourteen years old and Hayley's life hadn't been great from day one. Before that even, if one accepted the Chinese method of calculating age – from the moment of conception. Whoever believed that life should be fair should meet Hayley, she thought. She had forebodings about her future. If she had one.

She recalled one day, over the summer, when she had visited Hayley in her room.

Sometimes things were going so well it was tempting to return to a sunny, happier place.

She had never before been greeted by a smile from her. Certainly not one as bright and happy as this. She'd stood in the doorway for a while, wishing she could bottle it and take a sip every time things went wrong.

But that had been one of Hayley's last good days. 'I ate all my breakfast,' she'd said.

'That's good,' Claire said, and sat down beside her. This was an opportunity not to be wasted, Hayley in receptive mood. 'You know you've come close to dying?'

Hayley had shrugged and looked away, the smile already gone. And now, months later, Claire wondered. Had the girl been clever? Had the smile and reassurance been the smoke-and-mirrors manipulation of an anorexic to gain discharge from hospital? They were, after all, famously deceitful. She'd regarded her patient, who had suddenly taken an interest in her duvet cover.

'When can I go home, Claire?' Her eyes had been desperate to escape.

'You know the answer to that. When you reach your target weight.'

'What if I promise to eat?'

'It doesn't work like that, Hayley.'

Hayley was then detained under a Section 2. She had been an inpatient for three weeks when this conversation had taken place. They could keep her in for a further week. Longer if they transferred her to a Section 3. Claire had already known Hayley's case would take a long time. But for ever?

But then, taking advantage of the girl's temporary affability, Claire had made her decision. 'We'll see how you go,' she'd said. 'If by the weekend you're eating well, you've reached your target weight and there are no ill-effects, we'll think about home early next week.'

Hayley had tried to hide her disappointment by passing a hand in front of her mouth, but Claire had noticed the swift movement and had mistrusted the girl.

The plan had not worked then.

And now?

It looked as though her life teetered even more on the brink than usual.

She glanced at her watch. No time for reflection. Time for the multidisciplinary meeting about Stan. Another of her concerns.

She listened to one after the other of the reports.

As she had feared, Stan's paranoia had intensified and now was focused largely on the staff. He was convinced they were plotting to kill him and this had made him aggressive and difficult to manage. Claire was reluctant to sedate him merely to regain control. In fact the guidelines had recently tightened up over the sedation of difficult-to-manage patients. These days the old-fashioned 'chemical cosh' was actively discouraged, viewed as robbing patients of their human rights. But it could be difficult finding a compromise between protecting the staff of Greatbach and preserving patients' rights. It was a balancing act. Currently Stan was detained under a Section 3, for his own protection initially; but since his behaviour had become more aggressive, it could also be justified on the grounds of protecting the public at large. There was no question of him going anywhere. Physically he wouldn't cope. These days he could only be attended by two nurses at a time and was kept in the locked ward. But Claire had noticed his deterioration and had been wondering. Was Salena right? Was there another reason – apart from misuse of drugs – for his deteriorating condition and worsening behaviour?

And then there was the matter of that one, solitary fit he had suffered.

TWENTY-THREE

They were halfway through the case conference on Stan when Rita knocked on the door and whispered that DS Willard was outside, wanting to talk to her.

'Make him a coffee,' she whispered back. 'And tell him I'll be just ten minutes.'

Rita melted away and they continued.

Salena Urbi, her registrar, had previously worked at Broadmoor and was well used to the management of violent, paranoiac patients, so Claire let her take the lead on Stan. 'It's his unpredictability that makes him difficult to manage,' she said. 'One minute he's a charm offensive, quiet and polite, the next he's lashing out.' She frowned. 'It's a sort of blind fury. He doesn't target particular members of staff. It can be anybody.' She was thoughtful. 'It's only a matter of time before he causes someone serious injury.' She looked at Claire. 'I wondered whether we should consider referring him to Broadmoor. What do you think?'

Claire was silent for a minute then she held up a finger. 'I just want to run something past you all,' she said. 'Salena, Teresa, Astrid . . .' The forensic psychiatric nurse glanced across, impassive. Since Claire had spoken to her, relations between the two had remained strained.

'And you too, Siona.' She smiled. 'And you, Edward.'

Edward responded with his usual gentle form of politeness. 'I'm all ears.'

She had their full attention.

'When Stan was admitted, we knew that he had a long history of drug taking, both hard and soft drugs, heroin, cocaine, hash, meow-meow, ketamine and so on.' She couldn't resist a swift grin. 'He'd tried just about everything. And we also know that many of these drugs have long-term side effects – in particular, paranoia.' They were all listening with rapt attention now, waiting for her point. 'But once we'd sorted out the cold turkey bit, his mental state initially began to improve.'

There were nods of agreement and she continued. 'But over the last three weeks he's been getting worse. More unpredictable, more violent.'

Again nods of agreement.

'We know from his blood tests . . .' she gave a cynical smile, 'and the fact that he has no visitors that he has no access to further illegal substances here, so it isn't that.'

They all frowned, thought about it, nodded.

'And then there's that fit.'

Silence until Edward said casually, 'Could have been a result of withdrawal. It's not uncommon.'

'Yes – but . . . you know the old adage. Exclude the physical before you focus on the psychological.'

There were grudging nods of agreement and she continued. 'I just wonder if something organic is happening.'

Siona spoke for all of them. 'Such as?'

'I was considering two options,' Claire said. 'One is that he has some form of degenerative disease such as early Alzheimer's due to his substance abuse.'

'And the other one?' Again Siona spoke for all of them.

And this was more difficult. 'I'm worried he has a brain tumour.' She looked around the room and read varying degrees of surprise.

Salena Urbi was frowning. 'But I've seen no physical signs,' she said. 'No ataxia; his pupils are equal and reacting normally to light. His gait is normal.'

'Come on, Salena,' Claire said, 'you know as well as I do that Stan Moudel should have a brain scan.'

There was a pause for thought around the room and then slowly they all agreed. And, as they all agreed, they also knew that they would never be able to scan his brain without a general anaesthetic. There was no way Stan was going to keep still and allow himself to be subjected to a brain scan. It was going to be complicated. And then there was the question of capacity. Did Stan have the capacity to accept or decline a test? Would he understand the implications of a further diagnosis?

Probably not, so they were almost certainly going to have to make the informed decision for him.

But in the end there were nods of agreement right round the room. Claire stopped speaking. *Doomed.* Together with 'homeless', it had been the adjective used to describe Stan. She gave Astrid another hard stare. The nurse looked away.

These meetings were an opportunity to keep the staff up to date with all their patients. Claire drew breath. 'I'm afraid that Dexter Harding failed to turn up for yesterday's appointment. Felicity doesn't have a clue where he is. He's not been seen at the hostel since the weekend. He's still under a Community Treatment Order. As he has broken the terms of this, the police have been alerted and a DS is waiting outside to interview me. I don't need to tell you this is bad news,' she said. 'He's under our supervision and, considering his violently doltish history, I'm just hoping he isn't planning something as misguided and dangerous as before.' She paused, suddenly worried at her phrase. What exactly was Dexter up to? Why had he defaulted on yesterday's appointment when for two years he had never even been late?

What cataclysmic event was about to happen? 'I don't suppose any of you can shed any light on this?' But there were only shakes of the head and blank looks. She moved on. 'I had another DNA in clinic, who is less of a concern. Maylene Forsyte, a histrionic personality.' She frowned. 'I don't think any of you know her.' *The expensive butterfly.* Or did they? Again she focused a sharp look in Astrid's direction but again her face was bland – almost uninterested.

The others were more engaged, so she filled them in. 'She's never been an inpatient. She's a fantasist who has also lived a fantastic life. Her husband is extremely long suffering, but I don't have any concerns for her safety. And she's no danger to anyone.' She hesitated, reluctant to conjure him up. 'And then there is the newly married Jerome Barclay.'

She didn't miss the worried glances exchanged between the members of staff or their deliberate silence. Unlike Heidi, her predecessor, they had never seen Barclay as much of a threat.

None of them saw why he should be under *any* sort of supervision order, apart from a purely voluntary one; it had been partly due to their opinion that Claire had been persuaded to let him off the leash, realizing that there was no solid reason for – or benefit to be gained from – continued contact. She knew full well that she didn't have the backing or the sympathy of her colleagues, and her clinics were always overbooked. They were all urged by the Hospital Management Team to avoid following up patients unnecessarily so appointments could be freed up for new referrals.

Her colleagues had responded in various ways when she had mentioned she was going to his wedding. Astrid and Edward had wondered why she had been invited but had not ventured an opinion. The rest had responded with various degrees of interest – or lack of it. They all had enough of a caseload without concerning themselves with Jerome Barclay. On that one, at least, she was on her own.

Worse was the fact that she believed one of them had spoken to Barclay, given him details of some of her patients. This was not just unprofessional – in Barclay's case it was dangerous. So who, out of this circle of colleagues, was communicating with Jerome? Edward? She glanced at him. He returned a smile. No, surely not Edward.

Salena? She smiled as her eyes rested on her registrar. No way. She dismissed this without any thought. She would trust Salena with her life.

Teresa? She eyed the nurse with her long dark hair, slightly plump in jeans and a shirt. Teresa was looking thoughtful, frowning. But Teresa was a good sort. Reliable.

No, for her money, it was Astrid. The nurse had pointed features which tended to make her look angry. Disgruntled, envious, as though she should be earning more money, working less hard, having a more successful life, more recognition. She had a chip on her shoulder. Why had she left Broadmoor and moved here, to Stoke-on-Trent? She wasn't a native of the Potteries. She had not been promoted; she wasn't earning more money. She never seemed as though she enjoyed her job, so why was she here? What was behind this woman? More importantly, was this chip large enough for her to risk her career by leaking information to a psycho like Barclay?

All questions to be considered and then, if possible, answered.

But ruminating who was sharing information with Barclay was alienating her from her colleagues.

It was by planting these poisonous seeds to sprout and grow inside her brain that Jerome Barclay had successfully driven a wedge between her and them. But this suspicion not only isolated her from her colleagues – even she had to acknowledge that her behaviour was bordering on the paranoid. This is what happens when you do not know whom you can trust. You soon come to think you can trust no one, soon believe you are surrounded by enemies.

She returned to the present and their mainstream inpatients. 'Salena, perhaps you'll try and arrange Stan's brain scan?'

'I'll do my best,' she said, 'but I think he'll be passed from pillar to post. No one's going to want to pick him up.'

'I know that, but just remember after he'd been in and clean for two months, he was becoming quite a reasonable man. I was hopeful we'd be able to rehabilitate him, get him into Psyche-o-more, but we can't send him there while he's like this. We either have to sort him out and treat him, or consign him to Broadmoor. Let's just make absolutely sure we're not missing any pathology.'

There was a moment's silence before they moved on again.

She filled them in on Hayley's latest progress report and

watched all of them look reflective. Teresa spoke for all of them. 'What'll be will be,' she said. 'She'll eat or she won't eat. Live or die. We'll just have to see how she does, and if she does get well enough for us to discharge her again, she'll decide for herself.'

There was no answer to this. In the end humans do have a choice to live or die.

TWENTY-FOUR

4 p.m.

Detective Sergeant Zed Willard proved to be a bulky man with unruly dark hair and a pair of honest-looking large blue eyes that gave him a look of boyish innocence. He quickly got to the point, took down her details and made notes.

'When did you last see Mr Harding, doctor?'

'Two weeks ago yesterday. I have to see him every fortnight.'

'And the community nurse . . .' He consulted his notebook. 'Felicity?'

'She makes contact with Dexter every couple of days. If she's on annual leave someone else keeps an eye on him. And of course the hostel would report back to us if they had any concerns.'

The blue eyes fixed on hers. 'So what's his daily life like?'

Claire sighed. 'Not great,' she confessed. 'He's pretty much unemployable once we've disclosed his mental history. He lives at the hostel in Hanley and goes to a day centre a couple of days a week. The rest of the time he's supposed to be on a literacy course, but he often doesn't turn up.'

DS Willard looked up. 'Literacy course?'

'That's how we believe he torched the wrong house,' Claire said. 'He can't read numbers and certainly not words.'

'I see.' DS Willard frowned. 'So . . . mobile phone?'

'He gets a friend to punch in the numbers. He can't text.'

'Or travel?'

'With difficulty.'

'Can he drive?'

'Not legally,'

DS Willard drew in a long, deep breath and asked the million-dollar question. 'How dangerous is he, Dr Roget?'

'Claire, please.' She was warming to the detective's blue eyes; such innocence in a policeman was rather endearing.

He was waiting for her response.

'It's hard to say,' she said. 'He tends to lash out when disturbed or upset. The arson attack supposed to be on his ex-girlfriend's house was quite something for him – the planning, the buying of the petrol and even the act itself.'

Something seemed to strike Willard. 'The ex,' he said, frowning slightly, 'is she still around?'

'I believe so.'

'In your opinion, doctor, is *she* in danger?'

'I don't know,' she said frankly. 'The original crime was five years ago. He's certainly been compliant for the two years he's been under my care. But . . .' And she felt the heaviness of her job pressing like a lead weight on her shoulders.

After a moment's silence, Willard took out a Tablet and looked at her expectantly. 'Her name?'

Claire frowned. 'Sheridan,' she said. 'Sheridan Riley.'

Willard typed the name into his Tablet. 'She lives in Blurton,' he said. 'Maybe we should get over there, take a look . . .' his eyes met hers. 'Just as a precaution.'

She smiled acquiescence.

'Has he ever missed before?'

She shook her head. 'When he came here I spelled out in no uncertain terms what the conditions of his Community Treatment Order were. I told him then that if he missed an appointment the police would come looking for him and I had the power to detain him under Section Three of the Mental Health Act.'

DS Willard looked at her curiously. 'And how did he respond to that?'

'He didn't have much choice, DS Willard. He agreed to it.'

'You have a lot of power.'

She smiled wearily. 'It doesn't seem like power, Sergeant Willard. It seems like a responsibility, doing your best to protect the public in general.'

'So . . .' he said slowly, 'the public in general. Are they in danger now?'

'I don't think so but I can't be sure.'

'And Sheridan Riley?' he asked reflectively.

'If she's living in Blurton, he's had plenty of opportunity to contact her before now.'

'Maybe,' DS Willard said tentatively, 'something's happened to trigger him off?'

'Hey,' Claire protested, smiling now. 'Who's the psychiatrist here?'

'We're all psychiatrists,' Willard said soberly. 'In the Force we try to anticipate crimes, look into someone's actions, prevent crime if possible, look for motive and habit.' He made an attempt at levity. 'The old MO. You know what I think . . .' There was the tiniest hesitation and a small, tentative smile, 'Claire? I think we're all psychiatrists.'

She liked the blue eyes more at this comment and the regular white teeth even more than the eyes. 'That's a very profound thought, Detective Sergeant Willard.'

He looked embarrassed, then laughed. 'Oh, I'm deep,' he said self-deprecatingly. 'Deep as ditchwater. Now . . .' His manner became more business-like. 'We have a photo of him back at the station which we'll circulate. This—' he handed her a card – 'is my mobile number, station extension and email address. You can get me any time if he turns up. Umm . . .' He hesitated then grinned. 'I'll need some way of getting hold of you.' He tried her name out again, 'Claire.'

'Yeah.' She gave him her card with all her details, plus Rita's telephone number. He pocketed it carefully. 'Good,' he said. 'Thanks. I also have Felicity Gooch's contact details. If you or she hears anything, I would appreciate it if you would get in touch with me right away. But actually . . .' He looked uncomfortable. 'I've read the report of the house fire. I'm really not sure this guy should be out there at all, walking the streets.'

'Neither am I,' Claire confessed. 'I've always had my reservations, but he had a very powerful counsel who made much of his compromised mental state. An IQ of seventy, illiterate. Evoked some pity amongst the jury. And then there were the inevitable—' she wiggled her fingers – '"voices". Before we knew it, having basically murdered four completely innocent people, he was walking free.'

She was silent for a moment while DS Willard watched her curiously, wondering. The truth that lay beneath was her misgiving that the nationality of the murdered family, Iraqi Kurds, might have played a part in the light sentence. It was something Claire had always been concerned about. Human rights are human rights. They shouldn't depend on class, colour or creed. But it could be hard to treat all people exactly the same. Had they been a middle-class English family of four, she had always felt the sentence would have been life with no get-out-of-jail card – whatever his circumstances.

'And then he was out on the streets again under a Community Treatment Order.'

'So if he doesn't comply, you said the terms are . . .?'

'We can readmit him.'

'You can do that just on the terms that he didn't turn up?'

'Simply put, yes – though we can use our discretion. Say if he'd gone on holiday or missed because he was unwell, something like that, we can decide not to Section him.'

DS Willard nodded, understanding.

He seemed a reasonable person, someone intelligent. She decided to ask his advice. 'I wonder if you would give me your opinion on another patient. An outpatient.'

His eyebrows shooting up towards his hairline told her how surprised he was at this turn of events. Psychiatrist asking a policeman for an opinion?

'If I can.' His response was dubious.

'This patient is a male who has a personality disorder. He is attention seeking with a history of violence towards his ex-girlfriend. She dropped the charges.'

DS Willard nodded. 'They often do.'

'His entire family – mother, father and baby brother – all died in suspicious circumstances. I've never been convinced that he wasn't responsible for all three deaths, but there's no proof. Just the long arm of coincidence. But, unlike Dexter, this man is as bright as a button. I would say his IQ's at least 160. He can run rings around this department. He has recently married.' She moistened her lips. 'I was invited.'

Zed Willard interrupted. 'Is that usual – for a patient to invite his psychiatrist to his wedding?' He was astounded.

'Oh no. It is *not* usual. I was invited as a witness,' she explained. 'Purely to tease me. He knows I have my suspicions of his past and he also knows full well that I have no firm evidence, so can do precisely nothing about it except watch and wait and hope that at some point he makes a mistake and gives himself away.' She leaned forward, studying the inno- cence in the baby blue eyes. Innocence was not what she wanted now, but suspicious comprehension. 'Think of it as a cat-and-mouse game. It's one of the few pleasures he has in life. His wife is pregnant. On the one occasion he has attended here since the wedding, voluntarily I might add, and at his request, his wife had facial injuries which she claimed were . . .' The phrase was so clichéd she wafted it away with her hand and DS Willard met her eyes, understanding perfectly.

Willard opened his mouth to speak but Claire pre-empted his words. 'I know,' she said. 'If the wife won't testify, you practic- ally never have a proven case of domestic violence. It's only if another person witnesses it. And even then . . .' She left the sentence hanging in the air before plunging in again. 'His in-laws are lottery winners, worth about three million.' She knew by telling him these very specific facts that he would easily identify Barclay. 'He has just bought a boat and intends going off sailing in it. With my suspicions, DS Willard, what can I do?'

'If I call you Claire,' he said uncomfortably, 'I wish you'd call me Zed. And the answer is, I don't know. Don't you have any powers to control this guy's activities?'

She shook her head. 'No. He's never been convicted of any crime apart from minor misdemeanours. He's too clever for that.'

'I see,' he said. 'A slippery customer.'

'Very slippery.' She waited for his response but could see he was struggling.

He was silent for a long minute, his face mirroring his thoughts as he tussled with the problem as she had. 'I suppose,' he said eventually, 'that I would let him know I was on to him.'

She was frustrated. He hadn't quite grasped it. 'But, Zed, that's at least part of the thrill for him. He *wants* me to be *on to him*. He *wants* someone to applaud his cleverness. Just so long as he's not caught and convicted of anything. This guy has a couple of very minor convictions. Cheque fraud and shoplifting when he was young.'

'Oh shit,' he said. 'Then I would warn his wife and in-laws to be on their guard.'

She shook her head. That was not the answer. 'The in-laws aren't exactly the brightest buttons in the box – certainly not compared to him – and you'd have to meet his wife to understand. She's blinded by love. Devoted.' She paused. 'And pregnant.'

'In my experience,' he said seriously, 'women are devoted right up until they have a child to protect. And then mother-love kicks in and . . . Well, let's just say they change.'

Something in his voice pricked her. 'You sound as though you're talking from personal experience.'

He flushed. 'Yeah. Well.' He stood up. 'Keep in touch, Claire.'

'I will.'

He left awkwardly, bumping into the bookshelf on the way out, as though distracted by the turn their conversation had just taken, and she was left wondering. As always.

TWENTY-FIVE

Thursday, 23 October, 7.45 a.m.

Although she had plenty of problems to disturb her equilibrium, she had had a dreamless sleep and awoke with an unexpected feeling of optimism, many of her fears relegated to the back burner. And there was an explanation for her unwarranted peace of mind. She'd taken the bull by the horns. Late last night, feeling strangely calm and detached, she'd texted Grant suggesting they have dinner to discuss things. She'd desisted from signing off with a kiss, simply putting Claire.

Problem One – dealt with. Well, not quite. More like – faced up to. Now there were just the rest of them.

As she drove into work she tuned into Radio Stoke and kept the volume turned low. The day was dull and chilly, the city a uniform grey. But it didn't dampen her mood. She began to hum along to 'Holiday' by Madonna. Maybe that would be the next step. Where? Egypt to a dive site, Costa Rica, Sri Lanka, the world?

She was so preoccupied with this pleasant scenario that the eight o'clock news headlines hardly registered.

A couple have been found dead in their homes in Biddulph. Police have released no further details until relatives have been informed. A post mortem has been scheduled for Friday.

Biddulph, she reflected. A little close to home, but there were no names and so she drove on.

There was a brief mention of Kate, Duchess of Cambridge; her clothes, her hair. One story after another scrutinizing the poor girl in the minutest detail. Claire knew she wouldn't have swapped places with her for all the money in the world.

Thinking of large fortunes brought her neatly back to the Trigg family and Jerome, and her concerns started up again. What, she wondered, was he up to? There had been no further communication from him, which was both a relief and a cause for anxiety. Like a mischievous toddler, Barclay was at his most worrying when he was silent and absent. She wondered when he was planning to sail away into the sunset. What sunset? Whose sunset? It wouldn't be Barclay's. The sun was not about to set on him but possibly on his wife, their child and her family.

But when she arrived at Greatbach she was greeted with the news that the Royal Stoke University Hospital had been in touch. Hayley had deteriorated during the night.

Not a great start to the day. And it was about to get worse.

10.30 a.m.

DS Willard rang to say Dexter had still not been found and the search had been stepped up. There had been no sign of him, no word of him. No sightings. On the plus side no crimes had been reported. 'Just as a precaution,' he said, 'we're keeping an eye on Sheridan Riley. Provided her with an alarm.'

'But he's been an outpatient here for a couple of years,' she pointed out. 'If he'd wanted to try and get to her, he's had ample opportunity.'

'He's breaking the rules, Claire,' he said gently, as though speaking to a primary school child. 'You might be careful of yourself too,' he said, almost as a bluff afterthought, but she was touched by the kindness – the care – in his tone. His protective attitude reminded her of the way Grant had been with the unknown girl, the stroking of her cheek. She squeezed her eyes tight shut. What was she doing? Looking for love and care from just anywhere? Pathetic. But when they had finished the phone call, it wasn't Zed Willard or Grant or the unknown girl who was occupying her mind but her missing patient. The significance of Dexter Harding vanishing underground was just beginning to hit her. Were DS Willard's misgivings justified? Was there something sinister behind Dexter's disappearance? Where was he? Why had he vanished? Barclay's intentions were subtle, hints and jibes, but Dexter's assault was likely to be full frontal. A brutal bludgeon. Now she was recalling the description of the aftermath of his arson attack. The pathetic remains of four people, two of them children, bent and burnt, buried in a land foreign to them because their own had been considered unsafe. Unsafe? Stoke could be unsafe when Dexter Harding was on the loose. What would be next? Another attempt on Sheridan's life?

'*Leave it to the police,*' she muttered to herself. '*It's their job now. Their responsibility. Not yours. You've done your bit. Focus on your role.*'

And she did. Under duress, Stan's brain scan had been booked at the University Hospital of North Staffordshire, with the conditions that the procedure should be carried out under a general anaesthetic, that he must be accompanied by two of Greatbach's staff to supervise him, and that he be returned to the psychiatric unit as soon as he was conscious. Claire agreed to all three conditions – no more or less than she had expected.

The news from the hospital about Hayley was not reassuring. Stable but critical, the charge nurse said. They were monitoring her cardiac, liver and renal function and she was being drip-fed and with a feeding tube inserted into her stomach. She couldn't tolerate a naso-gastric tube and vomited anything put down it. There was enough accusation in the nurse's voice for Claire to pick up on her finger-point of guilt – as though the unit had not done enough for the child. Because in the eyes of the law, that was what Hayley Price was – a child. But they had kept her alive this far. Claire had some sympathy for the hospital staff's point of view. She had worked with enough patients in this state to have a picture of her, lying virtually helpless in bed. Nothing like a normal fourteen-year-old, who should have been out clubbing with her friends or working towards GCSEs. Having fun. A life. Not this. But Hayley had been cursed from her very conception. And now who cared for her except Greatbach? Not her parents, that was for sure. Mother dead, gone the way of most heroin addicts. Father unknown. Behind Hayley there was not exactly a stable, loving family. It had been a shit start to a life which had slowly got worse. Now all they could do was hope.

And so another day passed.

Claire checked her phone a few times but there was no response from Grant. So he had bobbed up, briefly, and now had gone underground yet again.

Outpatient clinic, Greatbach Secure Psychiatric Unit
Friday, 24 October, 2 p.m.

In that week there was one bright star in her sky. David Gad attended his clinic appointment accompanied by his grandson, the dark-eyed boy she had seen visit him on the ward.

He walked into the room slowly, leaning heavily on the boy, eased himself into the chair before meeting her eyes with a grave smile. 'I think you've already met Ephraim,' he said.

The boy didn't smile but fixed his gaze on her with almost scientifically detached curiosity. He was around fifteen years old, tall and skinny, a *kippah* on his head, worn without self-consciousness but proclaiming his race and religion as surely as a turban on a Sikh or the hijab on a Muslim.

Claire turned her attention on her patient, aware that he had been discharged nearly two weeks ago. Significantly there had been no suicide attempt since then. The longest period between attempts for years.

'How are you, David?'

He nodded his response. 'Still alive, as you see.'

The boy's arm jerked towards his grandfather's, almost staying him from saying more.

Claire remained calm. 'And will you remain so?'

His nod was more an acceptance of his fate than an enthusiasm for life. 'If God wills,' he muttered. But Ephraim held his head up high, staring straight ahead as he addressed her.

'My grandfather has told me the story of the burnt bread,' he said, with stolid dignity. 'I have told him: "One day, grandfather, I am going to be a film director".' Said with huge confidence. 'One day I will make a film of this story and children will see it.' There was something almost evangelical in the light in his dark eyes but also something endearingly mischievous. 'And maybe then they will stop casting the Israelis as the bad boy of the world, the bully boy of the Middle East.'

Claire said nothing. Politics in a consultation room was strictly taboo.

Instead she turned back to the old man. 'Will I be seeing you again, David?'

'No.' It was his answer and she knew it held the sanctity of a promise made with his hand on the Torah.

'OK,' she said. 'Then you're discharged. Goodbye.' She shook them both by the hand. David grasped hers, met her eyes and said nothing. It was the boy who spoke for both of them. 'Thank you,' he said, then, 'look out for my film.' He gave another sweetly naughty grin. 'And who would you like to play your part in this?'

She gaped. She had no actress up her sleeve ready to produce.

'I don't know, Ephraim,' she said. He grinned at her. 'I'll think
of someone.' David smiled and they were gone.

The Jew – haunted no longer – free of his ghosts.

Whatever Jerome's taunt at the man, David Gad and Ephraim
had risen above it.

Claire watched the door swing behind them. She would
look out for the boy's work. Something in her recognized his
determination and conviction. One day he would make that
film and it would be entertaining, interesting and without self-
pity. There would also be something new in the old story of
the holocaust. A different angle, maybe showing the long
shadows of terrible acts, but also the unexpected fallout. Would
he, she wondered, perhaps even touch on the terrible stories
of his grandfather's repeated suicide attempts? Would he peer
into the long shadows that were still being cast today by other
extremist groups?

Then she had a sudden thought which brought a smile to
her face and a quick giggle, hand over her mouth. Why hadn't
she suggested Jennifer Aniston or Scarlett Johansson play her?
Even Keira Knightley?

Damn. She clicked her fingers. Missed opportunity. She
caught sight of her laughing face in the mirror above the sink
and reflected. She hadn't looked like that for months.

Then she peered a little closer, still laughing. 'You didn't
suggest them, Claire Roget,' she said severely, 'because they're
far too bloody glamorous.' And she stuck her tongue out at
the too-truthful reflection.

But the encounter seemed a portent for an improvement in
her life. On the surface, at least, Greatbach seemed to be
succeeding with at least one of its patients. But the day – or
the week – was not quite over. She still had a pile of notes
and patients to see. However, she had ten minutes' grace before
her next one was due. She drew her mobile phone out of her
bag. The little icon was flashing. Before she pressed the button
she already knew it would be from Grant.

He'd left a message. She listened dispassionately. Not
appealing for her forgiveness or understanding. His voice was
unemotional, matter of fact. Realizing the situation had
changed irrevocably, he simply said: 'Yes, Claire. We need to

meet.' And then, in typical Grant manner he said, 'I umm . . . I umm,' then an embarrassed laugh. 'I have some explaining to do.' *Not really. Not now. Too late.* She rang him straight back. The sooner this was dealt with the better.

He agreed to meet her so they could talk things through.

The arranged meeting was for this evening, again at the tapas bar. It was convenient, not far from Festival Park, Greatbach or home. No point hanging around, wasting time. *Get it over with*, she muttered. *Then you can move on.*

She finished her clinic, and once she'd completed her dictation she pushed the problems of Greatbach – and its wider community – to the back of her mind. She focused not on the missing psycho or Barclay about to set out on his boat, family in tow; not on Hayley, teetering on the edge of life or death, or the black cloud that hovered over Stan Moudel. She didn't even consider the baker of Buchenwald and his charismatic grandson with grand plans for the future. For now only she and Grant existed.

It was enough.

She left work at six, needing to go home first to shower and change. But she didn't feel like dressing up. It didn't feel like she had anything to celebrate, so she wore a plain grey dress and black tights. With that she wore her favourite thick silver bracelet and pearl earrings, then finished off with some high-heeled black court shoes and a Hermès bag. The bag gave her a sliver of confidence, the feeling that she was in control of herself. But it was in reality simply a prop.

She finished the image off with a light spray of Kenzo.

There. Ready to go. Hot to trot. But the smile she gave herself into the mirror was wary and cynical – nothing like Keira or Scarlett or Jennifer. Just her. She peered closer and wasn't sure she liked this face. She preferred the other, the one that had laughed at her from the mirror. She stuck her tongue out.

As she drove the fifteen-minute distance to the tapas bar (again) in Hanley, she reflected. She was curious to know how she'd feel when she saw Grant again. Angry? Sad? Would she feel cheated or resentful? Would she feel that dreadful desperation to have him back at any cost? Was she about to make a huge fool of herself and fling herself at his feet? Or would she feel nothing but numbness and distance?

She didn't know.

7.30 p.m.

He was already sitting at a table, head down, clumsily trying to spear an olive with a cocktail stick. She smiled. She'd seen him do that on plenty of previous occasions, usually when he was uncomfortable about something. It was a distractive game. As she watched him she knew he was unaware of her, simply drowning in his own emotion. He looked as though he was carrying a heavy load, shoulders bowed under the weight, not like someone who has just fallen in love. She also knew that of all the emotions she had imagined she would feel, the one she actually experienced now was a void superseded by a wash of modified affection, as though she was meeting up with an old friend. Not quite someone as close as Julia, but an acquaintance of whom she was fond.

Fond? It seemed a weak word to describe the fire that had existed between them.

Like a bolt of lightning, she had a flash of his body next to hers early in the morning, hair sticking up, face towards her, arm thrown over her breasts. As they both surfaced, his arms had always seemed to find their way there, his chest hair prickling her nipples.

Shit, she thought, and banished the image to outer space. Somewhere beyond Pluto.

She covered the distance between them quickly and sat down, picked up the glass of red wine he'd already ordered. Even that pulled her up. He hadn't needed to ask what she'd like to drink. He'd already known. Of course he bloody well would.

He lifted his head heavily, finding it difficult to meet her eyes. His own edged away guiltily, as though he was ashamed of himself. It was a new attitude, one she hadn't seen before. She waited curiously, said nothing. There were too many ways to play this: affronted, outraged, indignant, confused, aggrieved. All of them negative.

So she simply waited.

His smile was tentative, then in a rush he said, 'God, Claire, it's good to see you.'

She merely gaped at him, mouth open.

TWENTY-SIX

He looked at her mournfully. 'Claire,' he said again, his voice husky. 'You look lovely.'

She couldn't think of a response. She simply continued to gape at him. What was all this about?

'I've made such a mistake.'

Oh – so that was it, was it? He wanted to backtrack, turn back time?

'No phone call,' she queried, then warming to her subject. 'No letter. No text. No email. No message at all? No explanation?'

'I didn't know how to play it.'

'Play it?' She couldn't keep the fury out of her tone now.

He tried to ameliorate the word. 'Manage it, then.'

He looked at her in that appealing, desperate way he had, brown cow-eyes begging, but there was something heavy behind them, as though he was carrying a terrible burden. Guilt, she remembered someone saying once, is as heavy and dense as lead.

'I had to go,' he said quietly. 'The days just went by. And she needed me.'

'She?'

She already knew, of course. Well – she knew what she looked like. She knew how Grant responded to her.

'I need to start at the beginning,' he said. 'Can I get you another drink?' She looked at her inexplicably empty glass, nodded and he strolled over to the bar, returning a few minutes later. He put the glass of wine down in front of her and sat down. 'I can't tell you how sorry I am.'

She wanted to tell him what she knew but she held back. She

needed to listen to all he had to say first, to know whether he would lie.

'I have a sister,' he said.

An odd quiver of hope rippled up through her like a finger of sunlight on dappled water, then it plunged right back down to the depths.

He cleared his throat. 'I've never mentioned her to you. There is a reason for this,' he added quickly. 'She's ten years younger than me. She has cystic fibrosis. She's ill nearly all the time. Sometimes we think she'll die. But then she recovers. She has it badly.' He frowned and looked down into his beer glass. 'Shit, Claire,' he said. 'I'm making a pig's ear out of this.'

She tried to smile some encouragement rather than simply nod, but she was confused and puzzled.

'I'd better start at the beginning,' he said. 'Mum and Maisie lived in Cornwall. I persuaded them to move up here, nearer to me, so I could help with her, but it didn't work. Maisie went into a crisis and then Mum couldn't cope.' He gave an apologetic smile. 'Dad never could. He buggered off years ago. But Mum was ill herself and I felt responsible. After all, I was the one who'd dragged them all the way up here. She wasn't too bad in Cornwall.'

'OK, Grant,' she said tightly. 'You had to go. Fine. But why not tell me? I wouldn't have had a problem with it.'

'You don't understand,' he said uneasily, looking away now. 'When we started making plans for our future, I was worried.' His eyes flickered. 'Frightened.' His eyes were holding nothing back from her now but held her gaze. 'I'm a carrier, Claire. I knew what life was like for Maisie. I couldn't have gone through with it with one of our own children. Don't you see?'

'No,' she said bluntly. 'Not really.' And she didn't. She didn't see at all why he couldn't have come clean or why his sister had commanded such complete devoted loyalty, loyalty that appeared to exclude her.

It made no sense to her. She was quiet for a moment, trying to work it all out. She suspected the sub-story was something quite different. Not a sick, needy younger sister, but someone greedy for his sole attention, someone manipulative, who didn't want her brother to have a partner who distracted him from his sibling duties, who might have a family of her own.

But even in her feeling of disorientation, she felt a tiny spark of triumph. 'So I take it the petite blonde girl I saw you having coffee with at the Potteries Shopping Centre a few weeks ago was her?'

Grant looked up, gaped. 'You saw us?'

She nodded, and for the first time she read into his eyes. *Desperate. Desperate?*

'That sounds like Maisie,' he said, crushed.

It was tempting to focus on Maisie – how old was she, why was she like this, but it would be a distraction, one she resisted.

The real question was: 'Why didn't you at least let me know what was happening?'

He dropped his face into his hands. 'She's dying,' he said.

She snatched back the *Aren't we all?* It would sound callous, petty and mean and . . . everything else she felt.

And her own selfish, private thought was: there is enough mess in my life as it is. My work is clearing up messes. I don't want my home life to be the same. I want my home to be a refuge.

'Look, Grant,' she said finally, when she'd finished her second glass of wine, 'I understand you have a very sick sister. I understand that you felt you should go to her. That's good. And I understand that at some point you and I would have had to face up to the fact that we should have genetic tests before even considering starting a family. But these problems aren't insurmountable, so why no word for eight months? *That* I don't understand.'

'Maisie was—'

And then it had come out from her like a burst boil. Hot, angry and painful. 'I don't give a fuck what Maisie wanted. We were an item, Grant. We'd been together for over five years. You never even mentioned her. You kept her a secret. You didn't confide in me. I don't understand why not. I'm a doctor, for goodness' sake. You think I can't deal with sickness?' Now she'd started she could not stop. It all poured out of her, poisonous as pus. 'There was the small fact that we'd bought a house together. That's a huge financial commitment.

We'd signed the fucking mortgage over twenty-five years. We'd been through thick and thin together. I don't know what was in your mind but I do know what was in mine. Yes, I thought we might be married one day. I thought we might have children.'

'Don't you see?' he said, lifting his eyes, and now she saw an answering spark in them too. 'I carry the gene, Claire. How could I bring that curse to a marriage? I'd watched Maisie suffer from day one of her life. It was shit. Physio twice a day, intravenous antibiotics, surgery. Tablets, antibiotic resistance.'

'*Both* parents have to carry the gene, Grant. *Both* parents. They must have told you that.'

'And I'd ask you to have the test?'

Again she could hit back. 'Even if I too carried the gene, who knows what life will be like in the future, Grant? Already these patients are living longer. There may be gene therapy. There may be new treatments. The future *will* be different. I do know that.' She met his eyes. 'I thought we'd be together. And then one day you were . . .' She angled her eyes up towards the ceiling. 'Poof,' she said, throwing her hands out. 'Gone.'

He said nothing. His eyes flickered over her. He was looking pained, hurt.

He was hurt*?*

'Maisie said you'd understand,' he grumbled.

Claire had no answer to this but a big jaw-drop. 'Maisie doesn't know me,' she said quietly. 'We've never met. I don't see how she could possibly imagine that I'd understand you going AWOL for eight months, not even replying to my texts and then popping up again like a jack-in-the-box.'

He gave it one more try. 'Ever since she was born, Maisie has had to come first. I'd drop everything if she was crying or poorly.'

'So how come you've kept this from me for five whole years?'

He smiled. 'With difficulty, but they were a long way away. Mum coped really well and sometimes I'd go down and see them for a couple of days if you were away or on a course or something.'

'You know what,' she said, 'I can't believe how you've kept this secret so well. In fact,' she said, 'I find it rather worrying.'

He looked ashamed. 'Mum and Maisie thought it best. They didn't know how you'd deal with it. And I . . . I didn't know what to do.'

She was silent for a moment, her thoughts and emotions tangled in an impossible knot. *He was so weak* was her initial thought, but then she realized – that had been part of his charm. Grant *was* lazy, easy-going. Someone who could be manipulated. And now look where that passivity had landed him – and her – because she could not separate herself from this mess that was, in reality, no more than a family problem, a hill they had to climb. Then she gathered herself up and continued in a voice she hardly recognized as her own: prim, tight-mouthed, unemotional, business-like. 'I'm thinking of selling up. You're on the deeds so I'll need your signature.' She managed a friendly smile. 'You've done virtually all the work. I'll get a tradesman to complete it, so if we make any profit I suggest we split it fifty-fifty?'

He looked stunned. His lovely dark eyes bruised as though she'd slapped him. His mouth was slack, uncertain. He'd run out of words. 'Claire,' he appealed. 'Please.'

Heart tumbling over head, head tumbling over heart. She was dizzy, then *that* voice came out again.

'I don't want to go through all this ever again,' she said. 'I'm sorry about Maisie. I'm sorry she's having a shit life, but I also think she and your mother between them were wrong. And so were you.'

He reached his hand out but she snatched hers away.

'Claire,' he appealed, 'I'd try to ring but she got worse. She was in Intensive Care and got upset if I said I should speak to you.'

'You should have confided in me, Grant, had more confidence in my humanity.' She paused. His face was frozen but he was also shamefaced.

'I don't want you just coming back,' she said. 'Let me have some time to think, to adjust. I don't know my own feelings and I don't know what's fair any more.'

He opened his mouth to speak then shut it again.

She finished her wine. 'If you can just give me a current address,' she said, standing up ready to leave, 'I'll be in touch.'

Then, stupidly and against her better judgement, she bent down and kissed his cheek. He put his face up to hers and then it was their lips that were touching. What was worse was that she was responding with a warmth that came from deep inside. The very core of her soul. And perhaps he recognized this.

'Claire,' he appealed again, a raw edge in his voice that she'd never heard before.

She moved away as quickly as though she'd touched a hot plate and was gone without looking back.

As she drove home she recalled her friend Julia's words, saying that men dance to their own tune while women accommodate and adapt to their partner's steps without even hearing the music. Her current instinct was to split the money down the middle and part. She had seen another side to Grant and she didn't want to be in a relationship with a man who felt he could pop in and out of her life like a rabbit in a conjuring trick. Neither did she want to be with a man who was at the command of his mother and sister. Then she realized something. If his father had abandoned the family soon after Maisie was born, Grant had had to act up. He would only have been ten years old, already the man of the family. And all at the command of a sister who had enough of a hold over him to convince him of her completely barking suggestion that he simply vanish from her life, and that she, Claire, would *understand*. Unless Maisie was completely out of sync with the rest of humankind, she must have known that Claire would *not*. She must have known that Claire was doing exactly what she would have predicted – dumping her brother. It stopped her up short. Was that what she wanted to do? Act out Maisie's selfish little play for her?

And then, as she neared Burslem, inexplicably her focus changed and she began to make plans for her future. It was as though waiting to find out why Grant had simply gone had caused a hiatus in her life. And now she knew she could move on if she wanted to. She could get decorators in to complete the renovation work and then she could put the house on the market. Fingers crossed she came out of it with a few thousand in her pocket. She would divide that with him. Then she would buy somewhere else . . .

Or else . . .

She drew the car up the drive, picked her bag from the passenger seat, climbed out with difficulty (she'd parked too near the wall again), and walked towards the front door with its sensor switch to illuminate her progress.

Someone was leaning up against the gatepost. For a second – no more – she thought Grant must have followed her home. Similar height, similar build.

Her second thought was that it was a punter waiting for his pleasure of the night. Was even forming the phrase, *Wrong place, mate.* Then she realized.

'Hello, Claire.' The voice was cold and gloating. He knew he'd rattled her.

It was Barclay.

All her instincts were to run to the door, insert the key and hide inside, but instead she turned and faced him with a coolness that impressed even her. 'Oh, hello,' she said, injecting her tone with boredom. 'I thought you'd gone sailing.'

'Not yet,' he said. 'Soon. Very soon.'

She wanted to tell him not to try any funny tricks, that she was *on to him*, but before she could get the words out, Barclay put his face next to hers. She could smell aftershave, soap and that ever-present cinnamon. 'You know too much about me, Claire.'

She felt a frisson of fear. This, then, was what he was like when . . . She backed away; her eyes shot over her shoulder. Where was the door? Could she make it before . . .? Before what? Why was he here?

He put his face close to hers, spoke in a hoarse whisper. 'I don't want you . . .' He stopped and she wondered what he was about to say. *Getting in the way? Spoiling my plans?*

Instead he put a hand on her shoulder and pressed it down, hard enough to hurt; then slowly he moved away.

She called after him. 'I suppose it was Astrid who gave you those little titbits about some of my patients?'

He looked cross. Then puzzled.

She had the upper hand? 'I'll be having words with her,' she said, carrying on as though she hadn't seen the flicker of fury that danced across his face. Rather than respond, he moved back, again put his face even closer. 'I wouldn't bother speaking to this Astrid person,' he said. 'I told you – I don't know anyone with that name. Wrong guess. Again.'

From the confident, swaggering way he said this, she had the awful feeling it just might be the truth. She was silent.

He spoke. 'You know why I like you, Claire?' It was his usual tone again, almost a cold caress, the threat milked away.

She didn't deign to answer but met his eyes now without even a flicker of fear.

He answered his own question. 'Because you are a worthy sparring partner.' He smiled at her. 'Watch this space,' he said. 'Things are about to get interesting. Or should I say, rough seas on the horizon?'

Then he turned and left.

TWENTY-SEVEN

The evening had been a splash of emotion, Barclay putting the final touch on the weird and macabre. His intention had been to unnerve her. She gave a wry smile. At least he'd distracted her from Grant's confession. Inside the house and feeling safe, Claire poured herself a glass of warm red wine, (kept right by the radiator for emergency use), sat on the sofa, took some deep breaths in and wondered. What had Grant really expected her to do tonight? Welcome him home with open arms?

Tempting thought. She took a sip of the wine and held it in her mouth, feeling the warmth and richness staining her tongue. Now she thought about it, he *hadn't* actually asked to come home. Only for understanding and forgiveness. Well, she could give him that. Grant, charming but weak, controlled by his mother and sister. So, if they did get back together, where exactly would she fit in to this pecking order?

And Barclay? What had he wanted, apart from to rattle her? Why had he waited for her tonight? What had been the point? She knew the answer. He wanted her to know about his sinister plans for his new family. He wanted her to worry and at the same time know she was powerless to prevent it, or even to bring him to justice. He wanted to assert his position. Either that or he wanted her mind to focus, to suffer, to worry and wonder. She groaned. She would do anything to have him right out of the picture, someone else's responsibility. She resented the place he occupied in her mind.

Why did these people spin around her, plucking at her skin, pricking her like picadors, goading her? Weakening her?

She finished her glass of wine. No answers there. Time to go to bed and try to sleep. She locked and bolted the doors both back and front, checked her mobile phone had enough juice in it. She would take it upstairs with her. It would be a comfort just to know it was there, that she could summon help – if she needed to. The house seemed ominously quiet tonight, haunted, ghostly, echoing – the empty rooms laughing at her, mocking her as she checked them through one by one. She felt her loneliness acutely, wrapping itself around her, distancing her from the human race. So this was what true loneliness felt like. A solitary monolith in a bleak and empty landscape.

She spoke only to her reflection in the bathroom mirror. *What are you waiting for, Claire? For Barclay to commit some act so he can at last be locked up?* She shrugged She didn't have the answer, only a statement of fact. *Well, he isn't here now and Grant is not coming back. Not ever.*

Well . . .

She slammed each bedroom door hard, hearing only the hollow sound echo round and around the house. She needed to fill the silence with something. Luckily she had a radio in her bedroom. She switched it on, tuned it to Radio 4 and listened to the bedtime story.

You can get through this, Claire, she whispered to herself, climbing into a bed which felt cold, too big and too full of memories, inside which she tossed and turned, one of her hands clutching at the other.

The weekend loomed ahead.

Empty.

But in the end the weekend was fine. She got up early on the Saturday, went into Hanley and bought herself some books and a DVD. That was her entertainment seen to. The weather was bright and pretty, so she went home, changed into her running gear and trainers and jogged along the canal towpath for a couple of miles. This was something she loved about the Potteries, the industrial heritage mingling with the fanciful. Etruria, for goodness' sake. About as far from the middle of Italy as was possible – unless you have a potter's dream. This Etruria was a rundown area peppered with bottle kilns, two derelict factories and a boarded-up pub. She ran on, along the towpath, passing some old factory wharfs. She overtook a decorated narrow boat sliding through the water. Holiday-makers waving at her rather than past workers loaded up with coal, china clay, finished wares. She stopped to catch her breath, hands on knees, and was passed by dog walkers and a couple with a baby in a sling. The baby's head was lolling. Practically asleep. One thing she was sure of as she straightened up; Barclay's baby would never pass the time in one of those, walked by Daddy. But what could she do about it? Really? The thought stopped her and she stood, breathing in the cool October air and came up with . . . nothing. She could not prevent a crime *before* it had happened. She hadn't exactly been successful alerting the authorities *after* he had committed a felony, so what hope?

None, and the knowledge that she was powerless depressed her.

Time to move on.

Back home she showered, cooked a meal of pasta, bacon, onion, tomato and cheese and sat through the film which had been a mistake from the first, *We Need to Talk about Kevin*.

It did nothing to lighten her mood.

On Sunday she had a late lunch with Julia and Gina at the house they were restoring. She left just after ten to ready herself for the week ahead.

Monday, 27 October, 10 a.m.

Khaled Farouk was good enough to ring her himself with the result of Stan's brain scan. 'Not good news, Claire,' he said. 'Poor old Stan. He has a frontal lobe tumour. A large one.'

'Primary or secondary?'

'We'll have to do a biopsy to see, but I think it's a primary, fast growing, as big as a walnut and unlikely to be amenable to either treatment or surgery. Particularly in the difficult circumstances of Stan's mental state and probable lack of cooperation and compliance with any treatment plan.'

Claire was silent for a moment. Stan Moudel was thirty-two years old. Unlike Hayley, his life had not begun terribly. He had had a chance. Once. Now it had gone.

This was the final insult to the person who had once been Stan Moudel, husband, father, working man.

'Dr Farouk,' she said, 'how long will he live without intervention?'

'Months,' he said. 'Possibly weeks.'

'Do you propose to do a biopsy?'

'I want,' he said seriously, 'to have a case conference before any surgical or radiological intervention.' There was a pause. 'Without any intervention he will certainly die.'

'So the sooner we have this case conference, the better.'

'Exactly.'

They made an appointment to meet up. He would organize the neurosurgical team and the radiologists and Claire tracked down the necessary colleagues who'd had most to do with Stan's case: Edward Reakin, Teresa and Astrid. She still didn't trust the girl, even if Barclay had denied knowing her. But Astrid had been subdued since the confrontation and Claire did not want to antagonize her, so she kept her suspicions to herself.

The wheels for a case conference were swiftly put in motion. They arranged to drive over to the RSUH on the following morning.

But first Claire felt she must speak to Stan herself. She needed to involve him in the decision – well, inform him at the very least.

As she walked along the corridor towards his room, she felt

nothing but sympathy and sorrow. Sometimes, she felt that her job was just too difficult.

She pressed the buzzer of the locked ward where Stan had had to be moved since he had become unpredictable, and was let in.

The rule was: no lighters, no mobile phones, no sharp objects or anything that might either be used as a weapon or might disturb the patient. As a member of staff she still paused underneath the notice. It looked so commanding. She put her phone on the desk.

Astrid was in charge of the ward. Uniforms upset patients, so the staff generally wore jeans and a baggy top. It seemed the most neutral of non-uniforms.

'I need to speak to Stan,' she said, tempted to add, '*the doomed homeless man,*' just to bait her and watch for her reaction, but she resisted.

Astrid must have caught something of her tone. 'What is it, Claire?'

'The scan did pick up on something.'

Astrid was no fool. 'So they're going to do what exactly?'

'He needs a biopsy. We're having a case conference tomorrow morning to decide.' Claire glanced along the corridor. 'I should speak to him,' she said.

Astrid looked concerned. 'Alone?'

Claire nodded. 'You can switch on the CCTV,' she said, with a watery smile. 'Keep an eye on me.'

'OK. He's been very quiet today.' She too gave an anxious look that skittered along the corridor, skipping along with guilt. 'Hope it's not the calm before the storm.'

Claire touched her arm. 'Let's hope it's not the storm before the calm,' she responded.

TWENTY-EIGHT

At first it seemed that Astrid was right. Stan was sitting quietly, looking out of the window. He could have been any of their patients, lost in thought. Or simply lost.

'Stan.' She spoke softly from the doorway. Since his condition had worsened (developed), loud noises or sudden approaches made him nervous, likely to lash out.

He turned his head.

Why is it that even the most unbalanced patients rarely look frightening? There is usually no clue in their demeanour to hint of the turmoil filling their heads.

Stan was a lanky man with prominent cheekbones and hollow eyes. He was dressed in jogging pants and a T-shirt, plain white except for the food that had been spilled down the front. Heinz tomato ketchup, by the looks of things.

She sat down opposite him and spoke gently, slowly, quietly, her words containing a lullaby rhythm.

'Stan, you know you haven't been well lately.'

He shook his head jerkily, as though impatient with himself.

'And you've had some headaches.'

He nodded. Head bowed, ashamed now, as though somehow he was to blame.

'And you probably don't remember it, but about a month ago you had a fit. You lost consciousness.'

He nodded abstractedly, still looking out of the window.

'Initially . . .' She corrected herself. 'At first we thought it was due to the alcohol or the drugs that you've taken.'

He dropped his head. Then lifted his eyes with a question.

'Claire,' he said, 'is something wrong with me? They put me to sleep to look in my brain, didn't they?'

She nodded, keeping her gaze on him, more sorry for him than she could bear. They hadn't dared use the word brain scan. Stan's behaviour was unpredictable at best; any member of staff who had been involved in his care would have known these particular words would have conjured up terrifying images in his damaged mind. A scan would imply an alien being drilling inside his brain ready to burst out at any opportunity, or some scientist watching him.

His eyes regarded her, expressionless. Not even asking the obvious question: *what did they find?*

'Stan,' she said, 'we think something's wrong inside your head.'

And with the combination of both unpredictability and

insight, he gave a lopsided grin. 'You're telling me,' he said. 'That's what I'm here for.'

Claire smothered a smile. Sometimes her patients could be unintentionally insightful, accidentally funny. This wasn't the first time one of them had made her smile with a comment.

'Stan,' she said, 'how would you feel about going back to the hospital?'

He looked at her blankly.

Capacity. It was the buzzword. If your patient has *capacity*, he or she must make their own decisions. The question was: did Stan really have the capacity to make this decision?

He bounced the question back to her. 'What do you think, doc?'

She didn't respond straight away but searched for the right words. It was another point that was drummed into them from the very first day at medical school:

Tailor your advice/suggestions to your patient. Don't talk over their heads by using too much jargon and words they will not understand. Likewise, do not talk down to them. Remember they are not children.

'I think it's possible,' she said tentatively, 'that you might become even more ill if we do nothing. The headaches might become worse.'

Something perceptive passed across his face and he moved a little closer. His clothes smelt of a combination of fabric conditioner and tobacco. It was not unpleasant and sparked a vague memory. Of her father? The French frog?

She shook her head to erase the memory, and Stan continued, 'But you can't promise anything, can you, doc?' His voice was raised now, his eyes bulging, his hands clenched into fists. She felt threatened, knew Astrid would be monitoring Stan's behaviour with concern, finger on red-alert button. But she must stick to the truth. She owed him that.

'No, Stan,' she said gently. 'We can't promise anything.'

His eyes were starey scary now. 'So what's the fucking point? What's the fucking point? What's the fucking point?' His body was rigid, movements stiff and jerky, his eyes staring at her in desperation. He stood up and moved quickly, his bony figure now between her and the door – her escape route.

She stayed sitting. And then the door was pushed open. Astrid and two orderlies stood there. 'Come on, Stan,' she said.

Claire stood up and Stan gave her a wicked grin. 'I had you on the spot there, didn't I, doc?'

She nodded and smiled. 'You did that, Stan.'

As she left the room she knew that this unpredictability would cost him his life. Biopsies, scans, radiotherapy, chemotherapy, surgery. Compliance. Capacity. The chances weren't great for anyone with this fat tumour inside his skull. And for Stan it was a hundred times more difficult.

She was not relishing the thought of the case conference.

TWENTY-NINE

Tuesday, 28 October, 10.00 a.m.

'So,' Dr Farouk said, 'who's going to kick off?'

During the car journey into the hospital they had discussed the difficulties of Stan's case. Struggling to understand some of the concepts put before him – sickness, possible side effects from treatment, the risks of surgery – let alone the notion of a biopsy, of something growing inside his brain that needed to be looked at and identified under the microscope. He would, quite literally, be capable of tearing his hair out.

What is in the patient's best interests?

It was another mantra they all abode by.

Khaled Farouk was courteous. He listened carefully to each point of view – Edward Reakin's considered *outcome* (another buzzword):

Inability to cope with the follow-on treatment.

The possibility of violence towards staff.

Removing stitches and dressings through difficulties with comprehension.

General poor health – renal and hepatic compromise, long term, poor nutrition.

Both Astrid and Teresa were nodding their heads in agreement.

Finally Khaled turned his handsome head towards Claire. And though she was distressed at the thought of the outcome after yesterday's encounter, she nodded in agreement. 'All those.'

Dr Farouk brought the scan up on the computer, giving them an entire picture before enlarging. 'You see,' he said, pointing it out to Mary Elgin, neurosurgeon, a newcomer to the case. She was a natural blonde with a pale complexion unenhanced by make-up, and with an apparently permanently fixed frown.

Only Claire knew this was not quite so. She had seen her at one of the medical dinners she had attended a year or so ago with Grant, and Mary Elgin, wearing no frown and plenty of make-up, tanked up to the eyeballs, had been frankly flirting with him. But then, Claire reflected, Grant had had that easy-going, relaxed sort of demeanour that invariably did attract women. She felt the knife twist in her guts. And one of those women who was susceptible to that attraction was her. Current.

Admit it, Claire, you still fancy the pants off him.

Mary was studying the scan result, taking careful measurements using a ruler, studying the tumour's proximity to the vital areas of the brain – in particular the Circle of Willis. In the end she would be the one to decide to operate or not to operate. To be or not to be. That was indeed the question. She turned to the roomful of people.

'In a healthy thirty-two-year-old,' she said, weighing each word up carefully, 'even in perfect health and with absolutely no previous medical history . . .' She gave a rueful smile. 'Even if it were someone who'd run the London Marathon last year, I'd say his chances would be slim.' She looked at Claire, who wasn't quite sure whether she had been recognized. 'Ethics,' she continued, 'demand that we treat all our patients the same and that we involve our patients in our decisions. Obviously in this case . . .' She let the sentence hang, unfinished, in the air, before jumping to the next point. 'But even if he was perfectly healthy and fit, I wouldn't be optimistic about the outcome of this.' She peered closer, the rigid ruler measuring its size. 'This is a very aggressive tumour.' She addressed her question to Claire. 'You say his symptoms have developed over the last few weeks?'

Claire nodded, feeling bad. Any change in Stan's behaviour had initially been put down to his unpredictable lifestyle and mental state. That would have delayed diagnosis by a month or two.

'And have you had any discussion with him about his diagnosis, possible prognosis and treatment options?'

Claire felt even worse. 'Not really,' she said. 'Not a meaningful discussion.'

'Then that's it,' Mary said decisively. 'If we can't guarantee his compliance with treatment, then I'm afraid surgery would be not only risky but a waste of time and resources.'

She stepped back.

The radiologist spoke next and put forward roughly the same argument.

So they were all agreed. No treatment. The result was documented, with their reasoning carefully compiled, and yet they would all leave the room with a sense that they had failed their patient. They hadn't even given him a ghost of a chance.

They started to file out.

As Claire was almost out of the door, Mary Elgin asked her casually, 'How's that gorgeous boyfriend of yours, Claire?'

So she did remember. Considering how tanked up her colleague had been, Claire was surprised.

Even more so at her own swift, unthinking response 'Oh, him? We're not together any more.'

Mary's eyes glittered. 'Oh,' she said. 'Really?'

THIRTY

After the case conference she went to the general medical ward to see Hayley, whose prediction of having tubes coming out of all orifices was proving to be true. She was heavily sedated and so was compliant with her treatment

rather than ripping everything out. Her eyes flickered when
Claire entered her room and sat down beside her patient.
'Maybe, Hayley,' she said very softly, 'we'll have you back
at Greatbach soon.'

Hayley returned a very watered-down smile. 'Maybe,' she
echoed. 'Maybe not.'

The hungry child.

It was such an apt description.

She was about to leave when her eye was caught by a card,
four plump women dancing across the front, instantly recog-
nizable as a Beryl Cook work. The women were having great
fun in tight shorts and T-shirts, plump and jolly, a singularly
inappropriate card to send to a young woman with anorexia
nervosa. Claire reached for it, but even before she'd glanced
at the inside she knew who had sent this and why. He would
use Hayley's deterioration to poke at her. Inside he'd written
a message guaranteed to goad.

So – which one are you? To preserve the mystery he had
not signed his name. He didn't need to. Underneath he'd added
advice:

You don't need to eat. It just produces this.

So Barclay was still influencing her patients. He just couldn't
let go of his malicious little game. What worried Claire was
what was he planning for the Triggs, his wife and unborn
baby? She looked from the card back at her patient. Hayley's
eyes met hers then dropped away, ashamed. Claire read the
evasion and knew she would not shake the truth out of her.
Jerome was very good at persuading people to keep his secrets.
And there was nothing Claire could say or do in this environ-
ment that would help matters. Even though Hayley was
sedated, she could tell the girl had been affected by the card.
Her eyes lingered over it, her face anguished. This was how
she saw herself, whatever Claire might say or do. Barclay's
influence was always stronger – evil triumphing over good
because his subject was so very susceptible. Claire wanted to
know whether she had ever met Jerome, and if so where?
How? She wanted to break the bond, stop the influence as
putrid and polluting as the old London smog.

'Friend of yours?'

Hayley turned her face away, shaking her head. 'Friend of a friend,' she muttered, closing her eyes.

Claire stood for a moment then turned and left. For now there was nothing she could do about this. She must leave the general physicians to deal with her patient's physical problems. Only then could she deal with this insidious influence and Hayley's mental state. Only when she was returned to Greatbach. If ever.

So Barclay was on the high seas plotting God-knew-what and Dexter was still missing. He had vanished into the ether.

Wednesday, 29 October, 9.30 a.m.

Even though the outcome for Stan was hopeless and Hayley was still in the general hospital, Claire felt that Greatbach and its patients were doing no worse than usual. But bad news had been hovering in the wings, waiting to make its appearance, flapping in its black cloak towards centre stage.

It was Rita who told her. 'I saw something in the *Sentinel* last night,' she said, and placed it, carefully flattened, on Claire's desk.

It was a small paragraph on page 4.

The couple who were found dead at their home in Biddulph on Thursday morning have been identified as Maylene and Derek Forsyte. Police are not looking for anyone else in connection with the deaths. Post mortems show that both died of gunshot wounds. A friend has been quoted as saying that the couple were heavily in debt and that Maylene had mental-health problems.

Rita looked up but didn't meet her eyes. 'She won't be needing that appointment then.' It was a gauche statement from one who had worked in this job for over twenty years and was a measure of her unease.

Claire looked at her then shook her head, her eyes drawn back to the brief paragraph.

That was all. Just a few lines. It hadn't even warranted a whole paragraph, let alone the front page. So that was it. *The expensive butterfly.* No more. And as though Claire had been there to witness the drama, she believed she knew exactly what had happened and why. Derek's desperation at the plight they were in, Maylene's complete refusal to acknowledge the reality of their debt and resistance to any attempt to alter her extravagance. And so Maylene had fluttered her last. Derek had finally snapped. Claire suddenly froze by the side of Rita's desk. What had made him finally snap? Claire picked up the phone and connected with the mortuary. She knew the pathologist, Caroline Morton, and had spoken with her on two previous occasions: one a suicide a couple of years ago and the other a patient's suspicious death at Greatbach, but which had turned out to be a death from natural causes.

It took a little while to connect with Caroline, but eventually, after a long wait, they spoke.

First of all Claire wanted to ascertain whether Caroline had performed the post mortem herself.

'Yes,' she said cheerfully. 'I had that unenviable task.'

'I just thought I ought to put you in the picture. Maylene, Mrs Forsyte, was a patient of mine.'

'Really.' From her tone she'd already known this.

'Oh yes – an outpatient. She had a histrionic personality disorder.'

'Well, she didn't die of that,' Caroline said baldly. 'She was shot at point-blank range. Scorch marks on her skin and clothes, wadding in the wound, I'm afraid. The verdict will be murder and suicide. *She* died of a single gunshot wound to the chest. Took out a lot of lung and extensive damage to the heart and major blood vessels. *He* put the gun in his mouth and pulled the trigger with his toe. The pair of them took ten, fifteen minutes to die. Not – quite – clean. A lot of blood loss and some dragging blood markings on the floor in the kitchen. We think she'd been trying to get to the phone. Apparently, they were over a hundred thousand pounds in debt. He earned £18K a year so it was going to take him for ever to pay his debt off. I guess bankruptcy would have loomed and, from what friends and family say, Derek was a proud man. That wouldn't have been his way out. He'd tried, poor guy. They'd remortgaged the house to well over its market value. They were in deep financial trouble. And I guess that's that.'

Claire thanked her; told her she'd make a statement to the coroner.

'We do have evidence for understanding his state of mind,' Caroline added. 'There were some articles about bankruptcy together with bank statements and a particularly nasty text message on his mobile phone.'

Claire half closed her eyes. She could almost smell Barclay's presence.

Caroline continued. 'Basically telling him his wife would soon be off when the money ran dry.'

So it had been this which had finally pushed Derek Forsyte over the edge – the thought of losing the wife he adored. 'Do you know who sent the text message?'

'Pay as you go.'

Claire thanked her and put the phone down. Was there no end to his evil – to his spite? And where was he getting his information from? It was driving her mad. Was life after life to be ruined by his taunts?

One consultation with Maylene stuck out in her mind. She'd turned up to her clinic appointment a week late, flamboyantly dressed and apologizing profusely for having mixed the days up. Derek had been taciturn, staying very much in the background, staring at the floor, biting his lips, his forehead puckered with deep frown lines. Claire was thoughtful. Had the clues been there then, lining up like ninepins, ready to topple him into drastic action? Was he already in despair at the miserable dance his wife was leading him? And one final shove – a vision of his beloved wife abandoning him, leaving him with his scarred life of debt. To him bankruptcy equated with shame. As usual Barclay's rapier had hit home clean. The suggestion that he would lose his beloved Maylene had been all it needed to push him into this horrible double crime. And, as usual, no one would be able to prove anything against him.

Poor Derek. He had been besotted. Claire smiled. One thing about Maylene, she had brightened up the clinic days with her glamour, her outrageous clothes and her loud, extrovert ways – even if she did knock the appointment system for a six, turning up on the wrong days or at the wrong times.

Maylene had always been loquacious, full of stories (these days mainly about recent purchases including a new Smart television set they'd just treated themselves to and didn't seem able to work).

She had glanced again at Derek. His face had been a picture of misery. She should have picked up on it, that Maylene's character would be the destruction of her husband and herself. But the jaunty outfit Maylene had worn that day, looking like a supermodel (a tight, short, faux-leopardskin skirt, a jaunty red-peaked cap, black patent-leather knee-length boots with killer stilettos) had made a change from the usual patients' garb of jogging pants, sweatshirts and worn, smelly trainers.

Maylene had babbled on, inconsequential gossip, but Derek had remained silent. Ominously silent, she now realized.

The call to the coroner was a quick affair. At the moment Claire only needed to give her a sketchy account of her involvement with the couple, describe how Maylene had made life difficult for her husband and give the coroner her contact details. There was no point dragging Barclay's name into it. She had no proof, only a suspicion. The coroner's officer thanked her and requested a written report. Much of that would remain confidential and need not ever enter the public domain. But Barclay had already known anyway.

Claire ate her lunch alone in her office. She had letters to dictate but she felt alienated from her colleagues. Until she knew who had fed Barclay his facts, she did not know who to trust. There was no one with whom she could share her misgivings.

2 p.m.

The afternoon began with a phone call from DS Willard. She had a moment's confusion, wondering who he was. But the minute he said what he was ringing about, she was right there.

'We have a possible sighting of Dexter,' he said.

Dexter, who had slipped from her mind with the latest events. 'Where?'

'Blurton.'

That was when alarm bells jangled. 'Is it a definite sighting?'

'It was made by someone who knew him well,' he said seriously. 'Marietta Shaw.'

Claire recalled the name Marietta Shaw. She was an ex-girlfriend of Dexter's. A girlfriend who had escaped his more brutal attentions only because he had moved on to her best friend, Sheridan. Marietta would not have been mistaken about Harding. She knew him too well. If she said she had seen Dexter, it was the truth. Claire had never met the girl but it was documented that when Harding had defected to her friend, Marietta was quoted as saying she'd had a 'lucky escape'.

'Shit,' Claire muttered under her breath, then: 'What's he doing in Blurton, for goodness' sake?'

'Well . . .' He gave an embarrassed little laugh, then. 'You're the psychiatrist, Claire.'

She wished she had a pound for every time that particular phrase was wheeled out, but she managed an answering snigger. 'I may be but I don't understand why, if he's still in the Potteries, he's felt the need to go underground. He's behaved himself for two years. Turned up regularly, so what's happened?'

Zed Willard spoke, more confident now. 'Well,' and she caught hesitance in his voice. 'We're hoping it's coincidence . . .'

'But,' she prompted.

'Sheridan Riley is due to get married on Saturday at St Bartholomew's Church in Blurton.'

For a moment she couldn't speak. Then, 'Shit,' she said, then, 'Sheridan?' She was silent for a moment. It did supply a reason why he might have gone underground, but something pricked her thoughts and she wondered why she didn't feel right about this. There was something she wasn't under-standing; it felt like it was obvious, something right under her nose, almost too obvious to see. She was tripping over it like a rolled-up carpet, invisible underfoot, and she felt as though she was about to fall flat on her nose. Hard.

She ran through events in her mind. Sheridan was the girl who had dropped him. It was that that had resulted in the fatal arson attack, which in turn had led to his initial incarceration and current Community Treatment Order. Facts as she knew them, or at least as she understood them.

Zed Willard's voice was deadly serious. 'Are you still there, Claire?'

'Yeah. Sorry.'

'How dangerous do you think he is?'

'Potentially very. Unpredictable and dangerous.'

'Just to Sheridan or the wider public?' He sounded anxious.

'I don't know,' she said. 'But what are you—'

DS Willard answered her unfinished question. 'We've put extra police on the streets – and we're going to have a police presence at the wedding. Claire,' his voice was strained, 'what do you think he's likely to do?'

'I . . .' She was at a loss for words. She conjured up the bulky guy, bullet head, tattoos everywhere; that mean, hateful expression which – combined with his bovine stupidity – made him so dangerous and unpredictable. But DS Willard was asking her to predict the impossible – how do you assess unpredictability? You cannot. It's written into the word. 'I think,' she said, feeling cold with the impossibility of this task and remembering his lack of remorse for the family he had slaughtered. 'He might . . .'

Willard took the words out of her mouth. 'You think he could attack her – or him – or just spoil the day?'

Spoil the day? It sounded like a child having a temper tantrum at a birthday party. Dexter would do more than simply *spoil the day.*

Claire wished she did not have the sort of imagination that supplied missing pictures: Lorna Doone, blood staining the pure white of her wedding dress. Roxanne, the wine spreading across her bodice, a smudge over the spot where her poor, misguided little heart was.

She shook the images away. She needed to be practical now – not imaginative.

'Have you spoken to Sheridan? Warned her?'

'Umm.' Now she understood his hesitation – and the tone of the phone call.

'You were hoping *I* would?'

'Yeah.' He sounded relieved.

'OK,' she said. 'Dexter was my responsibility. *Is* my

responsibility. *I* will speak to her. In fact I think it might be an idea if I spoke to both her and her fiancé together.'

'Yep,' Willard said cheerfully. 'Sounds good to me. He's in IT, works for one of the local pottery companies. He has a good job. Nice guy. I've met him once when I told Sheridan that Dexter was unaccounted for. He's very protective. I was impressed with him. He works all over the world. Might have to work in another country for a few years.'

'That might be a good thing,' she said drily. 'Put distance between him and Sheridan's past lover.'

'Right – well we'll keep looking for Harding. I suspect he's holed up somewhere, either with a friend or sleeping rough.'

She tried to picture this and failed. Dexter staying with a friend? No way. Sleeping rough. She tried to convey this to DS Willard. 'I can't think of any friends he has.'

'So – sleeping rough?'

'It's more probable.' DS Willard gave her Sheridan and Richard's contact details, two mobiles and a landline, wished her luck and replaced the phone.

So he had firmly planted the ball in her court. She still didn't understand why Dexter had gone underground. It didn't make any sense. The two words that kept popping up like targets at a fairground stall were: Why now? Why now?

She remembered her sympathy for the psychiatrist whose patient had gone on the rampage in Cardiff, with an axe. Even at the time she'd thought it could have been worse – far worse. She could well imagine Dexter doing something just like that, wielding an axe, Braveheart style, at the wedding. And this time it was her responsibility. She was the psychiatrist who was in charge. She picked up the phone with an uneasy feeling. She was not looking forward to this conversation one little bit. How do you warn a bride of this?

She connected on the third try and recognized Sheridan's voice straight away. It had a husky hesitance that she recalled well from her one previous encounter when she had inherited Dexter's case.

'It's Dr Claire Roget,' Claire said, not sure whether Sheridan would remember her after only the one encounter. 'I'm from Greatbach, the psychiatric unit.'

Understandably Sheridan's response was instant alarm. 'I remember. What's happened? Why are you ringing?' And finally, 'Not . . .?'

'Are you OK to talk now, Sheridan?'

'Yes. Yes. Tell me. What's happened? Why are you ringing?'

'I'm sorry about this. I'm sure you don't ever want to hear Dexter Harding's name again.'

'Too right,' Sheridan said bitterly. 'I bloody don't.'

'You know that I've been seeing him on a fortnightly basis, that he's on what we call a Community Treatment Order?'

'Yes,' she said, sarcasm leaking into her voice. 'I heard.'

'That he's also under the closer supervision of a community psychiatric nurse.'

'Yeah, I heard that too.' Now impatience and perhaps concern were sharpening her voice.

Claire knew what she was thinking. *So what's the phone call about?*

'I have to tell you,' Claire continued, 'that he didn't turn up for his last appointment which was a little over a week ago.'

'Oh.' And even in that high-pitched short expletive, Claire could hear the screaming panic. 'Sergeant Willard told me that. What's it to do with me? Why are *you* ringing?'

'The police are looking for him. He's left the hostel where he was supervised.' She was anxious to avoid the phrase, *gone underground.* It smacked too much of spy thrillers.

'So where is he?'

'He's been seen in Blurton.'

'Blurton? What? When? Who by?'

'Someone called Marietta?'

'Marietta Shaw? I know her. She's his old girlfriend. She used to be one of my best friends.'

'So I understand.'

And Sheridan echoed the conclusion Claire had already made. 'She knew Dexter well. She wouldn't make a mistake. If she said it was Dexter, then that's who it was.'

'Yeah. That's what I thought.'

'So what are you saying?'

'I know you are to be married on Saturday.'

There was a long silence from the other end of the phone

and then Sheridan's voice came back, frightened. 'You think he . . .?'

'I think he's unpredictable.'

There was a pause and then Sheridan's anger came out, spilling out, ugly, dark and destructive as a mud-slip. 'Why did they ever let him out? He's a fucking psychopath.' She drew breath to continue. 'I just want to get on with my life. With my wedding.' A pause, then more calmly and with some retrieved dignity, 'Dr Roget, I may not have a medical degree, but I bloody well know that Dexter Harding is a psychopath who should have been locked up for life when he murdered that family. I knew them, you know. When they first arrived we had a little welcome tea for them. We gave them clothes and things, bought the children toys. They were lovely people. He'd been a doctor, you know, in a small town in Northern Iraq. And they died in that horrible way.' There was a catch in her voice. 'And all because of me and that psycho. How do you think I felt, Dr Roget?'

There was no answer to this so Sheridan continued. 'And now you think he wants to try and ruin my life all over again? After . . .' She stopped short, overwhelmed by the horror, 'what he did?'

'The police are aware,' Claire said.

'Oh.' The one syllable reflected the general public's lack of confidence in the police force.

She followed that with, 'What do you think's going to happen? You think he wants to disrupt the wedding?' From the rise in her tone, Claire could hear that her fear was escalating.

She tried to diffuse it. 'Obviously I don't know, but the police wanted me to warn you.'

'To be on my guard? It's my bloody wedding day,' she exploded. 'You think he wants to ruin my wedding day?'

That, Claire thought, *is the least of my worries, that he will throw a glass of wine over your dress.* She wished she could banish the image of the mad axeman in Cardiff.

'We don't know,' she said. 'The police will be keeping an eye out for him.'

'Oh.' There was silence and then Sheridan spoke again. 'So I'm supposed to just relax, enjoy my big day?'

'They'll increase the police presence,' Claire said. 'They will guard you.'

'Yeah, like they did before. I had to walk past that wreck of a house with all the flowers outside, knowing that if Dexter hadn't been such an idiot it would have been *my* house and the flowers would have had *my* name on them. He wanted to kill *me*. And if other members of my family had happened to cop it too – well, that would have been the icing on the cake. He's evil, Claire.'

'I know.'

'Well then,' Sheridan said, showing some of the spirit that had helped her survive, 'roll on Saturday. I guess not too many brides have such an exciting prospect on their big day, a psycho-death-threat man the uninvited guest at their wedding. Maleficent left off the guest list.' Her tone was changing, sharp with irony. 'If the police – or you – do get hold of him, let us know, will you?' She was mocking the tone of a hostess asking if someone was coming to her dinner party. Claire bit her lip. The girl had been through enough, without this untimely reminder of the past and the systems that had let her down.

'Certainly will.'

'And thank you, Dr Roget.' Now she sounded sincere. 'I know you weren't part of the decision to release him.'

'No,' Claire said, 'I was not.'

So that completed her utterly shitty day. Maylene and Derek and now Dexter Harding. Sometimes this job was just far too hard. If not impossible.

She drove home, almost hating the golden sunshine that tried to lift her spirits. Waste of time, she thought angrily. But when she opened her front door (no one in the garden this time), it seemed fortuitous that on the floor was a leaflet from a local painter and decorator offering his services. His name made her smile.

Paul Mudd. Painter and decorator

At your service. Anything undertaken. Highest standards only.

Underneath the cocky little flyer was a mobile telephone number.

Claire rang it.

THIRTY-ONE

Thursday, 30 October, 8 a.m.

He was obviously eager for the work. An unprepossessing-looking man, medium height, slim frame. Large paintbrush, big glasses, and an even bigger cheerful grin.

She teased him about his name, which provoked a broadening of the grin. 'Yeah,' he said. 'But it makes people smile.' He wagged a finger in front of her face. 'They remember it.'

'True.'

He hadn't finished yet. 'Mudd sticks, you see.'

She giggled, then showed him round the house, apologizing until he put his hand on her arm. 'Just tell me what you want done, duck,' he said, and she liked him even more. She explained her situation, that her boyfriend had abandoned the job – and her – halfway through. He looked around, energy bouncing off him in shock waves, his grin ever present, a few quips up his sleeve and his thick-rimmed glasses peering into every corner.

Finally he gave her a rough quote for the job. 'You got four grands' worth of work here,' he said. 'What he's done he's done well, but even if I work a seven-day week, it's going to take me five, six weeks. I'll just about be finished for Christmas.'

She nodded and felt a huge relief. One burden rolling from her back.

It would be like old times, she thought. The smell of paint greeting her return home, rooms being transformed, the place ready to sell and then it could go on the market. If that was what she decided to do. With all the drama at work, she hadn't really sat down and thought it through: what to do about Grant. She could sell up, rent a flat for a bit then maybe buy again, maybe not. Somehow house ownership didn't seem anything like as attractive any more. In fact, she could even rent a hospital flat.

Mr Mudd agreed to start on the following Monday. 'Just got one small job I 'ave to finish,' he said. 'I'll be round seven thirty Monday morning.'

They shook on the deal and Claire felt instantly happier. Action usually works well as an anti-depressant. But the feeling was not destined to last.

Dexter was still on the loose.

9 a.m.

When she arrived at work she knew instantly that she had left behind that feeling of karma.

Rita was busily typing, headphones on, pecking away at the keyboard with unusual ferocity.

When she saw Claire she removed the headphones and stopped the machine. 'Roxanne Barclay's been on the phone,' she said.

Claire stopped in her tracks. Didn't she have enough to deal with?

'She sounded upset.'

'Did she say anything more?'

'Just left a number.' Rita handed her a Post-it note.

It was a mobile. Claire went to her office and rang her back.

'It's Dr Claire Roget here,' she said. 'What's the problem, Roxanne?'

As a blind man senses a shadow has been cast when the sun has gone behind a cloud, she instantly knew Barclay was there, listening in. Even the words didn't sound like the Roxanne she had seen. There was a stilted quality to the rhythm.

'How nice of you to ring back, Claire. Thank you.' The words she trotted out sounded wooden and unnatural. Was she reading from a script?

'What can I do for you, Roxanne?'

Silence.

Claire strained to listen but could hear nothing in the background. No breathing, no gasp, no sob. Nothing. No one. And it suddenly seemed that the silence was more ominous than any sound could be.

Barclay came on the line then, voice silky smooth. 'Where did you get this number from?'

She could not answer without probably putting Roxanne in a vulnerable position. So she did not reply.

He chuckled. 'Don't tell me Roxanne's rung *you* for some polite conversation?'

She could hear steel in his voice.

Shit, she thought. *But what else could I have done? How was I to know he would be there?*

'Oh, well,' Barclay continued. 'As you seem to be struck dumb, I guess I don't really need to come back and see you before we set sail.'

At that she gathered herself. 'Where are you going, Jerome?' she asked steadily.

'Oh, nowhere too adventurous,' he said.

'When?'

'In the next day or two, Claire.'

When he used her name she felt ice-cold prickles stabbing her skin. 'Should I be worried?' she asked, deliberately cool.

The question didn't faze him. 'That's completely up to you,' he replied without even thinking about it. 'But we are having a professional sailor with us, so I don't expect the boat to sink. Though, of course,' he laughed, 'there is always some risk in setting sail. Water can be *sooo* dangerous.' The malice in his voice was goading her to worry.

As she put the phone down she wished that she had been able to speak to Roxanne alone, even if it had been for only a minute.

The next event in her already eventful morning was a phone call from DS Willard, who sounded embarrassed. 'Umm,' he began.

Don't give me more bad news, Claire thought. *I've enough to worry about.*

But it was.

He began by clearing his throat, then umming and aahing – always a bad sign from a policeman, particularly when combined with noisy clearing of the throat. 'Hrrmmm.'

'Have you got him?'

What a stupid question. Of course they hadn't got him.

'No,' he said baldly. 'He was spotted in Hanley on the CCTV cameras, but we haven't caught up with him yet.'

'Look, Sergeant Willard, Zed,' she said, 'I don't want to tell you your job or point out the obvious, which you've already worked out for yourself, but Dexter Harding has complied with the conditions of his discharge for the two years he has been under the CTO. For some reason now he's flipped. It doesn't take a very big bunch of neurons to work out that the reason may well be that his ex-girlfriend, Sheridan, is about to get married. Now I'd say – not being a policeman of course – that given his history his non-attendance is a strong indicator that he may well wish Sheridan harm.'

She had to hand it to DS Willard. He retrieved control of the conversation. 'We're aware of that. Claire,' he said testily, 'we are using all our resources to make sure that Sheridan's wedding goes off without a hitch. If Harding is spotted in the crowd we'll be there.'

She almost wondered whether to confide in DS Willard, tell him about the mad axeman in Cardiff, decided to keep it to herself.

He continued. 'How did she respond, by the way, when you spoke to her?'

'She's a plucky girl but very frightened of Harding. She feels he should have been detained for much longer than he was and should never have been released. And, as you know, I agree with her.'

'OK.' She could hear the smile in his voice. 'Claire,' he said earnestly, 'you know Dexter Harding well. You'll recognize him. Can we rope you in to be an extra pair of eyes at the wedding?'

She hesitated. Hardly her role, but she did have a certain responsibility.

He sensed her hesitation. 'If I said please?'

She sighed. She didn't want to go but she felt she had an obligation. 'OK,' she said, resigned. 'What church is it?'

'St Bartholomew's,' he said. 'Three p.m.'

'OK,' she said again, 'I'll go.'

'Good. Thank you, Claire.' Then, 'Keep in touch?'
'Yeah.'

It was only when she'd put the phone down that she wondered where she'd put his card. No card; no number. No means of contact.

Distractions. There were always distractions. Another patient, another problem. And she always seemed to be facing the wrong way.

Stan's condition was deteriorating almost in front of their eyes, on a daily basis now. He looked tired and wan and these days kept to his bed most of the time. He'd had two further fits. They'd reduced his medication and moved him from the locked ward. He didn't need sedating any more and wasn't a danger to anybody. Claire had had a few brief talks with him and explained that they weren't going to operate, and he'd looked back at her as befuddled as a hundred-year-old patient with advanced Alzheimer's. He wasn't understanding any of it. Maybe it was a good thing. She sat with him for a while, tried to talk about other things, but his eyes stayed unfocused. She left when she realized he didn't have a clue what she was talking about.

And so the wheels went round.

Too much going on in my life, she decided, and worked through the rest of the day feeling she was never quite coping.

But after the usual drive home, something was waiting for her. On the doorstep was a large bouquet of red roses. She looked at them without feeling anything.

But when she read the card, his words did touch her.

I'm so sorry. I did the wrong thing, listened to the wrong people. I love you, Claire. Please, please, let me come home. Signed 'G' XXXXX

She picked them up, let herself in, stood the flowers in water and sent him a text.

Flowers are lovely. Will be in touch soon. Someone called Mudd is finishing the decorating. Hah hah. She signed off *C XX*

At six she had another surprise, a phone call from Adam, saying that he and Adele (what a pretty name) were going for a curry tonight nearby and would she like to join them? She accepted, enjoying this new relationship as though she had only just discovered she had a brother. (Half, anyway.) She suspected that they had come up to the Potteries to see his (and her own) mother. Her relationship with her mother had cooled to freezing point years ago. Weekends spent visiting her were certainly not on the cards, and as for her stepfather she'd never liked him anyway, so Adam was really her only family. Her own father had returned to France and appeared to have forgotten he ever had a daughter. Like Dexter Harding, Monsieur Roget had also disappeared into the ether.

She showered and changed into tight black trousers and a pale blue sweater with a huge rollneck. The outfit was finished with some high-heeled black suede boots and a signature Osprey handbag. She slicked on some lipstick and brushed her hair. There – ready.

The curry house they were going to was just half a mile from her house, which would soon be back to its role as decorator's shop. She walked up the hill to the restaurant, glad of the exercise and the distraction from her numerous work problems.

She'd given up trying to connect with DS Willard. She'd lost his card and with that his personal mobile and land office number. She'd tried to ring him more than once at the station, avoiding giving her name, but it was obvious that the Force guarded their officers' privacy. He had not returned her call. The wedding was the day after tomorrow and she'd promised she would attend, but she hadn't shared her fear that there would be another madman on the rampage, as had happened in Cardiff. Did she really think she could stop Dexter from carrying out whatever horror it was that he was planning, because she had no doubt that he had gone underground for that very reason. But why? It had been the default on his CTO that had alerted them that anything was amiss. In typical Dexter fashion, by going underground he had drawn attention to himself. Or was that what he wanted? Like Jerome – was fear his weapon? Had he wanted to spoil the build-up to Sheridan's big day? She walked faster, telling herself that it was a police matter. Not her responsibility. When someone defaults on their CTO, it is the *police* who track him down. Not the psychiatrist. And with this knowledge her quick steps up the hill seemed to have a rhythm of their own:

It's not all up to you, Claire. Sometimes you have got to hand it to someone else. Else you'll crack up, darling.

Again it was Grant's words, spoken about a year ago and accompanied by a long, lingering kiss, that comforted her. And after the kiss?

She squeezed her eyes tight shut, against Grant's particular brand of love-making, lazy but passionate and very arousing. And now she had reached India Cottage. She pushed open the door, caught the wonderful aroma of spices, and spotted Adam and Adele in the corner, heads close together, sharing secrets? He spotted her and stood up.

'This,' he said proudly, 'is my sister.'

No half measures here. Claire could have cried.

THIRTY-TWO

Adele was one of those sweet-looking, petite, frail girls, who look vulnerable – a physical and mental lie in her case. Claire would soon learn that her appearance belied a steely character, awesome intelligence and a white-water-rafting hobby. She stood up, held out her tiny hand, and appraised Claire with a smile. 'I've heard a lot about you,' she said. Her voice too was sweet.

They sat down, started chatting, ordered drinks and poppadoms and studied the menu. Adele turned out to be a solicitor who specialized in family law. 'Mostly divorce and custody battles,' she said, making a face. 'And believe me, they are battles.' She snapped off a piece of poppadom and spread it with mango chutney, finishing with sliced onion. 'And you wouldn't believe how tricky it can get when one of the parents is a native of another country. Crossing borders, child abduction.' Then she started laughing. 'Heaven alone knows why I chose that particular speciality when I could have done something so much simpler and less emotive.'

'Such as,' Adam challenged, grinning. Claire knew they were going over old ground here.

'Well, company law.'

Claire ventured her view. 'Don't you think it would turn out just about the same? Aren't companies a bit like a family?'

They all laughed at that.

They were just about to start eating when Claire's mobile went off. A mobile number she didn't recognize. 'Excuse me,' she said.

It was DS Zed Willard and he sounded relaxed – considering what might be happening on Saturday. 'Well hello there, Claire,' he said, sounding jaunty. 'Did I hear you've been trying to get hold of me?'

He'd obviously taken it personally. Completely the wrong way. 'Yes,' she said, 'I was.'

'Sorry.' Instant apology. 'I'm sorry to ring you so late. I expect you're—'

'Yes, I am,' she responded, 'at an Indian restaurant. With friends.' *Make of that what you will, Sergeant Willard.*

There was a brief, awkward silence while he did just that. Then, 'Well what *did* you want to get hold of me for?'

'I realized I had no contact details for you,' she said. 'If I spot Harding in the crowd or even going into the church, how would I get hold of you?'

He chuckled. 'My card?'

'Well actually—'

He butted in, unabashed. 'Lost it,' he supplied. 'Well you've got it now – my personal telephone number. It'll be on your phone memory.' He laughed again. (What was the guy on?) 'Don't go handing it out to just anybody, will you?'

'I won't.'

'No, really.' There was a little more urgency and less merriment in his tone this time.

She matched it with her own tone. 'I promise I won't, Zed.'

'Good. See you Saturday. At the wedding. Unless, of course, he turns up beforehand.'

He won't.

His jauntiness irritated her, particularly as both Adam and Adele were munching on their poppadoms, pretending not to be taking any notice. But then she had to remind herself that DS Willard didn't know what a nasty, stupid piece of work Dexter Harding was. He'd never met him. He probably didn't know anything about the Cardiff case; neither had he been involved in the house fire and its grisly aftermath, or the complexities of the subsequent kangaroo court case. He probably didn't have a clue how dangerous Harding really was; probably thought they were all making a big fuss about nothing.

Well – he'd soon see.

She put her phone away. Adam was watching her, sympathetic but curious. 'Work, sis?'

She nodded. 'I'm sorry,' she said, and tried to return to the conversation and the excellent curry that was now on candle burners in front of them, but there was little doubt the call had taken some of the joy out of the night.

She was dreading Saturday.

THIRTY-THREE

Saturday, 1 November, 9 a.m.

It was bright and warm, one of those days we don't expect in mid-November, which is, generally, a month associated with dullness, sulky skies, rain and chilling winds. Just to get you in the mood for winter. But today it was sunny, crisp and beautiful. Not a cloud in a sky of Wedgwood blue. It should have been a perfect day for a wedding. The service was at three, so Claire had plenty of time to take up her position at the church. What she really thought would happen was unclear or unimaginable. Did she really think Dexter would march up the aisle wielding an axe, stab or shoot Sheridan in her wedding dress? Was that really what she expected, a Lorna Doone drama? She sat at her kitchen table musing, wondering whether the seconds were ticking away towards some terrible bloodbath. It was hard to imagine in her quiet kitchen, the clock ticking on the wall a solemn reminder of time passing. And she tried to understand the reason why Dexter Harding had gone underground. Even he would have had a curious logic in his actions, and for once in her life she was afraid of the unknown. Not for herself but for Sheridan and Richard Hadley, the man she hoped to marry. What Claire hoped to achieve by her presence she also had no idea. Throw her body in front of Sheridan's? Save her life in melodramatic Victorian style? She shook her head and simply knew that she had to be there.

She didn't need an excuse to stand outside. Weddings are popular. The general public like the spectacle. Families enjoy themselves and plenty of friends would wish them well. Why shouldn't she be there? But what no one except the police would know was that this wedding would have an uninvited guest, the added frisson of a psycho on the loose, a heavy police presence, and herself standing on the sidelines feeling somehow to blame. Because she knew as sure as sure that Dexter would be there.

She had met Sheridan Riley in person only the once. She would not have recognized her on the street, but that one encounter with her had exposed the danger Dexter posed. Sheridan wasn't a stupid girl; neither was she timid or weak. But Dexter, even with his bovine stupidity, had made her afraid. He had infected her mind and controlled her; not in the way that Jerome Barclay controlled those around him, with subtle, sly jabs, needling his way into their subconscious with hints and innuendo, but with the blunt instrument of terror. Harding's was a physically frightening presence. Claire recalled a petite girl with frightened eyes. A girl completely intimidated. Terrified. The relationship and arson attack had been five years ago. Yet it was only now that Sheridan was getting married. What had happened in the intervening years, Claire had no idea. She recalled the girl's words and the feeling that she'd understood the situation.

'I met him at a party. I wasn't really enjoying myself that night. I wanted to go home but the party was one of my best

friend's and I didn't want to offend her, so I sat on the landing, pretending to drink, and Dexter came up and sat beside me. I didn't like him. From the first I didn't like him. There was nothing *about him that I liked. His blunt manner, his rudeness.'* She had dropped her head into her hands. *'His awful language. Every other word a fuck or a – well – even worse.'*

And yet, Claire had thought, you ended up with him?

'He seemed rough and, quite frankly, he smelt, but he could see I wasn't enjoying myself and he offered to drive me home.'

She had turned dark, troubled eyes on Claire. *'I just wanted to leave. You know how it is when you're in a crowd and don't want to be there?'*

Claire had nodded. She'd been to that particular place many times herself.

'Trouble was,' Sheridan said, *'because he'd given me a lift home he now knew where I lived and he pestered me. Just turning up any old time. Sometimes with flowers, sometimes it was threats. A bottle of wine, a takeaway, a thump, a slap. It was all the same to him. He'd just turn up and I couldn't stand up to him. He'd cancel any engagements I already had, ring people up, just say I wasn't coming. Little by little my friends bled away. They didn't like him either.'* She'd met Claire's eyes. *'They were afraid of him too. He'd suddenly just smash his fist into something. Break a glass, start shouting. It didn't seem to matter how much I said I didn't want a relationship, he just kept coming. He took no notice. It was as though I hadn't spoken. I was always frightened of what he would do. He was always there. And at irregular intervals. Sometimes every night, sometimes not for a week or even two weeks, but I was still afraid to go out. This went on for nearly a year and then I met Richard, someone I really did like. Just a nice ordinary guy from work.'* She'd worked in an office in the city. *'And I really wanted to be with him.'*

Her eyes had stayed unfocused. *'Dexter didn't seem to mind. He just said, OK. But I saw something in his eyes and I knew it wouldn't be OK. I knew something would happen.'*

She'd swallowed. *'And then that happened. Dr Roget, I felt responsible for the family's deaths. They'd had an awful life. I knew them a bit. They were Iraqi Kurds. The children were six and four.' She'd smiled. 'Babar and Harika. They were lovely. They'd fled death and . . .'*

It was only now, as Claire was dressing in a blue wool dress and navy coat, that she realized something she should have understood years ago, when she'd first taken on Dexter Harding's case. She'd had it at the back of her mind lying dormant, itching her brain, yet somehow she had skipped right over it.

Dexter Harding had been to Sheridan's house hundreds of times. He knew where it was. Even as stupid as he was, he wouldn't have made a mistake and torched the wrong house. He'd set the fire as a warning to her. A statement: This is what I can do. And as for the family he'd murdered, they could have been picked deliberately or been a random choice. But now, Claire understood. He'd known Sheridan was fond of the family. He had set that house ablaze – not hers – to teach her a lesson she would never forget. That was Dexter's way of thinking. He never had had any intention of killing Sheridan. He'd merely wanted to teach her a lesson. Why hadn't the original hearing taken this into account? Why hadn't *she* realized the significance? She was a psychiatrist, for goodness' sake. He was, as Barclay had said with more insight than she, *the stupid clever.* Claire looked at herself in the mirror, pale now with apprehension.

She understood now.

Sheridan's intimidation had only stopped because Dexter had been in custody, and then in prison, arrested within hours of the arson attack. With typical Dexter stupidity, he had been picked up on CCTV at the petrol station from where he had bought his petrol just a hundred yards from the scene. He hadn't physically had any chance to get at Sheridan after the fire. So she'd been safe, protected from his attentions. Then, when he'd been released, he'd pretended to abide by the rules of his CTO, kept away from her, lulling them into a sense of false security which Claire had never quite believed in. Had Sheridan read the message behind his crime? Part of the terms of his release had been an injunction not to approach her. And so, with patience most unlike Dexter, he had bided his time, waiting for what? A special day. So what was he planning in that clumsy, limited mind of his? Why had he suddenly gone AWOL when even he must have known it would end up in his being arrested again? What made this risk worth it?

Claire forced herself to concentrate. She was his psychiatrist. She had seen him every fortnight for two years, except for the couple of weeks when she'd been on holiday and her locum or Edward Reakin, the clinical psychologist, had seen him instead. If anybody could understand his mind and anticipate his actions, it should be her.

But her mind was a blank. She only knew she was apprehensive. And if she had been Sheridan today she would have been terrified.

Scared stiff.

2.30 p.m.

Her feeling of foreboding persisted as she drove towards Blurton, that this tranquil happy scene, a young couple marrying in a city church, would be transformed into horror.

She lectured herself. *Look, Claire, there's no point shrinking into a corner. You've got to make a plan.* So she did.

The best strategy, she decided, would be to mingle in with the crowd outside the church, invisible, acting the part of a curious bystander, a nosey wedding-watcher. And maybe, knowing him so well, she would have an opportunity of pointing him out to the police before he had a chance to go inside. Then they could deal with him, bundle him away and the wedding could proceed as normal, perhaps even before Sheridan knew anything was amiss.

That was the plan.

And so, for the second time in as many months, she found herself apprehensive at the wedding of one of her more worrying patients, uncertain what the outcome of the nuptials would be.

Should she ring Zed Willard? She fingered her mobile phone, found his number in the call log – and put it back in her pocket. He might think she was overreacting.

Her worry was that she was not.

She parked at the bottom of the hill, in the supermarket car park, and walked up to the church, arriving early, giving herself twenty minutes before the ceremony was due to start.

She stood on the edge of the few gathered people and observed the arrivals.

The groom made an appearance at a quarter to two, a good-looking young man, immaculate in a grey morning suit, eyes looking nervously around him. Claire watched him. Simple bridegroom's nerves, or something more? How much did he know about his bride's troubles? What exactly had Sheridan told him?

Richard Hadley was a little under six feet tall, with a sharp new haircut and shiny brown hair, strong shoulders and a clear gaze. No bridegroom hangover evidence from the stag night. And – something else which comforted Claire – he looked brave, one of these clear-eyed, challenging sorts who would shoulder responsibility and slay the dragon.

He didn't recognize her, of course, which gave her an advantage. She could observe him without being noticed as he posed for the obligatory photographs, jiggling nervously from foot to foot.

She watched the file of people, all in wedding finery. Hats and suits and some very smart clothes, the women like a flutter of butterflies. What a very appropriate collective noun that was. And, like the women whose movements and outfits did indeed flutter like butterflies, so too did Claire's thoughts, flying around, settling on one anxiety and then another.

Superimposed by Dexter Harding's character, dark as a crow's.

If butterflies fluttered then crows murdered.

She scanned the smiley, happy faces, all waiting for the bride. No Dexter.

Yet.

After a few awkward photographs (best man, ushers in attendance, very like Jerome Barclay's wedding – aren't all weddings the same? Not *all* weddings. Not *this* wedding), finally the groom disappeared inside the church. Safe for now – at least *he* was. She heard the organist playing a Bach cantata, the music sombre, cadences as threatening as storm clouds.

The ushers hovered outside, showing some more self-consciously smartly dressed people to their seats. Passers-by gathered, hovering expectantly. Waiting for the bride.

The organ continued playing, now another Bach cantata, which rippled out on to the pavement as a white Rolls-Royce pulled up and two bridesmaids in midnight-blue dresses tumbled out. The crowd shuffled and made a slight movement towards them. Claire hung back and looked around anxiously.

Still no sign of Dexter.

The car behind was another Rolls, silver this time, with white satin ribbons over its bonnet, and here she was, Sheridan Riley, looking gorgeous in an ice-white, huge-skirted dress, crystals dazzling in the sunshine, train trailing, face veiled, helped by her father in a grey morning suit, a splash of a red carnation with untidy petals on his lapel, just over his heart, pinned like the scrap of material meant to help soldiers take aim at a victim in a firing squad. *Please no.*

The bridesmaids patted Sheridan's wedding dress down, pulled out any creases, extended the train to its full, glorious length, holding it just above the pavement so it retained its sparkling, pure whiteness. Sheridan scanned the crowd but didn't appear to recognize Claire or see anyone else to concern her. So she focused on the wedding. There were the obligatory photographs. Flowers in the foreground, Sheridan flanked by the two girls in blue, both of them giggling self-consciously but looking ethereally happy. Claire remained in the background, her focus not on the bride, her nervous father or her pretty bridesmaids, but scanning the rim of curious members of the general public, the uninvited ones. Maleficent: the one who could cause havoc. Dexter.

She tried to spot the police in the crowd. No one obvious. Certainly no uniformed presence and not a sign of DS Zed Willard. She fingered her mobile phone in her pocket and felt let down. Something *was* going to happen and they just didn't care. They hadn't taken the threat seriously – or her warning. She should have warned them again. Now, when that something happened, they wouldn't be there to protect anyone. Had they not realized that Dexter Harding was a mad bull? She felt angry now as well as apprehensive, and kept her head down.

She felt nothing but relief when the bride finally disappeared inside the church to the strains of Wagner.

For a moment Claire could breathe. Nothing had happened. Sheridan was safe and the ushers had checked everyone who'd entered the church. Perhaps the police had briefed them to be extra-vigilant and considered that was enough. Perhaps she had been wrong. Maybe Dexter had vanished for another reason. Claire stood still and wondered. So many possibilities.

The sounds of the service drifted out on to the pavement, plenty of members of the public hovering, hoping to catch another glimpse of the bride. The crowd was gathering, waiting to see the happy couple emerge.

'*Dearly beloved* . . .' 'Ave Maria' . . . 'Trumpet Voluntary', as they (presumably) signed the register. And then she saw him. Well, the truth was, she *felt* him, *smelt* him and knew he was there. Somewhere behind her, not far away. The back of her neck felt ice cold.

Perhaps part of her had been watchful all the way through the service. And now she saw a couple of uniformed police, bright in their hi-vis jackets, cross the road towards the church. She saw them scanning the watching crowd, communicate on their walkie-talkies, speaking surreptitiously into microphones attached to their lapels. One of them had a head-cam and was sweeping the images somewhere. Back to a central station? So they *were* taking the threat seriously. She made a silent apology to DS Zed Willard and watched.

Dexter was hovering on the periphery of the onlookers, standing at the very back of the crowd, a bulky figure in jeans and donkey jacket. He was standing quite still and yet giving out vibes. Maybe it was his appearance or his animal scent – or the pungent smell that Sheridan had complained of. A few people glanced across and moved away from him. Just a step or two, but enough to put them beyond arms' (or fists') reach. She lifted her gaze to his face. He was fixed on one spot – the church door through which the happy couple would soon emerge. She inched closer, staring at the floor, pulling up the collar of her jacket, making herself appear smaller, insignificant, invisible.

Some hope.

Had the police spotted him? She couldn't be absolutely sure. There seemed no urgency in the two officers' casual stroll. She focused back on the arched doorway. Still empty, then risked another look at Harding. His chin was jutting out, his expression determined, his hand in his pocket.

What did he have in there? Not an axe. A knife or a gun or even acid spray for the girl who had spurned him. Whatever he was planning, in minutes, she guessed there would be no happy couple but a scene of destruction, devastation.

She manoeuvred herself next to one of the uniformed officers and spoke in a low voice.

'I'm Dr Claire Roget,' she said, hoping he would have been briefed so she wouldn't need to go into any explanation.

He looked down at her. He was young. Twenties maybe, oddly innocent-looking for a police constable. She continued in the same low voice, 'I think some of you at least are here because of a previous boyfriend of the bride?'

He turned surprised eyes at her.

'I know him,' she said. 'He's a patient of mine who has absconded. He's here,' she said. 'At the back of the crowd, in a brown jacket and jeans.'

The constable looked around.

'You mean that guy there?'

She turned and looked straight into Dexter's eyes. He'd moved right behind her. It would be futile to pretend she hadn't seen him. 'Hello, Dexter,' she said, smiling. 'You missed your last appointment.'

The look he gave her was one of utter contempt, and she knew then that her initial instinct – for him to remain in prison or Broadmoor for ever – had been right. He was not someone who should ever have been released. It had been a terrible mistake. And now there would be a terrible price to pay.

Dexter shoved his way through the crowd towards the front, while the policeman spoke into his lapel microphone. She could hear the strains of 'The Arrival of the Queen of Sheba'. The newlyweds were leaving the church and there was no way to stop them. Claire wondered if she could dart forwards and slam the door. Keep them in the church – safe. She again had that terrible Lorna Doone flash – a wedding dress and a spreading stain – and stood paralysed. Afterwards she was full of remorse. She should have warned them.

She had said nothing, done nothing, except alerted one policeman to his presence. And Dexter knew she was here. Now he was warned. Probably carrying a weapon. She should have told the officer he might have a knife. He's dangerous. But all she felt was panic. Then events happened fast. By the time she had formed these thoughts the constable had rallied two of his colleagues and they were closing in on him.

As the bride and groom emerged, laughing in a cloud of confetti, underneath the ancient arch of the church, Dexter lunged, knife in hand, slashing. And at the same time the three officers in their Day-Glo hi-vis jackets also lunged. The young officer clutched his chest and Dexter was on the floor, spitting and cursing, while the bride in her still beautifully spotless, perfect white wedding dress and the groom, swanky in his morning suit, blue cravat, white shirt and winged collar, simply stood, gaping. For a further minute, Dexter spat and struggled on the floor, the crowd frozen at the drama, not understanding. Then Sheridan née Riley, now Mrs Hadley, threw herself into her husband's arms to the cheer of the crowd, who still didn't understand what was going on. The cuffing of Dexter, the frog-march to the police van and the flashing blue light and screaming siren seconds later almost went unnoticed in the joy and romance of the occasion and the clicking of cameras and phones.

Headline news.

But Claire was not looking at the arrest, or the bride and groom, but at the young officer, face chalk white, and the blood pumping out of his chest.

Doctor clicked in. She pressed on the wound, shouted for an ambulance, checked pulse – a little thready, but then he was shocked. Better to keep the blood pressure low – less blood would pump out of his chest. 'We need the high-dependency ambulance,' she said, ice calm now. She looked up. 'What's his name?'

And then Zed Willard was by her side. 'Dylan,' he said. 'And you've got blood on you, Claire.'

She nodded, then heard the scream of an ambulance. A couple of paramedics were kneeling by her in seconds, an oxygen mask on his face.

'Dylan,' she said, 'you're going to be OK now.'

'Penetrating chest wound,' she said to the paramedic – a girl with a blonde ponytail. 'Arterial damage. You'll have to keep the pressure on.' She met her eyes. 'Ready?'

They switched roles. 'He'll have to go straight to theatre.'

Zed Willard touched her shoulder and smiled. 'We'll send a copper in with him to give details.'

Then she rested back on her heels. Her role was over. Job done.

And he was right. She had blood on her clothes. She didn't wait, not for the photographs with the lovely old church in the background, the sun sparkling on the crystals of the bride's dress, the yards and yards of train carried around the churchyard by the patient bridesmaids from one location to another, finally to be bundled into the car to the reception. Claire didn't wait for any of it. She just went home.

Her role here was over.

What, she wondered, would come next?

THIRTY-FOUR

Her mobile registered a call at six p.m. that evening. Shaken, she'd returned home, wondering what she could or should have done differently. It had been a close call. Armed with a knife Dexter, her patient, her responsibility, had been within yards of his prior girlfriend and might well have murdered a young policeman. It would be touch and go. If the police had been a little slower, if she hadn't been there, it could have been a different story. In her mind, Dexter would have knifed bride and/or groom. The beautiful dress would have been spattered with blood, just like she'd imagined, and somehow she couldn't rid herself of the feeling that it was, somehow, her fault. She was the psychiatrist in charge of his case, but her problem was always the same one: how do you anticipate a crime?

Hang on a minute – she just had.

She had a bath and discarded the bloodstained clothes. She probably wouldn't wear them again.

To distract herself she wandered from room to room, trying to move away from her thoughts, to focus on deciding the best décor for each room, and fire herself up to make a visit in the morning to the local DIY store. Do something calming like looking at paint shade cards, fittings and wallpaper books. But she couldn't stir herself and she had to acknowledge: she had no enthusiasm for the scheme, really. With Grant it had been fun building and feathering this little nest. Alone it lacked colour and excitement. She just wanted out. So when her phone rang she was glad of the distraction.

'Is that Claire?' The voice was male and tentative and she wasn't sure initially who it was. Then it registered.

'DS Willard,' she said, surprised. 'Zed. How is . . .?' she scratched around in her mind. 'Dylan?'

'Still in theatre, but alive as far as I know.'

That was when it struck her. Maybe Sheridan *hadn't* been the intended target. Maybe Dexter had simply wanted her to suffer – again. Maybe it had just been another warning. She was silent, then said, 'Well, you got your man.'

'Thank goodness you were there to point him out to our officers. He got pretty near.'

'Well I knew him,' Claire began, knowing she was sounding a bit prickly. 'He was under my care. Not surprising I recognized him.' Then she burst out. 'I knew he was dangerous, Zed. I fought his release into a Community Treatment Order but nobody was listening. I was always wary of him. I knew what he was capable of. This was my worst nightmare. And you nearly lost an officer.'

'Look,' he said, 'Dylan will be all right – thanks to you.'

'Thanks to me,' she said bitterly.

He butted in verbally to sidetrack her. 'Claire. Look. This might be a bit out of order.'

What on earth was he about to say?

'But . . . I er . . . I wondered . . .' He was having real trouble spitting it out. 'I was thinking of . . .'

She waited. For what, she didn't have a clue.

'I was thinking. I . . .' This was squirmingly embarrassing. 'Can I come round with a bottle of wine?'

She was so astonished that she did the usual, stupid thing and asked a stupid question. 'You know where I live?'

So stupid. He was a police officer, for goodness' sake. They could find out anything. Her address was probably one of the easiest, along with her mobile number (she'd given it to him anyway), her car registration, insurance status, tax and MOT.

'Ye-es.' He was quick to add, 'I mean, I haven't been snooping or anything.'

'When were you thinking of?'

'I could be round by seven.'

'OK.' She was still too surprised to say anything more – no platitudes, no *I'll look forward to it*. She was still gawping.

He gave a chuckle then an uncertain, 'Uumm.' Then, 'Red or white?'

In actual fact he was round in forty-five minutes, a bottle of Rioja under one arm, Sauvignon Blanc under the other. He held them out with such a boyish grin it touched her heart.

'I hope he's all right.'

'If he is it's thanks to you. You were amazing. You probably saved his life with your heroics.'

'Just my job,' she said. 'Any old doctor around would have done the same.'

He clinked glasses. 'Ah, but you were the one on the spot.'

'Not,' she reminded him, 'by chance.'

They were sitting in the garden, wrapped up in fleeces against the chill, drinking their first glass of wine.

'It could have been even worse.'

And then, like a boil, it had burst out, hot and furious. 'He should never have been let out, Zed. Never have been allowed to walk the streets. He is dangerous. Always has been and always will be. All his life.'

Then she raised her observation about the arson attack. 'He'd been to Sheridan's house on numerous occasions, practically stalked her. Yet he torched the wrong house?' Then, as he didn't appear to have grasped her full meaning, she continued, 'He murdered that entire family deliberately, just to teach her a lesson, to terrify her. Today was another . . . lesson. Her wedding day.'

Zed Willard leaned back in his chair, seeming to absorb this fact. Then he sat up. 'So obvious,' he said. 'So why . . .?'

'Mistakes are made,' she said wearily. 'Even I didn't think of it until today.' She turned to him, hands holding the wine glass, warming the Rioja to blood heat. 'If he hadn't missed that appointment, I wouldn't have been alerted.'

'So why did he miss when he'd turned up regularly for a couple of years?'

She gave a sour smile. 'I've been pondering this point,' she said. 'I like to think it's because he believed I would know something was up. He always had a belief that psychiatrists had almost psychic powers and could read minds.'

'Well, after this, he won't be walking the streets again. Ever.'

She turned on him then. 'I wouldn't bet on it, Zed. You think you can go against someone with their FRCPsych., and argue that he is and always will be a danger, when they're saying, under their treatment, whatever it might be, that he is cured of his malady and safe as the family Labrador?' Anger was making her voice tight. Zed Willard put a hand on her shoulder.

'Hey, Claire,' he said, 'loosen up.'

He was right. 'I'm sorry. I just think – because of Dexter Harding's evil nature and fixation – that your young officer could so easily have lost his life and Sheridan's wedding day has been blighted.'

'No it wasn't,' he said. 'She and her husband will be OK.'

He touched her hand. 'What more could you have done – really?'

She took a long deep draught of wine. 'It's not enough,' she said. 'Never enough. I knew Dexter was dangerous, but I couldn't do anything to prevent this.'

Just like Jerome Barclay.

Zed Willard was silent.

They poured their second glass and the conversation shifted gear.

DS Willard looked embarrassed. 'Claire,' he said, 'I don't know if I should say this.'

She raised her eyebrows. 'What?'

He looked even more awkward. 'I mean – are you in a relationship?'

She shook her head. She didn't want to go into it. 'To be honest, Zed,' she said, 'I'm not really sure.'

'Oh.' He looked about as confused as she felt.

Twenty minutes later he stood up, mumbled something about drink-drive limits and left.

She finished the bottle of wine alone.

Dexter had been taken care of. So now she only had Barclay to worry about. Was he planning something similar? A murderous attack on wife, baby, in-laws? Only, Barclay being Barclay, it would not be a visible knife attack in full public view. Nothing so obvious. Oh no. It would be something much more devious and subtle, hardly visible on the surface as a crime and impossible to prove. Was she equally powerless to prevent it?

THIRTY-FIVE

Sunday, 2 November, 10 a.m.

A day off but she wasn't relaxed at all. She felt fidgety and anxious. She had intervened in the Dexter case but the young police constable had nearly lost his life. If she hadn't been there he probably would have died. He still might do. Without opening up his chest she was aware his injury had been life threatening. Had Sheridan been his real target, she wondered, or the policeman – or just anyone? What was certain now was that Dexter was not currently a danger to the public. He was in police custody.

Not so Barclay. He was out there, on the loose, plotting

something. She felt depressed. She might know what was in her patients' minds, but she couldn't be everywhere, with everyone, to try and stop them. How could she protect Roxanne, let alone the unborn child, even her parents, when Barclay was luring them possibly to their deaths?

What if Jerome Barclay was as dangerous as her worst fear and the whole situation ended up like that of Dexter, with a fatal showdown? She sat and pondered the sixty-four-thousand-dollar question. How responsible was she? It was a point that troubled many psychiatrists who deal with forensic patients. They run a constant tightrope between protection of potential victims and preserving the patient's right to remain innocent until proved guilty. It was all guesswork really. An inexact science. And if they got it wrong, they were culpable in the eyes of the law.

But for guilt to be proved you first had to have an actual crime, or at least clear intention to commit one. Planning, stalking, acquisition of weapons, etc. After Dexter's murder of the Kurdish family, at least a second felony had hopefully been averted. She might well not be so lucky with Barclay. He was brighter than Dexter and, she hated to admit it, easily her equal. Capable of outmanoeuvring her.

If Roxanne and her parents hadn't been that lethal combination of naive and wealthy. And if Roxanne hadn't been exactly Barclay's sort of girl: compliant, easily intimidated and vulnerable, she would have let them work the situation out for themselves and hope that no harm came to them. She would trust they could protect themselves and that Roxanne would protect her unborn infant. At least there were three of them against Barclay's one. But the near tragedy on Saturday with Dexter had thumped home to her the responsibility of her position. She had actually seen what a violent patient could do – first hand. She felt a certain anger and frustration. She was not a magician; neither was she a medium or a visionary. She could not peer inside her patients' minds and anticipate death. She could not grade evil on a scale of one to ten and incarcerate anyone scoring over a five. Patients could be devious. She was supposed to be able to foresee the future, but she had no supernatural powers to call on. Only simple psychiatry. She spent half of Sunday tussling with the problem of what to do about Barclay, and the other half moving from room to room, trying to work out how best to present the house and sell it quickly and for a good price.

And was that what she really wanted? She didn't even know that.

As a consultant one was, to some extent, a lone worker. She needed someone to talk to about Barclay but she couldn't trust anyone in the hospital. Someone there was feeding Barclay his information.

Would, she wondered, DS Zed Willard take her a bit more seriously now if she raised the subject with him?

It was worth a try.

Feeling instinctively that it wasn't a good idea, she rang him. She knew it had been a bad idea when a woman answered. She bottled out and apologized for having rung a wrong number.

Monday, 3 November, 7.30 a.m.

Paul Mudd was as good as his word. In fact his knocking at the front door was what got her out of bed. Predictably she'd had a restless night imagining all sorts of scenarios, as well as recalling the young PC's face as the knife had driven home. She saw again and again his colour leach away, felt the thready pulse, watched him slowly lose consciousness. In her nightmare she watched him die, arms pinned behind her back, powerless to save him, while Dexter drove the knife home again and again. And then her mind took her to the sea, to a boat bobbing on the waves. Roxanne and family – and Jerome Barclay sliding on the deck as wave after wave hit. She was in the front seat watching a disaster movie, eyes wide open.

Paul Mudd's cheery face was a good start to the day, particularly as he told her, in business-like terms that he would 'start at the top, Claire, and work my way downwards. OK with you?'

What did he think?

Even better, he'd brought some shade cards with him so she could choose her colours without even having to trawl the

DIY shops. And even better than that, he assured her that he could get a 'very good trade discount'.

Happy, she left the house.

8.30 a.m.

One of the first things she did on arrival at work was to ring the hospital and ask how PC Dylan Salisbury was. The bright mood intensified when she was told he was out of danger and back on a general ward.

Thank God, she thought.

Next she searched out Edward Reakin. He was a few years older than her and more experienced. Not only that but his viewpoint, as a clinical psychologist rather than a psychiatrist, was different; she needed his perspective to help her to understand what she should do next to avert further tragedy. There was another benefit. He knew Barclay, had met him on a number of occasions as he covered her clinics when she was away. Bearing in mind that he might be the mole, she would be guarded in her questions.

She found Edward in his office and gained entrance with a tentative knock.

He grinned across at her. He was a friendly guy, very approachable. Of all the people in the hospital, she least wanted him to be Barclay's informant. She couldn't imagine him being friends with a worm like Jerome anyway, so she thought she was safe trusting him. She was really fond of him. He was about forty and had suffered a very traumatic divorce a year or two ago when his wife had publicly flaunted an affair. At that time he had lost weight and looked older and anxious and very unhappy. It had taken many nights out at the pub and a lot of heart-searching, but he had eventually settled down and now he appeared content.

Today he looked the part, dressed in a smart grey suit, cream shirt, blue tie. Not the usual work garb for a psychologist who tended, as a group, to dress like Freud or Einstein – in baggy tweed jackets and old trousers, sometimes completing the picture with scuffed suede shoes – rather than like the CEO of a major company. Edward was a slim man with long bony legs, and a thin face which easily looked tired, even haggard. His best feature, in Claire's opinion, was his eyes, very clear and grey, set wide either side of a sharply hooked nose. He also had a warm, genuine smile. The other thing she really liked about him was his gentlemanly, almost public school, manners. He stood up smartly as she entered. 'Claire,' he said gladly. (That was yet another thing to add to the list: he always looked glad to see her.)

Please, she thought, *don't let it be him.*

'Have you got a minute, Edward? I could do with some advice.'

'Of course.' His grin was warm and genuine as he patted the chair in front of the desk. 'What is it? You look bothered about something.'

'That's because I am,' she responded, sinking into one of his very comfortable chairs.

As succinctly as she could, and without emotion, she related the drama that had surrounded Saturday's wedding and she watched his face deepen into worry. He put his hand out and brushed hers in sympathy. 'Every now and then, Claire,' he said, 'we come across the real meaning of our job, don't we?' His eyes lit on hers. 'The bit about protecting the general public?'

She nodded and he continued.

'It's beyond us. I mean, how can you possibly know how far some of our patients will go? They brag and get expansive. How can we know when their threats will translate into action?'

'It was all there in the past for us to read, Edward,' she said. 'I should have realized. I've been really stupid.'

He raised his eyebrows. 'How so?'

And again she explained what had been staring them all in the face. 'Dexter had been to Sheridan's house on numerous occasions. He was not going to target the wrong house. If he did it was because he wanted to. It wasn't stupidity that murdered the family.' She tried out Barclay's phrase. 'He is the stupid clever.'

Edward didn't respond, except to frown, which put her mind at rest. The phrase meant nothing to him. She continued. 'It was pure evil. He knew that Sheridan would read the message and that she would be terrified.'

Edward was watching but not comprehending.

So she spelt it out again. 'An entire family were murdered just to teach her a lesson.'

Edward sat still; appalled as the implication of this bald statement slowly sank in.

'And you and I know full well that as a psychopath he ticks all the boxes; he isn't quite as stupid as he makes out. Now he's in police custody, and as his psychiatrist I can point this out. I don't think he'll ever be free again. But,' she said, her eyes full on his face, 'I have another problem patient.'

'Let me guess,' he said uncomfortably, shifting in his seat. 'Jerome Barclay?'

And she knew her case was lost.

Her colleagues had always believed that both she and her predecessor, Heidi, had overestimated Barclay's danger. They saw him as a self-preening narcissistic personality disorder, no real threat to anyone. All puff, boast and brag. When she had pointed out the poor life expectancy of his nearest and dearest, and the vicious assault on Sadie's life, they had argued that he had simply used facts for his own ends – to make her believe he was responsible.

Nothing she had ever been able to say or do had altered their opinion. And her misreading of Heidi's murder had underlined their opinions.

She sat still for a minute. She'd always liked Edward and had hoped that he, at least, had not judged her, but she could see now that she had been too optimistic.

This is just a waste of time. She could read it in his clear eyes, the dim flicker of disappointment in her.

She smiled, mumbled something and he watched, silent and embarrassed.

She stood up. So did he, almost a reflex. 'So . . .?'

'It's OK.' She forced herself to smile, thank him, and she left, very disappointed. She'd needed someone. Someone to listen properly to her misgivings. But now she knew. She was still on her own, unable to warn Roxanne of the approaching danger.

THIRTY-SIX

Later that morning

S he couldn't think of a way to do it, stop the train, avert the tragedy.

All she had were Jerome's mobile number and a land-line. No address. There was no way of bypassing him.

She sat in her office, door closed, disappointed in her colleague's response, feeling alone in her apprehension and sense of foreboding. She leafed through Jerome Barclay's file, searching for something that would point the way. Prove it. There it all was: his confessions (false?) of torturing animals. The allegations (unsubstantiated) of GBH, the assault on his previous girlfriend, Sadie Whittaker, who had not only left him after the assault that had landed her in hospital, but had deliberately terminated her pregnancy, as though she could not bear to harbour the devil's spawn. Claire read through the notes she had made after she had met up with Sadie.

'It was all there in his lovemaking. He enjoys inflicting pain . . . The sex act means nothing to him unless it involves terror. Bondage. Me being helpless. And . . .'

'Verbal threats . . . "I could cut a slice off those thighs . . . I could rape you and make you scream" . . . A hard pinch of the nipple . . . Sometimes I would pretend to be more fright-ened than I was but he knew. He always knew, as though he could bore into my mind.'

Unusually Barclay had had insight into his condition. And that had made him doubly cruel, triply clever and quadruply perceptive. There was no fooling him. Which was why he was so slippery and difficult to catch out. He was thirty-five years old and his criminal record was minimal.

To provoke him she had deliberately asked him on more than one occasion how he felt about the termination of his

child and had watched his features harden into hatred – one
of the few times he had let his mask slip. He had ground his
teeth and said nothing. But his eyes had burned with fury. She
had watched and felt unnerved and uncertain. Was he furious
that Sadie had cheated him of another vulnerable human being
to hurt, or was it remotely possible that he had at last felt
some affection for another human being – albeit his own, evil
spawn?

Claire stared into space, trying to find a path through this.
Relieved, of course, that Sheridan was safe, probably just
setting off on her honeymoon. But now there was Roxanne
and her family to worry about. Was there an endless supply
of cruelty in the world? Of course – just look at the news.

Probably, she reasoned, at the moment, Roxanne was
already being subjected to minor threats, both physical and
mental. The trouble is that people adjust to intimidation. Like
burning over scar tissue, they stop feeling the pain or recognizing the behaviour as pathological. Abnormal becomes the
normal. And, as the saying goes: no pain, no gain. This is
certainly true for the psychopath, whose distorted pleasure
can only be achieved through another's suffering. And so the
intimidation must escalate if your psychopath is to keep
feeling pleasure.

Her thoughts were going round and round. The injuries
Roxanne had displayed before the outpatient appointment were
typically inflicted somewhere visible, purely to keep her aware.
If she was to have any chance of averting disaster, she must
be able to speak frankly to Roxanne, bypassing Barclay. Maybe
probe at first, find out just what he was up to. But that would
never happen if he was listening.

There wasn't a lot of point in summoning him back to clinic.
He would see that as a triumph; he would know she was
powerless to do anything. No one listens to suspicion.

From Grant she heard nothing more and knew the ball was in
her court. The roses hadn't lasted very long – they never do,
which is probably why they are the recognized emblem of
romance and love. The trouble was, she understood the situation only too well. Grant had been manipulated and she knew

enough about the human psyche to know that this was how it was going to be. It was built into his personality. He was largely passive. She always went for the same sort of man: someone easy-going, commitment-phobic, unambitious. Maybe because they were the antithesis of her. But the trouble with Grant was that his strings were being pulled by someone else, and that someone was busily dancing him away from her. She recalled one of Heidi's lectures. *Fear the weak*, she had said. *Because manipulation is their strength. Don't underestimate that power.*

With all her skill, his sister was using her illness to manipulate him.

Wednesday, 5 November, 6 p.m.

She entered the house to the sound of tinny pop music and the smell of paint. She wandered upstairs into the spare bedroom and was entranced. Paul Mudd was doing a wonderful job, working his way methodically round the room, whistling and singing – songs from the musicals: *Evita*, *The Sound of Music*, *Phantom of the Opera*, *Les Misérables*. All mixed up, sometimes, into one confused song which she struggled to identify. But it was better than silence.

Anything was better than silence.

The house was coming alive again. The rooms were starting to look bright and cared for. Added to that he was turning out a whizz with the floor sander, and had transformed the ancient floorboards in the dining room into beautiful flooring. Claire had found a local firm who measured, made and fitted curtains, and the place was soon going to look good. Still a weenie bit under-furnished, but even there she had an idea. There were a few antique shops in Leek. When all the decorating was finished, she could take a trip out there. Then she stopped. It would all have been so much more fun if she and Grant had chosen pieces together. She stayed in the dining room, thinking it would make an excellent study, facing south and with a view over the garden through French windows. She loved the high ceilings, the original plasterwork, the square symmetry of all the rooms.

Paul Mudd was standing in the centre, paintbrush in hand. 'It'll fetch a good price, doctor,' he said, 'it's a lovely place,' and she felt an unexpected snatch at her heart. Did she really want to sell up?

'Noticed the wedding invite,' he continued, sounding impressed. 'Aren't they the ones that won the Lottery?'

'Was it common knowledge?'

'Oh. Ah. They went public on it. Lucky buggers.'

So easy for Barclay to home in on them then.

She opened the French windows and, ignoring the fact that it was dark and the grass was damp, walked out into the garden, sat underneath the gnarled apple tree (goodness knows how old it was), ran her eyes over the pots stacked on the terrace ready for geraniums next summer and, at the end of the garden, the high brick wall smothered in ivy. Even though the house was surrounded by other properties, it was silent and peaceful. Many of them were businesses: a dentist's, accountant's and a solicitor's office. She turned around, saw Paul Mudd's stocky frame silhouetted in the doorframe. 'Maybe I'll stay,' she said, surprising herself.

Paul Mudd stood still, paintbrush in hand, and simply smiled, like a wise old Chinaman. ''Appen you will.'

Her next thought was how much she would have to give Grant to buy him out. Maybe she should wait until the place was finished and then get a valuation and decide. Or should she make her move now, *before* it was at its best?

Make your move now, the little voice whispered. *Cut the thread. Sever the connection. It isn't going to work. Do it, Claire. Do it.*

But she didn't want to be unfair to Grant. He'd been a good boyfriend – one of the best. She'd had a few fairly rubbish ones, but Grant had been different and she'd thought they'd be together for ever. When he'd gone so abruptly from her life she'd mourned, felt damaged, angry, bereaved. But, like grief, one works through it and slowly one heals. She'd just been going through that process when he'd reappeared. Like bloody Lazarus rising from the grave, she thought crossly. So now what?

She couldn't decide. And so she did nothing.

Monday, 10 November, 12 midday

She'd been summoned to a meeting about Dexter Harding. Present were the CPS, his solicitor, and DS Zed Willard, whose eyes she could hardly meet. Her number would have shown up on his mobile phone-call record and he would have known it was not a wrong number.

She retrieved her professionalism, began by pointing out that Dexter was dangerous and would continue to be so – if not to the public in general, then to specific members of it.

'The trouble is,' she said, 'that in his obsession with that one girl, she is not safe and never will be. Neither,' she added, 'will people around her.' Eyebrows were raised. 'How so?' Amanda Cavendish, representative of the CPS asked.

Claire described Dexter's method – that of hurting people near to Sheridan – as a vicarious form of punishment designed to upset her and make *her* feel responsible for his actions. The solicitor moved uncomfortably while DS Willard met her eyes, opened his mouth to speak and closed it again.

'The Kurdish Iraqi family,' she continued, 'were murdered purely as a warning to Sheridan. She had built up a friendship with them. Was fond of their children, bought them toys. At Sheridan's wedding it didn't matter who died, just as long as he spoiled her day. That is a measure of Dexter Harding's psychopathy.' She paused, but no one else seemed to have anything to say so she carried on.

'If he is allowed to walk free, even on a Community Treatment Order which, let's face it, has failed, at some point he will attack again. Sheridan will always be a focus for his aggression. His brain is stuck on her.'

'So what do you suggest?' Amanda Cavendish asked.

'Personally I think he should go to prison for life for the attempted murder of the policeman, but that probably won't happen as he claims to have heard voices.' She scratched the air at the overused phrase.

Amanda Cavendish interrupted. 'You don't believe that?'

'Not for a minute.'

'OK,' she said slowly. 'We'll put him in Broadmoor for the

moment and ask the psychiatrists there to assess him. Are you happy with that, Dr Roget?'

'Yes and no,' she said. 'They're expert at dealing with true psychopaths and the more dangerous spectra of schizophrenics, but I'm not sure about their expertise in dealing with personality disorder.'

Amanda Cavendish smiled. 'I'll point that out,' she said. 'And I can assure you that he *will* be detained for a number of years and *not* released until he is deemed to be no danger to this poor girl or to any other member of the general public.'

The occupants of the room looked at one another. They all knew this meant his release would not be for a very, very long time – if ever.

Two days previously, Claire had liaised with another psychiatrist and they had both interviewed Dexter at length.

Dexter hadn't played ball. He'd stayed quiet and sulky, angry he hadn't succeeded in *'splitting that cunt's face'*.

It took them under a minute to place Dexter Harding under a Section 3, and now they could arrange to transfer him to Broadmoor. Initially for six months, and after that for annual review.

Job done.

She could wash her hands of him.

An inquest had been held on the deaths of Derek and Maylene Forsyte. As expected, the findings had been murder and suicide while Derek's mind was unbalanced. Their money problems were aired. There was no mention of the text which had probably goaded him into those final, violent acts. Barclay had slithered away again.

But at least Dexter had been put away. She could focus her attentions on her other patients.

Stan was dying, slipping away slowly but peacefully. Apart from the odd verbal outburst, he was too sick for any aggression and lay in a state of semi-wakefulness. Claire would sometimes sit with him, as did the other nurses, but it was sad to watch. Soon he would have to be transferred to the hospice. In the days since he had been ill, he had had not one visitor – no one to care for him. Stan would soon slip out of the world unloved and unmourned. Claire had rung his ex-wife, Annie. Surely she would remember a Stan before all this? But Annie was unforgiving. 'He cocked up our lives,' she said harshly. 'Me and Stacey had a rough time with him. I don't feel no affection for him.'

'And Stacey? He would love to see her. He is her father.'

'Listen, you psycho-whatever you are. I don't mean to be rude,' she'd said, 'but I've remarried. The guy is steady and *he* is a father to Stacey now.' There was a bitter laugh. 'A kid of eight don't need two fathers. I don't want her knowing her real dad died in a mental hospital 'cos he'd taken too many drugs. The world'll be a better place without him. See?'

No, Claire thought, *I don't see* – but she could do no more except appeal.

'Annie,' she said, 'Stan is dying of a brain tumour. Not drugs.'

There was a shocked silence. She had no response to this.

Claire put the phone down. Maybe Annie needed to do some thinking.

But she was with him one day when he opened his eyes and, with a lucidity she hadn't seen for months, asked again to see his daughter. 'I want to see Stace, doc,' he'd said to Claire. 'I know Annie probably feels that I let her down, but Stacey's my little girl. Can't you persuade her?'

'Not really, Stan,' she said, and she didn't tell him she'd already tried.

Sometimes the life of a psychiatrist is just too hard. For Stan to see his daughter she would have to have summoned the courts and forced Annie's hand. Was this a good idea? Did she have time?

Again she turned to Edward Reakin for advice.

She could tell he was relieved that, for once, the conversation was not centring on Barclay. 'Does he still have bouts of violence?'

She nodded. 'Verbal.'

'And are they predictable? Could you guarantee the little girl's safety? Could you guarantee that he wouldn't have an outburst with her?'

She shook her head.

Edward smiled at her. 'Then you have your answer, Claire. I should leave well alone.'

But time was slipping away.

On the following day, Stan was transferred to the hospice.

There was one ray of hope in those days and one piece of good news.

The good news was that PC Dylan Salisbury had been discharged from hospital, pronounced fit and well. He would be returning to the Force.

The ray of hope was that Hayley Price had returned to them, looking reasonably well and with a tiny pot-belly from the food she had been managing to eat. Somehow the Royal Stoke University Hospital had weaned her off the tubes and machines and her liver and kidneys had recovered to some extent. They would never be 100 per cent healthy, but they could see her through a normal life span. If she ate. Simple as that.

Claire spent time with her one dull November day and found her more amenable than before.

Did anorexics, she wondered, do this – push themselves to the very brink, and once they had reached that then draw back, knowing now exactly where the boundary lay so they would never scrape quite so close again?

Perhaps.

Hayley had reached her target weight. Already they were making plans for her to be discharged to one of the safe houses. From there she would be taught on a one-to-one basis until it was felt she could once again return to the home and go to school like any other normal fourteen-year-old.

So now Claire's problems appeared reduced to one patient: Barclay.

THIRTY-SEVEN

He lay at the back of her mind, taunting her with memories. Slippery as an eel; worrying her. He was like the family Rottweiler – you knew there was a potential for trouble, but trusted that the instinct would remain quiescent.

Who are you kidding?

She knew what he was planning. A sailing accident from which he would emerge unscathed and a hero. He was going to get control of that money one way or another, and the Trigg family – Roxanne and the baby included – would be lucky to survive.

Barclay tended to get what he wanted.

And however much she knew she could read his mind, anticipate his actions, even she was powerless to stop him.

But just over a week later she had what appeared to be a stroke of luck.

Friday, 21 November, 9 a.m.

It was her habit to meet up with Rita three times a day: early morning, lunchtime and at the end of the afternoon. Rita was the one who took all the phone calls, chased results, answered queries, typed the letters.

Also, being Claire's secretary, Rita knew how her boss felt about Jerome Barclay. She had taken phone calls from him and arranged appointments. So it was Rita who handed her a message. 'Mrs Barclay's phoned again,' she said, handing Claire the Post-it note.

For a minute Claire was confused. For a split second Mrs Barclay was Jerome Barclay's mother, Cynthia, who was supposed to have committed suicide five years ago. Cynthia Barclay, who had adored her son, worshipped him and in the end died for him. Or by his hand. To her Mrs Barclay was already dead.

Then her mind cleared. Not Barclay's *mother*. Barclay's *wife*. The name on the note was Roxanne.

And the number, this time, was a mobile. She raised her eyebrows at Rita. 'This could be interesting,' she commented.

'I thought it might be.'

'Did she sound . . .?'

'A bit agitated. A bit upset.'

'Well I'd better ring her then. What time did she call?'

'Twenty minutes ago.'

Rita watched as Claire went into her office and closed the door, saying she wanted no interruptions.

Claire dialled the number and the phone was answered almost straight away. 'Roxanne? It's Claire Roget here.'

'I'm glad you called.'

'Is there a problem?'

The question provoked a silence.

And then, 'I'm not sure.'

'OK. How can I help?' *Why did you ring?*

'Can I talk to you?'

'Of course.'

'Without Jerry knowing?'

'Yes.'

'Even if it's bad things?'

Claire knew if she was to take any action against him, she would have to reveal her sources at some point. She could deal with that later.

'When can you come in?'

'Now?' Her voice was breathy. 'He's gone to the Boat Show at the NEC with my dad.'

'OK. Now's a good time. Just come to the hospital and ask for me.'

'OK.' She sounded enthusiastic. Excited.

Later Claire would remember that tone.

THIRTY-EIGHT

Claire hadn't really studied Roxanne before. She had only ever seen her with Jerome. The person she saw in front of her now was more attractive than she remembered from her first impression. More self-assured. She observed a small mouth, sharp little eyes. A trifle plump, but more a pleasing roundness than fat; the six-month pregnancy was suiting her. Short stubby fingers, her gold wedding ring embedded below the knuckle. Her hair was less brown, more caramel, with a couple of professionally applied blonde streaks and straightened like a sheet of glass. She looked less nervous than Claire would have thought.

Quite a bit more confident and less intimidated. Roxanne was changing.

'Thank you for seeing me.' She gave a tentative smile. Claire asked her if she wanted a coffee and Roxanne said she'd love one. So the ice was broken. Rita fetched a couple of coffees and they sat down to talk.

Roxanne began. 'You see, I don't know what's normal.'

Claire knew what she must avoid was putting words into Roxanne's mouth. 'In what way?'

The girl swallowed. 'In marriage,' she said quietly. 'I don't know how most people's marriages work.'

'But you know about your parents.'

The sharp little eyes met hers with a ping before dropping her gaze to the mug of coffee. 'My parents,' she said, 'are very different from Jerome.' She looked up, surer of her ground now. 'They're simple people, Doctor Roget. They go to work . . .' Quickly correcting herself to: 'They went to work.' She frowned. 'You know about their Lottery win?'

'Oh yes.'

Her gaze sharpened. 'That wasn't why he . . .' Her voice trailed off. Roxanne wasn't sure enough of this to say it out loud.

And Claire dared not prompt her. She had come to her, consulted her, sought her advice as a professional. Might this be her chance to incarcerate Barclay? Put him where he belonged; at the very least, place him under a Community Treatment Order?

'So what brings you here today?'

The girl's eyes shifted to slide along the floor and Claire wondered.

'He . . .'

She was not as articulate as Sadie had been.

'He's not very . . . affectionate.' She raised her eyes. 'He seems to want to be unpleasant to me. To . . . to . . . hurt me.'

No surprise there then. Now Claire had to choose her words very, very carefully because she would be documenting this conversation word for word. 'In what way, Roxanne?'

Claire gave her the quick once-over. No marks. No black eyes this time; no bruised cheeks.

'In what he says,' she added quickly.

Claire recalled Sadie's description: *I could hurt you. I could cut a slice off these thighs. I could puncture your throat. I could kill you. I could rape you.*

Hardly the usual pillow-talk.

'He seems to want to upset me.'

'And this is a worry to you?'

'Yes.' Said gratefully. 'I worry about me, but more I worry about the baby. How will he be with . . .' She rested her hands comfortably on her bump.

Barclay with the baby? Claire thought. *I dread to think.*

Roxanne continued, her voice slightly less timid now. 'I just wish he'd stop and be more normal.'

Barclay won't stop, Claire thought. *Not ever. He will never be normal.*

She looked at Roxanne. 'Roxanne,' she said, 'have you ever wondered why Jerome is under me, a psychiatrist?'

'He told me it was because he'd been distraught when he'd lost all his family, one by one.'

Claire was impressed. *Oh, Barclay*, she thought, *you are so neat. So clever. Clap clap clap.*

But she couldn't completely spill the beans. 'Put it like this, Roxanne,' she said finally, 'the way Jerome is with you is part of the reason why he was under my care.'

'Oh.' Her eyes were wide open. Claire wasn't convinced she had actually understood. She returned to the main subject. 'So what do you want me to do about it, this problem?'

'Speak to him?' It sounded almost pitiful.

'Don't you wonder *why* he speaks to you like this?'

'I have asked him.'

'And what did he say?'

'That it was part of his illness.'

Oh, that too was clever.

'It is, sort of. It's part of who he is.'

'So . . .' Her comprehension was slow. 'You mean he's not likely to change?'

Claire shook her head. 'It's unlikely. He might improve with time and age.'

'But now he wants us all to go on a sailing spree – my

parents too. And I'm . . .' She hugged her pregnant belly. 'I'm worried I'll go into labour and . . .'

Claire knew exactly what Barclay was planning. She could see it all, unfolding in front of her eyes like a roller blind dropping down a window. It was all in his plan: Roxanne, vulnerable and in danger, the in-laws there as witnesses. And, of course, if his plans included a tragedy to them, Barclay would stand to inherit.

The lot.

She knew exactly what he was planning. Or did she?

She gave Roxanne a sharp look, suddenly understanding much more.

'Did he send you here?'

Roxanne flushed and looked panic-struck. And Claire had her answer.

THIRTY-NINE

After that there wasn't much point in prolonging the interview. Roxanne had been a plant, Jerome teasing again. She felt annoyed with herself for being taken in.

Roxanne left, stuttering in embarrassment, and Claire started to document the interview. But halfway through she sat, chin in hand, and wondered.

She had choices. Barclay was attention seeking and manipulative. He wanted her to sit up and take notice. So, like a parent with a recalcitrant child, she should not pander to his whims. She should ignore him.

Dangerous.

Her colleagues were convinced that she was obsessed with Barclay, that he was not nearly as dangerous as she thought. They knew he'd committed a serious assault on Sadie Whittaker, his previous girlfriend, but that was years ago, they argued. He had been a young man. The assaults on his three family members had never even been investigated by the police. They were all classed as non-homicidal: his father and baby brother natural causes, his mother a suicide. And yet Claire feared Barclay more than she had Dexter. She found him much more of a threat. Dexter was in your face. Barclay behind your back.

6 p.m.

She tussled with the problem all day and finally gave in. She wanted to talk to someone – not one of her colleagues. She couldn't trust them. Besides, they were halfway to classing her as obsessed. And again, in spite of her earlier confusion, she thought of Zed Willard, detective sergeant. He'd given her his card, invited her to contact him if she had concerns. She fished it out of her purse and dialled before she could change her mind. This was pure business, she told herself.

She'd used the hospital phone, which blocked the number, so he was, understandably, wary when he answered.

But relieved when she gave her name. 'Nice to hear from you. I think I had a missed call from you the other day? My sister said she answered. It was a wrong number. But it *was* your number, Claire, wasn't it?'

'Yeah,' she said. 'But it wasn't important. I decided I shouldn't bother you.'

'Oh,' he said, brought up short. 'So what can I do for you now? Dexter's well out of it and . . .' he chuckled, 'likely to remain so. You've sewn him up all right.'

'Let's hope so.'

There was an awkward silence until Zed Willard prompted her. 'So?'

'It's a bit of a cheek,' she said, 'but I wondered if I could run something past you?'

'What sort of thing?' He was definitely wary.

'It's about another patient.' Now she was just beginning to feel silly.

'Your colleagues?' he suggested. 'Don't you discuss . . .?' He gave an embarrassed laugh. 'I mean – I'd love to be in your confidence. But I don't know how much use I'll be. It'd be great to see you again, Claire. I'm just not sure how my perspective will help you. I'm a layman. A copper.'

'I know,' she said. 'That's why I'm asking you. You see – I feel I'm being used.'

He gave a little chuckle. 'I'd rather speak to you face to face,' he said. 'Let's go for some pasta or something. What time do you finish?'

'In about an hour.'

'Do you know the Italian restaurant opposite the Regent Theatre?'

'I do.' She'd been there with Grant on a number of occasions. Good food and better wine.

'I'll see you there at seven.'

7 p.m.

She had had no time to change, so had to go in her work clothes – dark skirt and pink sweater – but she had a spare pair of black high-heeled shoes in the car so she could change into those. She cleaned her teeth, brushed her hair, splashed cold water on her face and freshened up her make-up.

He was already there when she arrived. She'd had trouble getting the change for a parking space, and walking in high heels is necessarily slow. But she'd finally made it.

He was sitting at a table, a smile on his face as he watched her enter. He stood up, his smile broadening. 'This is good,' he said, almost rubbing his hands together with the fun of it. 'The psychiatrist asking my opinion about a patient.'

She laughed, liking this teasing mood and the sparkle in his bright eyes. The waiter bustled up and she ordered a drink. And now she was not so sure that this was a good idea.

He sensed her hesitation and encouraged her. 'Come on, Claire,' he prompted, 'I'm dying to know how I can help you. Don't back off now. Please?'

So she told him the whole story, mentioning no names, simply calling Barclay 'a patient'. She left nothing out, even when it reflected badly on her.

It all spilled out: her suspicion that he had been involved in the murder of Heidi Faro, her predecessor; the deaths in his family; his mocking, manipulative behaviour, his brutal treatment of his ex-girlfriend, the invitation to his wedding and his wife being sent to unnerve her. Last of all she described the Trigg family, and watched his eyebrows meet when she detailed the Lottery win.

He was silent all the way through, making not even one interruption or prompt.

His only movement was in his eyes, troubled yet somehow innocent. Blue eyes often look like that, innocent.

She knew that he could easily find out who the person was by the history she'd given. There weren't that many unfortunates whose brother had died a cot death, father through an overdose of insulin and a mother more recently who had committed suicide. And it would be easier still to track down a recent Lottery win and a local wedding. She also knew that he wouldn't pursue this. He wouldn't break her confidence. Blue eyes. There is something trustworthy and transparent about them too. Not like Grant's dark pirate's eyes, which had concealed so much.

She finished with her quandary. 'I don't know whether I should keep tabs on him,' she said, 'or how. Or what I *think* I can achieve by this, except pandering to his attention seeking. Do I have a duty to monitor his behaviour?'

He was silent, took another sip of wine, then smiled at her. 'And you want *me* to advise *you*?'

She lifted her eyebrows, splayed out her hands on the table, lifted her shoulders in a silent plea. 'The bottom line is, Zed, I think he's planning something. Why would he suddenly want a boat? And if he is planning something – how can I stop it? I can't be out there on the high seas. And I can't stop him going.'

'I don't know,' he said slowly. 'Let me think about it for a moment. Shall we order?'

She'd learned her lesson years ago. When on a date you don't order spaghetti. It might be all right for Italians to tuck their serviettes like babies' bibs under their chin and dribble their way through a meal, but it was not all right for her.

She ordered fusilli.

They'd almost finished when he put his fork down. 'You

really think he's going to hope his wife dies in labour and drown his in-laws for their money?'

Put like this, it sounded silly, and she risked appearing histrionic. She shrugged. 'I don't know,' she said. 'That's the trouble.'

'But, Claire, seeing him regularly isn't going to prevent any of this. You know what he's like. You can't stop him. As you said. You can't go to sea with him, can you? It appears that you have no access to the family except with him lurking or listening in the background. So what do you propose?'

He was so right. His gaze was on her. Of course she couldn't prevent Barclay from carrying out his plans. Could she warn the Trigg family – if not Roxanne, who was so completely under her husband's spell, then perhaps the parents? She put this to Zed. 'Well, you tried it with Roxanne,' he said. 'It didn't work there, did it?'

She shook her head. 'I don't know what to do,' she said simply. 'I can see what's about to happen and I can't stop it. But I have to try something.'

'What about,' he said slowly, 'the parents?'

That was when she made up her mind. That was what she would do: speak to the parents.

She smiled at Zed Willard and thanked him. 'I don't know why I had to bounce that off you. Why couldn't I see that for myself?'

'Because you're a psychiatrist. That's why.' His grin was genuinely warm. 'You make things more complicated than they need to be.' He reached across the table, his eyes meeting hers, and touched her hand.

And she knew, in that instant, that she wanted Grant back – sick-sister baggage and all. She smiled and moved her hand away and DS Willard sensed her retreat.

A few minutes later, when their plates had been cleared and they were drinking coffee, he asked her. 'So?'

'Yep,' she said firmly. 'I'm going to speak to his in-laws – at least warn them. I don't think there's any point talking to Roxanne again. She's too much under his influence. She'll side with her husband.'

Zed Willard nodded. 'Atta girl,' he said, and she knew he'd

recognized that moment when her heart had spoken loud and true. Banged like a church bell.

Tuesday, 25 November, 9.30 a.m.

Before she could speak to the Triggs, she had to formally discharge Barclay from her care. It would not do to be speaking to a patient's relatives without his permission, so she needed to distance herself from him. She dictated the letter. And, strangely enough, when she signed the typed version, she felt cleansed. He was off her hands. No longer her patient. Which changed the ground rules.

Three days later she rang Kenneth and Mandy Trigg and invited them to come in and talk to her. They were wary at first, but when she said that she had their interests at heart, as well as those of their daughter and unborn grandchild, they agreed to come in on the following Monday at 12 o'clock.

4 p.m.

She visited Stan at the hospice. He was sadly pathetic – sunken eyes, a grey skin tone; no flesh, only bones. He already looked like a corpse. The staff told her he slept for most of the time. It was obvious his tumour was growing rapidly and he wouldn't last much longer. He probably had just days to live. She was at least pleased she had made the decision to transfer him to the hospice. Their care for him was the best. Greatbach was not equipped to deal with such a physically sick person. They couldn't run drips or tube-feed him. Even a morphine pump was beyond them. The staff were trained in mental disorders and were poorly trained to manage this terminal physical condition. He was in the right place. She sat with him for a while and then the ward sister came in, bent over the bed, spoke to Stan and then addressed her.

'I was so pleased,' she said softly.

Claire struggled to see what could possibly please her in this situation. She raised her eyebrows and the sister continued, still speaking in that soft voice.

'His ex-wife came in with Stan's little girl, Stacey,' she said.

'The little girl was so sweet. They sat with him for a while and Stan was more lucid than I've seen him since he was admitted. The little girl kissed him and he knew what was happening. He smiled and later on that day he said to me, "I'll die happy, you know."' She looked down at his wan face. 'Sometimes,' she said, confiding in Claire now, 'I feel I can't do this job any longer. I feel so emotionally drained by the whole thing. Every day some new heartache, some new tragedy. Death—' she wafted her hand – 'all around. And then . . .' her hand moved down towards the bedclothes, 'someone like Stan is admitted and I think I can do it just that little bit longer.'

Claire nodded. 'I know just how you feel,' she said. 'Right down to *that little bit longer* bit.'

FORTY

Friday, 28 November, 6 p.m.

B ut she felt as though doom was moving inexorably forwards. Barclay's plans were heading towards fruition and there was no way she could put a stop to them. The letter discharging him would have arrived by this morning and she expected some response. But from Barclay, unpredictable as ever, there was nothing. She was just leaving the unit when her phone pinged with a text.

Are you very busy over the weekend? I'm off duty. If you fancy an evening out, give me a call.

Anytime.

Zed X

She was just about to reply when she had a crisis of conscience. She wanted to see Grant. It wasn't fair to play this game. She'd thought Zed had realized. Clearly she'd been wrong to initiate that last meeting. She had told herself it was purely business, but had it really been?

She liked Zed. He just wasn't for her. It is when you prepare to take on even a man's faults and baggage that you know you are truly in love. She wanted Grant lock, stock and two smoking barrels. She texted back:

I'm sorry. I'm a bit tied up this weekend. See you soon, Claire.

She put her finger on the Send button, but stopped and added, *X*.

Monday, 1 December, 12 midday

The Triggs were wary of her from the first and sat down on the edge of their seats, patently uncomfortable. She reassessed them.

Today both were smartly dressed, Mandy in a pair of well-fitting black trousers and a sweater and Kenneth in chinos, a shirt and jacket. No tie. They'd adjusted to having money, were learning how to spend it.

She greeted them and they waited for her to open the interview. *She* was the one who had summoned *them*. Something in their manner surprised her. They seemed more dignified, more in control. She looked closer. Had she initially misjudged them? Underestimated them?

'I feel I should warn you about Jerome. He isn't quite what—'

Kenneth interrupted. 'I don't understand,' he said, 'how you can discuss our son-in-law like this when he isn't present.'

Claire stopped in her tracks. 'I wanted to warn you,' she said. 'Jerome can be unpredictable.'

Mandy Trigg burst out laughing. 'We know that,' she said indulgently. 'He's fun. You don't always know where you are with him. He likes to tease.' A swift, merry glance at her husband. 'We understand Jerome,' she said, a note of steel in her voice, 'perfectly well. And we will protect our daughter and our grandchild from harm. Understand?'

Claire was silent. She was crossing a boundary and she knew it.

'Be careful,' she said. 'Jerome is a very intelligent and devious person.'

She suddenly noticed that Kenneth Trigg had gone very

quiet and was pressing his lips together. The classic sign of suppression. Something seemed to pass between the couple. Maybe since they'd won all that money they had become cannier, more suspicious and more wary. 'We *are* . . .' Kenneth said, deliberation in his words. 'We are *very* careful. We know Jerome has had . . .' he grappled for the word, 'issues. We know that events have occurred in his family. He's told us *his* version. Don't you worry about *us*, Claire. *We'll* be fine.' It was a verbal pat on the head.

They glanced at each other again, something unreadable but determined passing between them. Then they stood up as one and Mandy spoke, held out her hand and smiled. 'Our grandchild will be perfectly safe.'

And with that they left. Claire was bemused. *She* had orchestrated the interview but it had been *they* who had had the upper hand, and if she wasn't mistaken there had been a hidden message in their exchanges. She sat for a while, recalling all that had been said, the emphases on various words. Yet again she was missing something.

But she felt happier. She could wash her hands of Barclay. The Triggs had assured her that they could look after themselves.

And it was time to move on in more than one way.

The news came through that Stan had died, his ex-wife and daughter by his side. The news gave Claire a feeling of peace. One should die with one's family at one's side. And on the wings of that thought came an unexpected feeling of guilt. That was where Grant had been, at his sister's side, when he'd thought she was dying. His sin had been to exclude her from this scenario.

She had a pleasant three weeks, looking forward to Christmas in the newly decorated home. Paul Mudd was working wonders and had practically finished. On the Monday before Christmas, she met up with Grant, and they talked as they'd not talked when they were a couple. She was blunt and honest with him, telling him that his family, mother, sister, had obviously taken precedent over her and that that was a situation she would find hard to live with. She smiled at him. 'But . . . You're a great bloke, Grant,' she said.

He gave her a dark look. 'That sounds like a pre-dump line.'

She shook her head. 'No,' she said steadily. 'It's the line I draw before I meet the other two women in your life.'

He nodded.

'I should have met them before,' she said gently.

He nodded again. 'I'm sorry,' he said. 'I've played the whole thing wrong. Made a bit of an idiot of myself.'

She just smiled.

'I just thought . . .' he frowned. 'I just thought it was all too much for you.' He paused, frowning that dark, piratical scowl. 'You're right. I should have told you about Maisie before.'

She nodded, reached out for his hand. 'And now *I* need space,' she said. 'Some thinking time.'

His eyes were on her. 'Again, it sounds like the dump cliché.'

'I just need that time,' she said.

He shrugged. 'OK,' he said. 'Whatever. Not a lot I can do about it.' He'd finished on a grumpy note.

'I wouldn't want to be cut out of the loop again?'

'I promise.'

She continued. 'I've decided, now the decorating is almost finished, that I'm going to stay in the house. I've grown fond of it.'

'So?'

'So let's just see what happens. Eh?'

'Yeah.'

He seemed to have more to say and reached across to take her hand. He pressed her fingers to his lips and met her eyes. 'I'm so sorry, Claire. I'm really sorry I put you through all that. I did the wrong thing, listened to the wrong voices, and I feel terrible. But I don't want to be without you.' His hand reached out for her. 'At first I thought Maisie was going to die. I couldn't really deal with that. I was just distraught. I've always been the big brother, always there for her, you know? And then when she got a bit better, the weeks had gone by and I realized what I'd done.' He stopped. 'She just wanted me to stay with her all the time. She was frightened. Every day it became harder to get in touch with you and explain, Claire.' His face was contorted. 'I know I've been a shit,' he said. 'And a coward. You must think . . .'

She drew in a long, dragging sigh. 'Never mind what I

think,' she said. 'To be honest, I'm not even sure I know.' Suddenly all the fight and denial and strength had leached out of her. She wanted him back. But she couldn't do it right now.

She wafted her hand and Grant got the message and stood up. 'I'll leave now,' he said, 'but promise me.' His voice became impassioned. 'Please, Claire, promise me you'll . . .' And then his merry pirate look was back. He gave a cheeky grin. 'Ring me tomorrow?' She nodded. He bent and kissed her cheek. 'Goodnight, darling,' he said.

She watched him go, uncertain.

Was that what life was really all about? Uncertainty?

Christmas came and went. She didn't go home but Adam, Adele, Julia and Gina came round on Boxing Day. They played riotous charades and she cooked a duck with plum sauce and an actual on-fire Christmas pudding, which she produced to a flourish of applause. They watched a film companionably and left in the early hours.

She spent New Year's Eve again with Adam and Adele, having dinner at a local restaurant, which was offering an eight-course meal with entertainment. The entertainment proved to be a rather plump Elvis lookalike in a skintight white onesie, which only added to the jollity. They toasted the New Year in and made a solemn pledge to meet up at least once a month. From Grant she heard nothing, and tactfully neither Adam nor Adele asked any questions.

To try and find out what it was she really wanted, she met up with Zed a couple of times in January. They had a few dates – went to the theatre, the cinema, for walks, for dinner. She liked him. He was uncomplicated, honest, with a keen intelligence and sense of humour. And yet, although she was happy with him, it wasn't reaching the heights she had experienced with Grant and she believed it never would. Grant was proving a hard act to follow. He was quite a person. Much more Bohemian and unpredictable than the dependable and predictable Zed Willard.

Question: Why did the word dependable come up on the radar as enemy aircraft?

Zed *was* dependable. He was also predictable. Was that it? Were there to be no surprises with him? She wasn't sure. They

had not even become close to being lovers. She had to admit
it. The spark was missing.

Her house had been completed by the energetic Paul
Mudd. She had had an estate agent round and he had valued
the house at well over cost so, if that was the way forward, she
could split the money evenly with Grant. But although
she could now put a figure on it and knew he would agree
to whatever she suggested, she didn't write out the cheque.
She kept in touch with him and they met up a couple of
times, each time gently tiptoeing back towards their previous
relationship. But it wasn't the same, and Claire suspected
it never would be. The relationship had changed. One thing
she did know was that she had found some sort of settlement. She had renewed vigour in her work, socialized more
with her colleagues and had written an article on narcissism
and its consequences, which had been accepted for publication in the *British Journal of Psychiatry*. It felt like a little
feather wafting proudly in her cap. She'd even built bridges
with Astrid. They weren't exactly best friends and never
would be. The girl was too hard. But they had reached a
decent working relationship.

She thought life was settling down, forgetting that life itself
is turbulence.

Thursday, 29 January, 7 a.m.

The first she was aware of it was a phone call from Zed. She
was still yawning, sleepy-eyed, just about to make herself
some coffee and wake herself up. She hadn't even cleaned her
teeth. She looked at the number, surprised at the hour, then
answered.

'Claire,' he said, and his tone alerted her, 'have you seen
the news yet?'

'No,' she said. 'I've only just woken up. I haven't even had
my first coffee of the morning.'

'Put the news channel on,' he said seriously. 'I'm coming
over.'

Alarmed now, she put the news channel on and there it was,
in the ticker-tape along the bottom. Her nightmare. Sea tragedy.

Then the newscaster moved on to the story and Claire was confused.

This was not how she had imagined it.

She sat on the sofa, put her head in her hands and watched the news channel leak out more sparse facts until there was a knock on the door. She opened it to Zed. 'I've failed,' she said.

He wrapped her in his arms. 'No you haven't,' he said. 'You haven't. You couldn't have prevented this. Look at the facts, Claire.' He sat opposite her, his eyes full of sympathy. 'What could you have done? Roxanne came to you as his emissary. He sent her.'

That was when she began to see a fuller, clearer picture. 'She knew,' she said. '*They* knew. They've played me like a fish on the line. I feel such a fool.'

'Look at it this way,' he said. 'What else could you have done?'

'I don't know. I only know I was wrong.'

'We're never going to be able to prove anything. There's going to be no evidence. I'm just a DS,' he said. 'I'm not in a great position to initiate an inquiry. My relationship with you might compromise my position anyway, and this all happened offshore. Out of our jurisdiction.' He gave a weak smile. 'Not exactly Stoke-on-Trent.'

Her eyes moved back to the TV. The newscaster gave more detail on the main story. But Claire hardly needed it. She *thought* she could have written the text herself. *A boat tragedy, wife (heavily pregnant), in-laws. Missing bodies. The shipmate, Nic Benedetti, had, apparently, miraculously, survived and told a story of a giant wave capsizing the boat. In the Caribbean? Surviving hero had done all he could to save the family before somehow inflating a life raft and eventually being picked up by a passing ship. Brief news footage of Barclay, shivering, wrapped up in a blanket looking pale, pathetic and heartbroken as he spilled out to the world that he and his wife had not been married for very long and that she had been expecting their first child.*

But that wasn't the story at all. It had been *Barclay* who had gone overboard. *Barclay* who was dead, and Roxanne and

her parents, together with Nic Benedetti, were the survivors.
Claire had to recast villain and victims in this story. For the
moment she was too stunned to think clearly.

It was Zed now who spoke. 'The family will close ranks.'

'Unless . . .' she said.

He read her mind. 'Independent witness,' he said.

'The crew?'

'Nic Benedetti. He's our only hope.' He quickly translated
thought into action. 'I wonder if there's any chance we could
speak to him?'

She waited. Zed was silent for a minute or two and she
didn't interrupt his train of thought. Finally he spoke. 'I think
I might be able to do something.'

She hardly let herself be hopeful.

'I can probably gain access to something about Benedetti,
keep an eye on his phone calls, bank accounts and stuff. There
had to be a payoff. I think I can find out a few things.'

She couldn't believe this. What was she doing? Recasting
Barclay as victim? Barclay dead? It was an about-turn. She
was almost dizzy, as though watching the world while standing
on her head. Zed was looking at her, concerned. 'Claire,' he
said, 'what will you do if the Triggs contact you?'

'See them.'

'Will you contact them?'

Slowly she shook her head.

The television was still dancing out colour in the background
but she could feel Zed Willard was uneasy. 'Uumm,' he said.

'What?'

He looked really uncomfortable and she felt anxious. 'Zed,'
she said, alarmed, her hand on his arm, 'what is it?'

'Dexter,' he said. 'He's appealed. He's denying that he meant
Sheridan any harm.'

'He was carrying a knife. He almost murdered a police
officer.'

'He says he meant her no harm and the officer just got in
his way, that he had the knife because he was paranoid.'

She almost snorted her derision.

'And things got out of hand.'

'But . . .'

'He says it was in the heat of the moment, under pressure. He was frightened.'

'You don't believe that?'

'It isn't about what I believe.'

'But it's rubbish. He's a liability. He's dangerous.'

'He insists he just went to wish her well.'

'With a knife in his pocket?'

Zed Willard didn't even attempt to respond to this, and she felt herself cave in. 'Will I need to testify again?'

'I don't know,' he said.

'Are you holding him?'

'He's still at Broadmoor.'

'Thank God for that,' she said drily, 'as it appears my judgement is not quite sound.'

Even the news channel had moved on to other items.

Over the next couple of days more facts leaked out. The boat had been taken into port, where it was being examined by forensic experts.

Look the other way, Claire wanted to say to herself. This isn't your problem. You do not police the world. This happened thousands of miles from here. Someone else's responsibility. And yet, as though she had been a passenger on the boat herself, she could see what must have happened. And in one way she was to blame. She had alerted – or confirmed to – the Trigg family as to what Jerome was like. And they had acted to protect their daughter and their unborn grandchild. When they had assured her that the child would be safe, they had already been formulating their plan. Jerome, alive, an unprovable villain, would have rights over his offspring whether he and Roxanne were together or not. And that they couldn't allow.

And so when Claire watched the footage of the boat being winched into a dry dock in Bridgetown, she wanted to shout to the authorities: Look the other way. Not at the boat. Or a bloody big wave. The problem was in passenger and crew. Then she rose and switched off. What was the point? She felt defeated.

More reports leaked out over the next couple of weeks. What was left of Barclay's body had been recovered from the sea: evidence of scavengers, post-mortem changes consistent with drowning. No mention of unexplained injuries.

Game, set and match to the Triggs then.

The funeral was set for a month's time. Claire decided to go.

From the Trigg family there was no word at all. They were lying low, or maybe waiting for Claire to call them.

She didn't. She would wait. Watch and wait. Her thoughts were still in turmoil. But if she was in turmoil now, her biggest surprise was yet to come.

The day she learned of the tragedy, Rita asked to see her in her office. She looked upset but she also looked guilty. 'Claire,' she said, 'I feel I've let you down.'

Claire was bemused. 'Sit down, Rita,' she said. 'I'm sure you haven't. You're overreacting to something. What is it?'

Rita sank into a chair, her eyes focused downwards. 'It's Jerome,' she said.

Claire frowned, unable to see where this was going.

'I knew him,' Rita said softly.

Claire opened her mouth to speak. She wasn't sure she wanted to hear this.

Rita continued, eyes still on the floor. 'My mum lived next door to the Barclays,' she said. 'I used to babysit for Jerome when he was a little boy.'

'No.' It was a shock. Rita – dependable, reliable, truthful Rita, the traitor in the camp? Claire felt her mouth drop open.

'We kept in touch,' Rita continued.

And then Claire knew.

'He'd ask stuff.'

'And you told him.' She didn't need the confession. But this wasn't the time to read the Riot Act, talk about breaking confidentiality.

'The phrases,' Claire said. '*The hungry child, the doomed homeless, haunted Jew, expensive butterfly.* Where did they come from?'

'I couldn't use names,' Rita said, as though justifying her leak. Apparently explaining, defending. 'So I just called them stuff. I'd type your letters and think to myself. "A hungry child. The stupid clever." And so on . . .' Her voice trailed away. She

looked ashamed, but Claire wondered whether she would have
made this confession had Jerome Barclay still been alive.

'How did you know Stan was doomed?'

'I didn't. At least when I said he was doomed I meant in
his life. I didn't know he had a tumour. I couldn't have done.'

'And the expensive butterfly? Maylene?'

Rita smiled. 'I was in clinic one day, bringing some notes
down for you when she breezed in wearing a short, brightly
coloured dress. I was trying to describe her to Jerome. It was
just coincidence that . . .' She changed her words. 'What
happened to her. I'm not responsible. I didn't know he'd . . .'
She was struggling to find the word, 'Provoke them.'

She looked up then. 'Will I lose my job?'

Claire brought her hands up. 'I don't know,' she said,
surprised at how upset she felt. 'I don't know.'

It was another piece of the jigsaw, one she wished she had
not had placed.

She had trusted her secretary.

FORTY-ONE

D S Zed Willard tried his best to get some facts about
the sea tragedy but Benedetti had returned to his roots
in Sicily. They would find out nothing from him.
Omertà, the Sicilian vow of silence, appeared to have glued
his lips together and wrapped up his financial transactions in
a blurry fog.

Thursday, 26 February

The weather was freezing on the day of the funeral.

The service was to be held at Carmountside Crematorium
on the Leek Road in Milton. It was a place that had won
awards for its landscaping and, in particular, the children's
area, pretty with dolls and teddy bears, toy cars. It looked a
morbid playground.

Claire sat at the back, next to Zed, during the service.
Dressed in black, she kept her head down. She didn't want to
be noticed but to observe.

By the look of her, Roxanne was about to give birth, parents
flanked protectively either side of her. As the coffin passed
Claire she flicked her head round, gave her a quick, sideways
look. Then a serene smile, and Claire felt cold.

She couldn't believe that Barclay – Barclay, of all people
– had been outwitted by this clod-hopping family. She watched
Roxanne throughout the ceremony, which focused on the tragic
– Jerome Barclay, tragic life, untimely death; brother, father,
mother, all dead before their time. And now, on the cusp of
happiness, about to fulfil a lifelong ambition of bliss. Claire
frowned. Ironic that Barclay's crimes were now tangled up
for ever in his own murder.

FORTY-TWO

Wednesday, 19 August, Six months later

R ita looked up as she entered the room.
         Claire had done nothing about Rita, partly out of
loyalty for a loyal and competent secretary but also
because she knew if she reported the incident Rita would be
sacked, probably face criminal proceedings and never again
work in the N.H.S.. Also she knew she had been similarly
manipulated by both Barclay and the Trigg family. She had
spoken to her, and her secretary had assured her that she would
never break confidentiality again. 'Not ever,' she'd said but
Claire knew she could never trust her again. However for the
time being Rita was still in post.

'You're not going to guess who's rung up and asked if she
can consult you.'

Claire shrugged.

'Roxanne Barclay.'

'Really? What for?'

'She wants to talk to you. Grief counselling?' she suggested tentatively.

Just when you thought a patient had disappeared from your radar for ever, this happened.

Claire was curious. What would be the point of this? She couldn't guess.

Roxanne had the child with her, a little boy with watchful eyes who sat motionless in the pushchair.

Roxanne had lost her baby weight and was plainly and tastefully dressed in jeans and a blouse. She gave Claire a smile as she entered. 'Thanks for seeing me.'

'I'm not sure what I can do for you,' Claire said, still bemused.

Roxanne smiled and crossed her legs, almost ignoring the boy in the pushchair. 'Well,' she said, 'you knew Jerome.' She opened her mouth slightly so Claire could see a little pink tongue.

Claire nodded and met Roxanne's eyes. Hard, cold and somehow triumphant.

'You always thought *him* a threat,' she said, verbally poking Claire with her finger. 'I think you were worried for *my* safety. But in the end,' she said, the note of triumph even more evident now, 'it was *he* who died. And I,' she said smugly, 'am still alive. And this,' now she turned to the child, 'is his son. I have called him Cain.'

Cain? Was the child destined to be a murderer?

Claire studied the little boy, who regarded her with cold grey eyes. Claire was confused now. What was all this about? She grasped at a familiar straw. 'What have you come to see me about? Is it for grief counselling?'

'No. I don't need that.' There was a note of disdain in her voice now. 'I didn't come for that. I came to introduce you to our son. Jerome's and mine.' She leaned forward, her face malicious. 'You never had the measure of him, did you? He was too clever for you. But then . . .' Her face changed again. Smug smile this time. '*I* was too clever for *him*.

'And our child . . .'

The devil's spawn, Claire thought.

'Our offspring,' Roxanne continued, 'will, I'm sure, have as interesting and adventurous life as his father.'

And then she touched on the real reason for her visit. 'I know you've asked the police to look into the tragedy. They told me. But there isn't any point in your trying to get anything out of Benedetti. He won't speak.'

Neither did Claire. She looked at the child who stared back, unblinking.

Then curiosity got the better of her. 'Is he really called Cain?'

Roxanne shook her head, laughter bubbling out of her. Water from a spring. 'Not yet,' she said. Claire simply gaped and Roxanne left, leaving behind nothing but a vague scent of Estée Lauder's Youth Dew.

And so Claire was left in an empty room to reflect. Nurture or nature? Psychiatrists would argue over that point for ever. Evil was evil, wherever it originated from. And the merry-go-round would continue to turn. Maybe one day, she thought, she would meet this child again – or even Roxanne herself. She had the ingredients. But at least Jerome Barclay was off the scene – permanently. Maybe only death discharges a patient permanently from his psychiatrist.

Dexter would remain in Broadmoor for ever now. He had proved himself, displayed his right to be there. His appeal would fail.

Hayley might live for a few more years, but her reserves were low. She would not survive one more trip across the line.

Stan was dead but, in the words of the old films, *He died happy.*

Who can ask for more?

And maybe one day, Claire thought, she would go to the cinema and watch a film about the baker of Buchenwald and the fatal burning of bread.

Patients would come and go and she would do her best.

No one could do more.

Lightning Source UK Ltd.
Milton Keynes UK
UKOW03f1842080217

293944UK00001B/11/P